THIS

LITTLE

LIGHT

☀

THIS
LITTLE
LIGHT

LORI LANSENS

RANDOM HOUSE CANADA

PUBLISHED BY RANDOM HOUSE CANADA

www.penguinrandomhouse.ca

Random House Canada and colophon are registered trademarks.

Library and Archives Canada Cataloguing in Publication

Lansens, Lori, author
This little light / Lori Lansens.

Issued in print and electronic formats.
ISBN 978-0-7352-7642-0
eBook ISBN 978-0-7352-7643-7

I. Title.

PS8573.A5866T55 2019   C813'.6   C2018-905691-6
                                                C2018-905692-4

Book design by Kelly HIll

Cover images: (woman) © CoffeeAndMilk, (flame) © Sean Gladwell, both Getty Images

Printed and bound in Canada

2 4 6 8 9 7 5 3 1

Penguin
Random House
RANDOM HOUSE CANADA

For Allegra

THIS LITTLE LIGHT

BLOGLOG: Rory Anne Miller   11/27/2024—9:51 PM

We're trending. Rory Miller. Feliza Lopez. In this moment, on this night, we're the most famous girls in America.

Those pics you've seen in your feeds and on TV over the past few hours? Two fresh-faced teens in bridal couture on the arms of their daddies at tonight's American Virtue Ball? That's me and Fee, my best friend. The grainy footage from the school surveillance cameras of two figures in white gowns climbing up into the smoky hills after the bomb exploded at Sacred Heart High? Also us. It's true that guilty people run. Scared people run too. They're calling us the Villains in Versace.

What they're saying about us? First—who wears Versace to a purity ball? I wore Mishka. Fee wore Prada. The details matter. The truth—which is not somewhere in the middle as guilty people like to say—is vital. Like oxygen. The truth is that Fee and I did *not* try to blow up the chastity ball at Sacred Heart High tonight. We had nothing to do with that thing they found in my car, either. And we have no involvement whatsoever with the Red Market. We're not the spawn of Satan you're loading your Walmart rifles to hunt.

If I'm being honest? Totally honest? I've spent a stupid amount of time daydreaming about being famous, and how amazing it'd be to have millions of followers. That's normal, right? A shallow distraction from reality? I live in California, after all, where fame pollutes the atmosphere then penetrates your skin with the UV rays. But this isn't fame. It's infamy. And I feel like I do in my recurring naked-at-school nightmare—gross and exposed.

Careful what you wish for? Fee and I don't have followers so much as we have trolls and trackers. We're being flayed in the media. Convicted by social. And now we're freaking fugitives, hiding out in this scrap metal shed behind a little cabin in the mountains overlooking Malibu.

I'm so thankful for this old pink laptop—courtesy of Javier, who's letting us hide in his shed, which I'll explain later. I've caught up on the fake news and read all the hate tweets. Bombers? Religious terrorists? Red Market runners, trafficking stolen babies? It feels like a joke, but it's not. And to make it even more real, the rock evangelist Reverend Jagger Jonze just put up a million-dollar reward for our capture. There's a freaking bounty on our heads. So here we sit in this shed. No way to defend ourselves. Nowhere to run.

My throat hurts from swallowing screams. And the worst thing—I mean, worst is relative under these circumstances—but Fee is really sick. She's curled up beside me under a tattered blanket, not really awake but groaning. Whatever's wrong with her, it started at the ball, and once we got here, she basically collapsed.

Her forehead's hot. She's pale. Something she ate? She barely ate today. Flu? I don't know.

In order to remain calm-ish, I'm going to write our side of the story. I'm afraid we'll be tracked to the shed if I post entries in real time, so I won't submit until I know we're safe. This old laptop has had a long-life battery upgrade, thank God. I could write all night. Maybe I will. Wouldn't be the first time. Won't be the last. Writing? It's the only way I've ever been able to make sense of my life.

Just this afternoon, Fee and I were with our other best friends—Brooklyn Leon, Zara Rohanian and Delaney Sharpe, all of us students at Sacred Heart High School—getting ready for the ball at Jinny Hutsall's house. Hutsalls are beyond rich, so they hired a StyleMeNow crew to come over and do our hair, paint our nails, curl our lashes and plump our lips, which I did not hate. We sipped the champagne Jinny'd cadged from the fridge—a very unJinny move, now I think about it—and snapped a hundred pics of our virgin-bride splendor, while our tuxedoed daddies tossed back Manhattans on Warren Hutsall's lanai. The others got giggly, but slipping into my gorgeous Mishka, I felt nothing but dread.

It wasn't about the virginity pledge we were about to take. My friends and I weren't serious about that. Not really, or not all of us. The Virtue Ball was a swag grab, a couture gown, a brush with celebrity, a photo op. Or at least that's what we said. For me? As an atheist who definitely won't be saving it until marriage, it was also an opportunity to do some reporting for my blog. That's what I told myself, over and above the dread, which I'll explain later.

Driving there tonight, I still hadn't decided if I'd dig into the hellaciousness of vowing chastity to our fathers or if I'd go with a softer piece acknowledging the father/daughter bonding but include some solid stats to show that teaching abstinence doesn't work. I hadn't decided which angle would get me more likes. That's the truth. I hadn't quite got to the point where I actually was considering exposing the whole corrupt deal. Too scared, maybe?

Well, I know which way I'll go now. Though I couldn't have imagined I'd be writing about how Fee and I became outlaws hiding in a seven-by-eight-foot shed, crowded by a greasy lawn mower, a couple of leaf blowers, a tangle of fishing rods, three old suitcases and some fat white trash bags leaking lawn clippings.

When I look up, I can see the full moon and stars blinking through gaps in the aluminum roof, and the distant lights from passing planes. There are no doubt already bounty hunters out there looking for us in their MiniCops and GarBirds—those homemade flying jobbies people get shipped from China to build in their garages even though they're totally illegal. They're crowdsourcing our capture. It's all over the news.

There's a window at the front of the shed that looks out over the rocky cliffs, and from there I can see the neighbor's trailer a hundred or so yards away—an ancient silver Airstream, the front tow-hitch propped off-kilter on three big cinder blocks, a big blue tarp that was strung up to make an awning over the porch billowing in the breeze. Light from a television was flickering in the front window when I looked out before. No vehicle in the driveway, though.

I've seen a couple of drones whir by. Definitely looking for us. The new cam-drones are so quiet and acrobatic you don't see them until they're on you taking surveillance. I noticed an UberCopter pass a few minutes ago. Saw the police helicopters flying back in the direction of Sacred Heart High, where the bomb exploded. With the bounty, and the media firestorm, there will be a lot more of them tomorrow in the daylight. Unless the Santa Anas start blowing. The news is saying we should expect strong winds later tonight, and off and on tomorrow. Crossing freaking fingers. The winds will keep the air traffic down.

The cable stations are covering us round the clock like we're a weather event—a hurricane or severe snowstorm or a California wildfire so big and bad they gotta give it a name. Fox News is calling our story "The Hunt"—so ugly rhyming memes. My head's spinning. It's been torture to go online. But worse not to know. People say you shouldn't read the comments section. People are right. I seriously want to respond to each one. Like, I want to tell Twitter user @H8UevlGASHES—who suggested the insertion of a broken bottle into our life-giving lady parts—that he does not understand irony. And I want to tell that congresswoman from Texas who just tweeted that Fee and I should have our "eyes sewn open and be forced to watch a late-term abortion" that she should definitely kill the person who does her hair. The guy who started #rape'em1st? He just makes me wanna cry. And? The president tweeted out a White House dinner invitation to Jinny Hutsall and Reverend Jagger Jonze. It would be funny if it weren't too true.

Our "friend" Jinny is trending too. They're saying that what happened at the Virtue Ball tonight has ignited an "American Holy War." Jinny fucking Hutsall. Until that blond-hair, yoga-arm, apple-ass thigh-gap-in-a-tartan-skirt moved in next door a few months ago and joined our class at Sacred Heart High, we were just us. The Hive. Friends since we were toddlers. Now, two of us are the New Targets of Holy War. And the host of tonight's ball, Reverend Jagger Jonze—the one that put up the million-dollar bounty after everything went down in the parking lot at the AVB?

He's rocketed to superstardom. Just like that. Jagger Jonze is the devil. But more on that later.

First—the bomb. We didn't set the bomb. And if someone wanted to bomb the ball, why did they blow up the bathroom clear on the other side of the school's fifteen-acre campus? Nothing makes sense. It's all just crazy. We've been accused of being "runners" doing dastardly deeds for the Red Market. My mother's always said there's no such thing as the Red Market. She says it's a construct—evil alt-right propaganda. I don't know what to believe. I mean, people have been talking about the Pink Market since long before abortion was banned again. Everyone knows there's a Pink Market out there helping minors access birth control, and morning-after pills, and getting them to underground clinics and all.

But the Red Market? Supposedly it's a baby-stealing mafia that supplies product to illegal stem cell research labs. Even the media say "alleged" or "rumored" when they talk about it. Law enforcement officers and politicians are rumored to be involved in the Red Market too. Even if my mother's wrong, and people are actually that depraved, Fee and I are not, and never have been, and never would be, involved in such foul shit.

I'm scared. No, terrified.

When my father left us, I was scared. I thought my mother'd die of heartbreak and I'd be left alone. When the wildfires got close again last year, and we had to evacuate, I was scared for the neighborhood pets, and Mrs. Shea at the end of our street because she's deaf and takes too many pills. I remember being lost in the grocery part of Target when I was little, staring at the chevrons on a stranger's herringbone pants. So scared.

But this? This fear has fangs. I've never felt so awake.

Why are we targets?

Not for nothing—I'm Jewish. Spawn of two Canadian Jews twice removed through birthright and marriage outside the faith, which is why Jew*ish*, not *Jew*ish. My parents, Sherman and Shelley Miller, immigrated to southern California, legally, from Toronto, the year after they finished law school. My best friend and costar in this horror show, Feliza, is the daughter of immigrants too. Her mother's Guatemalan. Her father's from Mexico. Fee was born in Tijuana the day before their illegal border crossing. They used to call people like her Dreamers. Now they're Probationary Citizens. Procits for short.

We live in Calabasas, California, which is famous because Kardashians. For anyone who doesn't keep up with the Kardashians and might be reading this outside our bubble, you have to know that my town isn't a town the way people think of towns. Calabasas is spread out over fifteen square miles of coastal paradise: gated communities of big-ass mansions tucked into the nooks and crannies of the northwestern part of the Santa Monica Mountains, linked by scenic roads to tour-class golf courses and high-end strip malls and gold-label private schools. The sheriff's blotter in the local paper reports on crimes like: "a pair of sunglasses valued at $1,800 were stolen from an open convertible Maserati in the six thousand block of Las Virgenes Road." There's no smoking in Calabasas. No Styrofoam. No plastic bags. No straws. No fast food. No trash on the streets. No homeless. No ugly, basically. The rocky outcroppings, and the blurry ocean horizon and the chaparral-covered hills, make a stunning backdrop for the photos we post. We post a lot.

From the outside we must look like assholes. Maybe from the inside too. We have too much. We are too much. The student parking lots at all the schools are filled with the Beemers and Bentleys and Mercedes and Teslas driven by the progeny of all the entertainers and athletes who moved here for the clean air and good schools—second-generation superkids—super-good-looking, super-talented, super-rich. The Kardashians reign over us as we #Bless the crap out of our Maui vacays and shiny new cars like they all came straight from the Maker.

But wait. How can we be blessed? The way I understand the Bible from my Sacred Heart education, Christians are supposed to get their rewards in heaven. Like the Muslim martyrs with their virgins. And the Crusaders from history. Could it be that all the #Blessers might be setting themselves up for a hard drop at the Pearly Gates? Using up all their blessings on earth and leaving no bank whatsoever for the hereafter?

Afterlife? I can barely make it through presentlife.

The Internet's losing its shit with all the Kardashian references, and blaming Kendal and Kylie Jenner for the crimes we did not actually commit! They're speculating that Fee and I could have become involved in the rumored Red Market, because we needed money for our retail habits—our Balmain this and our Blahnik that—in order to keep up with the Kardashians. Not a crazy theory, I guess. They're comparing us to the kids from Indian Hills High who broke into celebrity houses and stole clothes and jewelry from Paris Hilton a thousand years ago. The Kardashians have offered "no comment" yet, although Scott Disick did drunk-tweet "The Mexican chic is sizzlin'."

Here's what I think. I know it sounds crazy. But I'm sitting here trying to put the pieces together and I think this whole thing must be a setup. By Jinny Hutsall, our resident Christian zealot Crusader. And her father's friend, Reverend Jagger Jonze.

Jinny Hutsall already loathed me for being Jew-y, and for being a heathen. Then I became a Category Five threat to that psycho

Jesus freak. I know her secret, and I'm pretty sure she knows I know, which makes me think that she and Jagger Jonze planted the bomb at the ball tonight. And they have something to do with that thing that was found in my car in the Sacred Heart parking lot too. It has to be that. What else could it be? And Fee? She's collateral damage, which slaughters me, because Fee doesn't deserve any of this. I'm the atheist blogger with opinions. I'm the one who just couldn't mind my own fucking business. Maybe this is my karma. Not that I believe in karma, but you still find yourself saying shit like that, don't you? Like the way we heathens say "thank God."

I've been staring at the pics of us all over the Net, of me and Fee and our best friends and families—pics I've never even seen before. This loop plays over in my head: Wait. What? Wait. What? Our friends? Bee? Zee? Dee? Our best friends in the world? They've turned on us. They've sided with Jinny Hutsall and joined the throngs of accusers calling for our capture. They're tweeting at us to turn ourselves in! How could they do that? How could our best friends think Fee and I would plant a bomb, let alone participate in that other atrocious shit? I love those girls. Brooky, Zara, Delaney and Fee have been everything—my life, my family—especially since my dad . . . I believed in them. A few hours ago I would've said I trusted them with my life. It's just such a betrayal.

We girls are more than neighbors. We're sisters. We've lived on Oakwood Circle in Hidden Oaks of Calabasas since we were buzzing little Beelievers—in matching yellow-and-black-striped T-shirts—at Sacred Heart Nursery School, where we got our nickname, the Hive. Someone's made a meme of us as an old-time-y United Colors of Benetton ad, which is not inaccurate. Brooklyn Leon, the beautiful, athletic black girl; Delaney Sharpe, the red-headed English rose; Feliza Lopez, the sexy Latina; Zara

Rohanian, the smoky-eyed Armenian; and me, not exactly a category you could name. Real people who are not my parents sometimes say that I am striking. I take after my father's side north of the neck—brown eyes, freckled face, dark, naturally fro-ish hair. South of the rib cage I'm mesomorph-y, the only physical trait I share with my blond, green-eyed mother.

All we know we girls have learned together behind the doors of our Mediterranean-style mansions, beside our blue infinity pools, under rows of date palms, in the heat of the big, boiling sun. We're double-gaters. That means after you pass the first security booth with armed guards named Marcus and Dax, you have to go through another set of gates to get to our cul-de-sac. The Kardashians are Hidden Oaks triple-gaters. The whole clan lives at the top of the hill now, in this massive compound because safety. We see the paparazzi swarming one of their vehicles most days. We care about them like they're our actual family, and have been KUWTK since, like, third grade, or at least we did, until Jinny Hutsall moved to Oakwood Circle. She called them Kar-douche-ians. We let her.

I keep hearing noises outside the shed. I tell myself, It's just the wind, girl, nut up. But my heart won't stop racing. I have to say, it would be tragically lame to die in a Holy War when I don't even believe in God.

Fee's breathing is shallow. When I shook her just now, she coughed a little and asked for water. She's so dehydrated. I thought about going to Javier's cabin to ask for more, but he told us not to leave the shed and I don't wanna make him mad. I also thought about going outside to look around, but I'm scared of the eyes in the sky.

"Maybe there's something in Javier's truck. Water bottle. Juice box," I say.

"Go see," Fee croaks.

"The winds are supposed to start up around midnight. The air traffic'll be grounded, so I'll go out then. Okay? I'll go out and look around then."

"Ror?"

"Yeah."

"Are we gonna die?"

"We're not gonna die."

"Smells so bad in here," Fee said.

It does. The shed reeks of gasoline, and rodents, and me. The floor is dirt, so bugs. I go back to the laptop.

"What are they saying online, Ror?"

She's too sick to hear the gory details right now, so I just say, "'Thank God for American Girls' is number one on the pop charts. Not the Christian chart—the actual chart."

She doesn't respond. She's out again. I have to find a way to get her some fluids.

I cannot believe that Jagger Jonze's rancid American Virtue Ball theme song has climbed from number 429 on iTunes to number 1 since this whole thing went viral. Oh my God, those lyrics . . . *She is proud, she is strong, and she knows right from wrong. Temptation will not find her 'cause she's just where she belongs. Thank God for American Girls.* Before Jinny Hutsall moved in, we'd all mocked that sexist dreck. If you never heard the song before, you've heard it by now, and you've seen clips of the Reverend from his *Higher Power Hour* Sunday TV show, belting out more lame Christian jams in his designer T-shirt and thousand-dollar sneakers. Lucifer in Louboutins. How 'bout that?

I just checked MSNBC, which has been showing a portrait of the whole gang of us—the five families from our cul-de-sac

gathered together for a backyard barbecue at the Leons' house—
with the tag "Portrait of Perfection?" In the background of the
shot is Miles, Brooky's older brother, with his band, Lark's Head,
led by my not-so-secret crush, Chase Mason. He of the long hair,
tragic eyes, shredded bod—twin of Jesus Christ Himself. My
mother recently wondered out loud, like she does, if my crush on
Chase means my Freudian slip is showing and that I still have
some unresolved feelings about religion. Nope. I used to believe.
Now I don't.

Chase works part-time at the Calabasas Library, where I've
done volunteer hours Mondays and Fridays since eighth grade.
I'm in his friend zone, which is grave. At Leons' BBQ, I remember I caught him watching me from behind his microphone, so I
tossed my blowout around, then grabbed Dee's little sister's hula
hoop and started gyrating with all this, like, fake innocence.
Thinking of it now, I might've looked more seizure-y than sexy.

My mother, a hermit since my dad left, had pulled herself
away from her computer and come for a while that day. Shelley
seemed like herself, laughing with the other moms, arguing with
Zara's dad about climate change, and that gave me hope. But it
didn't last. I saw her wiping tears from her cheeks as she slipped
out the side gate before dinner.

Mrs. Leon had piled so much food on the buffet table she
worried the legs were gonna buckle—Kobe steaks and fat shrimps
on skewers, salads and artisan breads and one of those edible fruit
bouquets, any kind of dessert you could imagine. But we hardly
ate any of the food because thin. Chase and Miles were crushing
it with the band, but we girls didn't actually dance because parents. And when Delaney's dad, Tom Sharpe, of Sharpe Mercedes
Calabasas—local celeb because of the commercials where he waves

at a customer driving off in a convertible and goes, "Lookin'
Sharp!"—well, when he said it was time to get jiggy with it, we
bolted to Bee's room to post the pics we'd been taking all afternoon. That was three short months ago. Labor Day. The week
before Jinny Hutsall slithered into Oakwood Circle.

Just realized I'm still wearing my pearl ring from the Virtue Ball.
I want it off my finger, but I don't know what to do with it—don't
wanna leave it here in the shed. Evidence. Fuck. I wish I'd tossed it
into the creek with our smashed phones when we ran tonight.

Fee never got to put on her pearl ring. Delaney's dad, Tom
Sharpe, was Fee's daddy stand-in tonight. He's basically been
her daddy stand-in her whole life because she doesn't have a dad,
and because Fee and her mom, Morena, Sharpe's housekeeper,
live in the guest house behind their pool. I'm no fan of Tom
Sharpe, but at this point I'd say he's been more of a father to Fee
than mine has been to me. Anyway, during the pledge tonight,
Mr. Sharpe tried to jam the ring on Fee's finger, but it wouldn't
go over the knuckle. He thought he might've gotten her ring
mixed up with Delaney's and they switched, but no. So Fee put
the stupid too-small ring in her Gucci metal clutch, which she
left on the counter in the school bathroom. No doubt it was
blown to bits along with the porcelain toilets and speckled tile
floor. Not that she should give a shit about the stupid pearl ring.

Poor Fee. She just barfed again. I'm really starting to wonder
if she was poisoned. Is that crazy to even think? But she seemed
fine today, until we got to the ball and she ate those little chocolate ganache thingies Jinny pushed on us. The ones I didn't eat.
Did Jinny Hutsall actually poison her? Did she mean to poison
me too? Or to poison me instead of Fee? Did Jinny and Jagger
Jonze wanna make sure I'd be stuck in that bathroom back behind

the gym, where she'd specifically told me to meet her, shitting and puking my guts out, when the bomb went off?

A breeze sweeps tumbleweeds against the patchwork walls of the metal shed. Not the Santa Anas yet, but twigs snap. Branches crack. My heart stops at each sound, wondering if we've been discovered. If what I'm hearing is the wind, or the stealth boots of some rude dude from the homicide squad, or a redneck with a rifle, or some white-collar with a pistol out to collect the bounty.

I'm also on edge over every crackle of noise because it's fire season. Well, I guess it's always fire season now. The drought is all the local news talks about between pauses to discuss White House tweets and the war in the Middle East. We've had only a few inches of rain in over two years. There was a huge fire in the canyon behind Hidden Oaks when we were in middle school. Shelley and I watched the twisting flames rise up over the hills, blazing the black skeletons of oaks and sycamores left for dead after a smaller fire years before. There was a mandatory evacuation so we grabbed the boxes and suitcases we keep in the closet by the door and hurried out to the car. Our friends on Oakwood Circle stayed—they always do—but I was glad my mother didn't think of a mandatory order as just a suggestion. I was scared.

If a fire started here in the hills, or someone tried to smoke us out, we'd be doomed. I wonder how much it hurts to die of smoke inhalation. Like drowning, only in smoke? And what about that? Whoever planted that bomb is lucky that the whole hillside behind the school didn't go up in flames.

Fee's passed out again. She looks corpse-y. This is bad. It's really fucking bad. But she'll feel better in the morning. Right? And we'll figure a way out. Hope. It's all I have, so I have to hold on to it. I have hope—no—I have faith that the truth will prevail. And it will. Right?

─☼─

Been looking out the window. The lights in Javier's little log cabin at the front of the property just went out. I don't know how he can sleep with two of America's Most Wanted hiding out in his toolshed. The TV is still on in the Airstream trailer next door, but no lights, and no car or truck in the driveway. No dogs barking. No coyotes howling. Just wind whistling through the slits in the shed.

I guess it's time to fill you in on Javier. He's the cousin of our gardener, who's also called Javier, and that's why I remembered his name. Not-our-gardener Javier lives in this cluster of half a dozen cabins and trailers on this weedy plateau in the hills a few miles from the coast. He was once a client of my parents and I was here before, a few years ago, a tagalong when my parents delivered Christmas baskets.

My parents used to be immigration lawyers, and they did a lot of charity work with procits, and helped newcomers settle into the area with food and clothing and electronics donations, all that. There used to be foreigners with dusty suitcases and peppery odors in our guest room for weeks at a time, back when my parents were soul mates and did good deeds together.

I remember that while I waited in the car for Miller Law to bring tidings of comfort and joy here, I noticed that the place seemed familiar. Then I realized the cabin was on the other side of a rickety bridge over a deep crevasse at the middle point of the seven-mile loop we run for cross-country; my school is on the other side of the hills. When the bomb exploded, Fee and I started running, and as we got deeper and deeper into the bush, the cabin was the only place I could think to go.

Once, about a year ago, while I was out on a solo run, I stopped to pee behind this shed we're in now. I checked the little cabin, and the old Airstream trailer next door, and couldn't see anyone around. No vehicles in the gravel patch driveway. No kids playing in the scruffy yard. I pulled my shorts down and squatted, then out of nowhere this huge black pit bull comes steaming straight for me, snarling and snapping and growling and barking like he was gonna murder me while I peed. He made it to spitting distance before the rusty chain attached to the frame of the Airstream yanked him back.

On the rocky path through the hills heading back to the school, I thought about that poor dog and the fucked things that must've happened to make him so vicious. I thought about that pit bull tonight too, as we got closer to the cabin. I looked for him as I dragged Fee across the rickety bridge, and listened for him as we pushed through the brush toward the clearing. But we heard nothing.

Fee and I didn't love the idea of waking up our gardener's cousin, basically a stranger, to ask him to help us, so you can imagine we were relieved when we saw the light from a television glowing in his little living room.

Moving closer to the cabin, I caught this horrible stench and at first I thought oh no the pit bull, then realized what I was smelling was me—wicked BO mingling with the copper-pot smell of my blood. It was like I was bleeding out, so much blood was running down my legs and pooling into my sneakers under my gown. My period arrived at some point tonight between the welcome mocktails and the explosion, maybe proving the existence of God after all, and that She has a gnarly sense of humor.

As we inched toward the cabin, I worried about the shifts in the wind and the satanic dog catching scent of my moon. If that beast started barking, the neighbors might come out and see us, or the police on our trail might hear.

The screen door to Javier's cabin was open, but we couldn't see anyone moving around inside. As we got closer, we could hear voices coming from the television. When you're a regular person, you don't expect to see yourself on TV, and even as I write this it still feels unreal.

It took a sec to grasp that the voices Fee and I could hear were our own. We stood on the porch of the cabin, peering in the screen door, watching ourselves in a montage of pics from tonight of our daddies in their white tuxes holding us close in our pretty white gowns, posed against a waterfall backdrop. Romantic, and twisted because Daddy. Then they cut to me in full-freckled close-up, footage from the interviews they'd done with us weeks ago at the orientation session for the ball. I was talking about the growing popularity of chastity events in America and what a great opportunity the ceremony was for father/daughter bonding. Just gonna say that listening to myself in that clip, I totally get why the Hive stings me about affecting a British accent when I'm trying to sound smart. "I think the American Virtue Ball experience is going to change my life," I said.

Not a lie. Yet, what a fraud.

We kept watching as Jinny Hutsall's face filled the screen, long fingers brushing satin hair away from her doll-blue eyes, explaining how Reverend Jagger Jonze and the AVB have changed the way she sees herself as a woman. I have reason to believe that. She's all, like, "The American Virtue Ball has armed me with the courage to be brave at a time when our country needs heroes most." Then she licks her lips like a porn star and goes, "My father thinks I'm worth waiting for. Yours does too."

The anchor on the TV interrupted the video with breaking news. An eyewitness claimed to have seen us get into a blue Honda in the parking lot of a Starbucks in West Hills. Another saw us in a black Escalade on the 405 south, heading toward the airport. The screen cut to an image of the bomb damage at Sacred Heart High—fire trucks everywhere, with men in black uniforms leading snarling German shepherds around the perimeter of the smoldering ruins of the blown-up bathroom. Then there was a shot of the shallow creek where we buried our smashed cell phones. Fee and I were just looking at each other, going, This is not real, it's not real. But it is. We are news. We are the biggest news around.

I reached out to rap on the door, hoping one of Javier's kids wouldn't answer, because we looked like brides of freaking Frankenstein, me especially, but I prayed—well—I wished that the man's wife was awake, because in addition to asking these strangers to hide a couple of teen girls accused of bombing a school and being runners for the Red Market, I needed a menstrual pad stat.

Then we heard a twig snapping behind us. Slowly we turned. There was a man, holding a rifle, looking nervous as shit. Our conversation went like this:

"Do you know who we are?"

He just stared.

"Es tu Javier? El primo de Javier the gardener?" I asked.

"Si."

He soon saw we weren't armed, like the media reports were saying, and we couldn't have looked very dangerous, since he lowered his rifle. "They say you detonada una bomba."

We spoke Spanglish to each other. "We did not detonada any bomb, sir. Believe me, por favor."

He had a dead-thick accent. "Villains in Versace."

I played my only card, and said, "Sherman and Shelley Miller son mis padres."

"Rory. Te conozco." Javier looked around, checking the woods for bounty hunters, the mountain road for vehicles. "Por qué vienes aqui?"

"We didn't know where else to go."

"We didn't do any of what they're saying, sir," Fee said. Fee doesn't speak Spanish. Her form of rebellion. "You have to believe us."

He believed us. I could see it in his face. He gestured for us to step inside the door, out of sight from sky surveillance.

"I came here a few years ago when mi mami y papi were delivering navideños a su familia," I said as he came in behind us and shut the screen door. "Thank you. Muchas gracias."

"No." He wagged his head back and forth. "You shouldn't have come here. Muy peligroso. For me. For you. Ustedes deben entregarse a las autoridades."

Fee shook my arm. "What's he saying? What's he saying?"

"He's saying we should turn ourselves in."

Still shaking his head, he said, "La recompensa."

"We know about the bounty. We saw on our phones before we ditched them."

"One million dollars."

There was a crashing sound from the direction of the trailer next door. A metal bucket taken down by the wind, or a raccoon? Maybe it was that vicious pit bull. Or worse—the human who owned it. Javier waited a long beat, watching the Airstream from the doorway until he was satisfied there was no immediate danger, then he turned back toward us and said, "You cannot stay here."

"We can't turn ourselves in, Mr. Javier. I mean—with the bounty and everything . . . ? We have to wait until it all dies down and people come to their senses, right? All the bounty hunters, and the Crusaders?"

He nodded.

"Who can we trust? The police? Hay una razón por la que los llaman Triggerheads."

He nodded.

"Please. Please let us stay? Just for tonight, until we figure out our next move. My friend here? Feliza esta muy enferma. We've been corriendo a través de las colinas para siempre. Just, if you had a little agua? And maybe I could use your phone to call my mother?"

"Your mamá was detenido," Javier said. "Detained."

Wait. What?

"Her mother too," he said, pointing at Fee. "Morena Lopez. The Guatemalan."

"Why would they detain my mother? What have our mothers got to do with anything?" Fee was shocked.

"Los documentos de immigracíon fueron expirados." Javier shrugged. Nothing more to say.

"Oh my God," Fee said. "She's gonna kill me."

"What about my mother?"

Javier paused to study my face, then said, "Your mamá is being held on suspicion."

"Suspicion of what?"

"They say she helped you plant the bomb. They say she's involved with the Mercado Roja. Red Market."

"Okay, well, that is insane. Actually insane. I don't even believe in the Red Market. There's no proof there IS a Red Market."

"I don't believe this of her either," Javier said.

Obviously. I mean, Jesus, Shelley's barely been out of the house in three years! Is it because she went to a rally with Aunt Lilly one time and shouted, "Get your laws off my body"? Because she did consulting for an organization trying to secure safe abortions for victims of rape and incest? Now she's being accused of trading in fetal tissue and selling babies for the Red Market mafia? Sincerely?

"And what about my father?" I asked. "Has my father been detained?"

Javier shook his head. "Police say Mr. Sherman is helping with the investigation."

Helping with the investigation? I've barely seen my father since the beginning of eighth grade. Sushi dinner every few months and only because my mother bribes me with Sephora. I cannot look at him, my mother's soul mate—he used to say that all the time—without seeing the biggest hypocrite on the planet. I hate hypocrites more than anything. And he's the worst. A straight-up liar who lies. My father knows nothing about me now. How in the fuck could he be helping with the investigation?

"Please don't call my father," I said.

I had no doubt that Javier knew what had happened between my parents. People knew. After they split, Sherman married someone semi-famous, so his wedding was semi-news.

Javier nodded. "I won't call your papá."

"We can stay?"

He pointed outside. "You can stay in the shed tonight. Tonight only. If someone comes—if they find you—nunca he visto."

"Gracias," I said. "Javier, I'm sorry to . . . but I have to . . . Is your wife awake?"

He looked at me strangely. "My wife? No esta. She is deported."

Fuck. That was sad to hear. Plus, this made my next question super-awkward, because I couldn't figure out a way to describe to this savior of ours my urgent need for a sanitary napkin and my hope that his deported wife might have left some in the bathroom.

I looked at Fee, dead pale and clutching her gut, but somehow she had my back. Or my vadge in this case. We tried to string together the Spanish words—not in this order—*woman—rag—pad—blood*.

Javier took a hard look at Fee beside me and said, "You don't speak Spanish?"

Fee shook her head tragically. "No hablo español."

I explained to him in Spanish, but I'll write it here in English. "Her mother is a housekeeper and Feliza was raised with an English family since she was a baby. She grew up with us in Hidden Oaks. She doesn't speak much Spanish."

But Fee somehow remembered the Spanish word for bandage. "El vendaje," she offered, pointing at me.

I remembered a word too. "Putacachuca."

Years ago, my parents had a client who shot her husband in the foot for calling her a dirty putacachuca. My mother, hearing the word but not the definition, thought it'd be a cute name for a cat. Mommy.

Javier made me repeat—twice—"El vendaje para la putaca-chuca?"—just to make sure he was hearing right. Rough translation? A bandage for my whore's vagina. Then he checked the sky, black and empty but for the moon and stars, opened the screen door, motioned to the shed and said, "Go now."

We ran.

He could have been a rich man right now if he'd shot us, or tied us up and called the authorities, instead of giving us shelter, even if it's just this dirty toolshed. Plus, he waited out a search copter arcing over the mountain toward the beach, and then he ran out to the shed with two old blankets, and a sleeve of Saltines, and two bottles of water and a paper towel roll with, like, five one-ply sheets left. His wife had left no stash of la venda para putacachuca.

Before he closed the door, Javier warned us in no uncertain terms not to leave the shed. Then, pointing to the silver Airstream trailer next door, he warned, "Don't let him see you."

Fee and I both drank the water Javier'd brought us in one long gulp. Fee's came right back up. All of it, in a foamy mess on the ground beside us.

I was seriously about to cry, for the first time all night, because hiding in a shed and menstruation and my mother's detained and Fee's puking, but the shed door creaked open, scaring the shit out of me. It was Javier again. He pulled the pink laptop I'm typing on now from under his arm, saying, "The signal reaches out here. Puede ver todas las noticias. It's better to know. Don't try to contact anyone. No use sus medios sociales. They'll track you here if you do."

I figured the laptop must belong to one of his kids, because pink, and then I flipped it over and saw there was a Miller Law sticker with the password written in Sharpie. *America321*. A gift from Sherm and Shell. Serendipity.

———

Fee just lifted her head and asked me to stop typing because the noise is hurting her ears. "I'm so thirsty, Ror."

"I know."

"What is even happening?"

How can I answer? I do not know. "It's okay, Fee. Try to sleep. You'll feel better in the morning. And we're gonna figure it all out. Don't I always have your back?"

Fee nodded and closed her eyes, but before she passed out again, she whispered, "Malibu Sunset."

I laughed, then felt queasy, as I always do, at the mention of our most secret secret. Back in sixth grade, Fee pocketed a red lipstick at the mall drugstore. It was just the two of us running an errand for her mother, while she was running errands for Tom Sharpe. I didn't know what Fee'd done until the bald security guard grabbed us both by the arm and yanked us into this tiny, windowless room at the back of the store. He told Fee to empty her pockets and she set the gold tube on his desk. The old dude picked up the lipstick, turned it over, and read "Malibu Sunset" from the sticker on the bottom. Then he shook his head tragically, saying he had no choice but to call the police, and our parents. Store policy. He sat behind his desk, and must have hit some unseen button, because the door suddenly locked behind us.

We waited, trembling, as the guy sat there watching us squirm. Finally he goes, "I don't want you girlies to get in trouble for one little lipstick. I wonder if there's something we could do?" I dug into my pocket and found the fifty-dollar bill I'd grabbed from my jewel box on the way out the door. I was eleven yet understood extortion.

The old dude took the bill and slipped it into his shirt pocket, and told us he'd keep the police out of it but he still had to call our parents. "Or," he said. "Maybe there's something else you two girlies could give me." Fee and I shared a look. We didn't need to discuss. We turned back to the old perv, lifted our shirts and gave him a three-count flash of our tender buds in their little cotton bralets. When we pulled our shirts back down, he hit the button on his desk. The door unlocked behind us, and we bolted. We ran through the drugstore and into the mall, then out to the parking lot to Morena's empty car, and sat scream-laughing in the back-seat, imitating the slurry way he'd said, "Malibu Sunset." The ickies, as Fee called the feelings, would come later. I cried in my bed that night for betraying my boobs.

We didn't tell our parents about the drugstore perv. We would've had to say why we'd ended up in that windowless room. We didn't tell the other girls because they'd have judged Fee for stealing. I never asked Fee why she lifted the lipstick when I had money in my pocket and would've bought it for her. "Malibu Sunset" became our code for when shit was getting all too real.

This laptop is my savior. To be able to write about what is happening right now? While I'm living it? Not to mention the access to information. Knowledge really is power. I cannot even imagine, as bad as this is, what it would be like to be sitting here in the dark, in the dark.

Sherman Miller. My fucking father is helping with the investi-gation. I'm kinda tripping on that right now.

I've looked online, but Sherman's not out there shouting that I'm innocent, or calling on people to put down their guns. Like, how would Sherman be helping? By throwing my mother under the bus like he did when they split up? He did that. Threw her under, ran her over, then backed up and rolled over her again, and again, until she was flattened, like in cartoons.

I was beginning eighth grade when my father slipped away. He was suddenly gone a lot, and when he was home, he was cold and distracted. He'd go out to the patio at night to smoke cigars and talk on his phone, and I'd crack open my window and listen as he confided to my parents' friends, and associates and clients, and family members, "Shelley has lost her mind. She's gone off the deep end. She's accusing me of having an affair! How crazy is that? I think it's the menopause. She isn't sleeping. Hardly eating. I'm so worried about her, and about how all of this is affecting Rory." The game my father was playing was fucked, and fascinating.

Because my father *was* having an affair. And in between sharing his deep concern for my mother and her menopause, he was whispering baby talk to his lover. I heard it all, every repulsive, disgusting thing, but I never told a soul. Not my mother. Not even Fee. I didn't wanna break the spell. I didn't want Sherman to stop talking beneath my window, even though it sickened me, and I basically stopped eating. I wanted the truth—craved it like a drug.

My mother knew. Or at least she was suspicious enough to search through Sherman's desk drawers, and coat pockets, and phone and computer while he slept. She discovered the texts and pics and hotel receipts and perfumed notes signed by "Sugar Tits." I'm still not over that gross nickname. I heard my mom tell her sister, Lilly, on the phone, "My whole life feels like a lie." When I heard those words, something shifted at my core. If her life was a lie, then mine was too.

One Sunday morning, while the neighborhood was at church, Shelley confronted Sherman, as I eavesdropped from the landing on the stairs. My father's rage was so hot I thought it'd set the curtains on fire. Even with the evidence spread out over the glass

coffee table in front of them, he called my mother crazy. *Crazy.*
That word. Over and over. Shelley was insane and Sherman the
indisputable victim of unfair persecution. It went on like that for
weeks, as I listened to Shelley's firm prosecution and Sherman's
flimsy contradictions through the AC vent in my bedroom, which
connected to the one in theirs. And night after night, hiding behind
the curtains at my window, I held my breath against the smoke
from his Cubans and the stench of his lies. Hysterical/dramatic/
volatile/bitter. He used all the woman words. "And she's gotten so
hostile. I'm afraid she's headed for a complete psychotic break."

Sherman left less than two months after Shelley discovered
his non-affair because, as he told everyone and his mother, he
couldn't handle another day of his soul mate's crazy accusations.
He told my mother that her emotional fragility was bad for business and asked her to stop coming to the office. She actually did.
Instead of lawyering—doing the thing she loved—she fused with
the sofa, day-drinking vodka from a coffee cup, inhaling reruns of
Dr. Phil and crying for all the other cheated-on wives. She stopped
socializing with the neighbors when she realized she'd been the last
to know—another fucking cliché—and saw it in all of their faces.
Not to mention that the dads stayed bros with Sherm. He still
skulks back onto the cul-de-sac the first Saturday of each month for
poker night at Big Mike Leon's house. I heard my mother asking
Aunt Lilly on the phone why one of her friends didn't tell her. "They
are my friends, Lilly. They are."

My mother didn't have a psychotic break. She brushed her
hair and put on clean clothes most days. She made meals neither
of us could eat, asked me about school, and about the Hive, took
me shopping, did car pool and groceries. But much of the time I
had the urge to snap my fingers to remind her I was there. Or that

she was there. She was flustered by everything, and clumsy. She missed steps, missed beats, like her operating system had a bug. She looked like my mother, but when Aunt Lilly came to visit from Vancouver, she noticed it too: the Shelley Miller we knew had been all but extinguished, her light barely a flicker.

A couple of weeks after he left us, Sherman moved in with Sugar Tits—that toothy actress who sucks hairy-ass in those UpTV movies. Soon after that, he shuttered Miller Law and went to work with the actress's father in a Christian-owned entertainment corporation on Wilshire, one of those companies that make God-themed inspirational movies. My father also, hilariously, converted to Christianity. Atheist Sherman Miller even got baptized at a box church in the OC. They got married in Montecito before the ink was dry on the divorce. When I refused to go to the wedding, Sherman blamed my mother for turning me against him.

Poor Shelley. Her confusion over it all broke my heart. To be honest, it also plucked my fucking nerves, because she couldn't seem to make sense of the most obvious and basic shit. At the beginning of this semester in Psych One we learned the term *cognitive dissonance*—the confusion that arises in a person when what they believe and understand about life doesn't line up with what's happening in front of their face. My father's affair. American Holy War. Cognitive dissonance. I get it.

My aunt Lilly, my mother's little sister, has been her adviser, and therapist, because she had been cheated on too. Lilly understands what they call the Shattering. Apparently there's a shorthand for survivors of betrayal. Hope I never need to learn it. Just wanna say that I do not believe, in spite of all evidence to the contrary, that every guy out there is a cheating dick. I think there are actual human males in the world who wouldn't betray their partners. Just, I might have to move to a different zip code.

I'm glad my mother has Aunt Lilly. Especially in those early days, I was so relieved when she came to visit us, because I couldn't stand when Shelley would stop in the middle of dinner and say things like, "Remember, Ror, how Daddy would hold my face and say, 'You are mine, Shelley Miller.' He did that. Didn't he do that?" It was like she'd lost confidence in actual reality. What could I say? Yup. I remember, Shell. I mean, Sherman did things like that all the time. I'd loved that cheesy, cornball crap between them. I believed in it.

Shelley cried so much that first year. Out of nowhere, she'd just start bawling uncontrollably. I heard her describe it to Aunt Lilly as a crygasm—full-body waves of intense, gut-wrenching pain. But really? Soul mate. Soul mate? What a laughable and tragically naive idea. Are you fucking kidding me? *You are mine. I am yours.* Words. My father wanted to have his cake and eat it too, and in the end he decided he preferred the young actress slice over the aging soul mate slice.

Aunt Lilly, whose husband left her on their fifth anniversary for a girl he met online, says people like Sherman and her ex—not just men but all people who cheat—commit love fraud. She thinks there should be jail for that. Like, why does a guy who lies and cheats in business have to compensate for the losses but cheaters in a marriage get off scot-free? I see Lilly's point, but ethics jail is a scary idea.

When I think about it, though? Sherman did commit murder. He killed something fundamental in my mother. And definitely arson. He torched my family. Grand theft? He stole my innocence, which has nothing to do with my virginity.

I turned to God when Sherman left us. I was still a believer back then, just like the rest of my hive. I went to the chapel every day for weeks, praying for my daddy to come home. Praying for my mommy's heart to heal. And for the fiery death of Sugar Tits. When prayer after prayer went unanswered, I got kinda pissed. I should've just made voodoo dolls and put my faith in those badass Santería gods. Anyway, I never caught up with Christian God. He was no doubt slammed, as usual, with major American sporting events.

After a while my mother and I didn't talk about my father except when she asked me to please see him for dinner in hopes he'd put an overdue alimony check in my hands when he dropped me off from Sushi Planet. He's a bit of a deadbeat. Forgets to send money. Thank God Shell got the house in the divorce. Thank God she didn't sell it, even though I know she wanted to move. Aunt Lilly couldn't understand why we stayed in Hidden Oaks. She wanted us to come home. By home, she meant Canada.

"Too much. Too soon," Shell had said. She knew I'd die if I lost everything at once—my dad, my house, my best friends. She put me first. Like always.

Over the past couple of months my mother's started working from home, sitting at her computer for hours on end. At least, I think she's working. She says she's helping a colleague from the old days with immigration consultations. She almost never talks on the phone, except to Aunt Lilly. I admit I've been avoiding my mother lately, because sadness. Just. So. Done.

It's been a while since I last looked online.

The Internet keeps slurping Jinny Hutsall and Jagger Jonze through a fat fucking straw. Does no one sleep?

People Online just called them the Sexiest Christians Alive. With the hair and the lips and the cheekbones, and that voice, Reverend Jagger Jonze could convince the world he's the Second Coming.

Is that his plan? "Thank God for American Girls" is holding at number one. People gotta be hate-listening that shit. And Jinny Hutsall? All those pose-y shots of her in the stunning off-white Monique Lhuillier with the bloodstains? "Ethereal beauty." "Lit from within." "Modern-day Joan of Arc." The media's calling the two of them the Divine Duo. "Touched by God." "Sexy Saviors."

Jinny Hutsall? This whole fucking nightmare started when she blew into Oakwood Circle with the Santa Anas, also known as the devil winds, the second Sunday of September.

We'd been expecting her—the new girl who'd be joining our class. Trucks had been coming for weeks, bringing boxes and trunks and furniture protected by plastic and crates. Jinny Hutsall had no social accounts for us to creep, which we wondered about, but lots of parents won't allow their kids on social these days, and kids have to make fake-name accounts. We didn't think that much of it.

All we really knew was that the Hutsalls were relocating from Chicago. Our parents, even my mom, had been curious about the new neighbors, especially after they googled Warren Hutsall's net worth. Super-rich. Super-connected. Import/export king, but also kinda private and mysterious. My mother said he sounded more triple-gater than double-gater, and wondered why he'd be slumming. Good instincts, my mom.

We girls were hanging in my room that random Sunday when Delaney looked out my front window and goes, "Oh my God. The new neighbors."

We all dashed for the window as this Town Car pulled into the cul-de-sac. For a long time, no one got out. By the time the driver came around to open the back passenger-side door, the anticipation was killing us. One long leg followed the other, and Jinny Hutsall stepped out of the car. She arrived alone, which did seem a tad odd. Nothing else about her was odd, though—long flaxen hair, lean yet curvy body, huge blue eyes and plump pink lips and a tiny, perfect nose. Brooky whispered, "She looks like a sex doll."

Our faces pressed against the window, we watched Jinny juggle her big Louis tote and too many shopping bags. She must have sensed us there, because she turned to look up. We held our breath. She smiled and waved.

Zara opened my window and called down, "Wait there!"

We didn't oh-my-God the situation, or hang back and discuss, like, how nice we'd be, or if we'd be nice at all, or what Jinny Hutsall's arrival would mean to our sisterhood. We had no game plan whatsoever. The others skipped down our spiral staircase and spilled out the door, but I held back, stopped by crushing waves of panic. Like, the sound of my footsteps should've been scored with some dread-y suspense beats.

By the time I got there, the Hive were throwing themselves at the new girl. *We're so stoked you're moving in. Is that the new Louis tote? We gotta tell you everything about Sacred Heart High. We'll help you catch up with the work you've missed.* I stayed quiet, evaluating her in close-up. No makeup. But those lashes gotta be extensions. That complexion. Does she have no hormones? Bow lips. Shimmering hair. Cheekbones. The thing is, the Hive officially worships beauty, and Jinny's beauty is colossal.

"Oh my gosh, you guys," Jinny said, pretending to be flustered by the attention.

I stepped forward then, and introduced the girls one by one. "And I'm Rory Miller."

Did I see her flinch when I said my name? Maybe I'm just imagining that, in hindsight.

"Jinny Hutsall," she said.

"So you were in Chicago before this?" I asked. It was an innocent question. Just breaking the ice.

But Jinny narrowed her eyes and goes, "Oh my God—did you, like, google me?"

"Um, no, I just—we heard you were moving here from Chicago."

She threw her head back and laughed in this very actressy way. "Good, because I was feeling so violated."

The Hive giggled along with her to defuse the tension, even though they google too.

"Was your last school all-girls?" I asked.

"I've only ever been to all-girls," she said.

"Christian schools?"

"Of course."

"In Chicago?" I asked.

"Oh my goodness! Do you wanna know my Social Security number too?"

I think I already had her number. She was evasive, and phony, and beautiful, and I hated her. All I could do was smile hard.

"Would it be okay for me to carpool with you girls tomorrow?" she asked. "My mother's out of town for, like, months, and my dad's busy with the move."

Shelley was driving that week. Fuck. "Sure," I said. "We leave at eight from my house. That one." I pointed.

Jinny goes, "I'm excited about Sacred Heart. I met Pastor Hanson. He seems like a big ol' teddy bear."

Brooky cocked her head. "Headmaster Handsy?"

Delaney sighed. "More like grizzly bear."

"His paws are definitely furry," I added. "You'll find that out when he strokes your thigh by accident during skirting at chapel next week."

Skirting. Ugh. All the Christian schools do it. Row by row, we're called up to the stage and made to kneel in a line, then the Pastor takes his yardstick and bends down to measure the distance from the floor to our hems, girl by girl. If we're showing too many inches of thigh, we get detention. Skirting starts in middle school. In sixth grade you're still too dumb to know dude's copping a feel. In seventh you're too embarrassed to admit you know what copping a feel is. When you're in eighth, you and your friends laugh about it because you don't know what else to do, and by frosh year you're just sick of having feels copped. At least I was. That was when I told Shelley about Pastor Hanson's roving paws. I asked her to, like, do something, and she confessed to me that Sherman had recently decided to stop paying the monthly bill at Sacred and she'd have to "tread lightly." That's the day I found out I'd become a scholarship kid.

On the morning that Shelley went in to tread lightly with Pastor Hanson, we girls waited in the hall, listening through a crack in the office door. I was so proud. Then Shelley started to talk and I wished I were spying alone. She spent the first part of the meeting thanking the Headmaster for the financial aid, which I hadn't told the Hive about—so humiliating. Then she dropped her voice and told Handsy she'd heard murmurings about the girls feeling uncomfortable about his bare hands on their bare legs during skirting.

We all jumped back when we heard Pastor Handsy's chair hit

the floor; he must have stood up so fast he knocked it over. We froze in the hallway as he started raving about how skirting was necessary for modesty, and discipline, and Shelley must understand that he was like a clinician, a doctor. The idea that someone might think his intentions were anything but righteous enraged him. Shelley assured him it was just a rumor she'd heard on Parent Day but thought he should know. I can appreciate she didn't want this confrontation, which was no confrontation, to come back on me, but there was a part of me that wanted that fucker to know I told. Shelley chilled him out, oh-so-gently suggesting he needed to change the skirting practice or, better still, eliminate it altogether if he wanted to avoid the rumor mill.

My mom came out of the Pastor's office smiling like she nailed it, and we all just looked at her. Like, without even discussing it, we were all thinking the same thing. Thanks, but wha. . . ? She didn't call him out for the perv that he is, and she left with no resolution.

The girls and I managed to avoid Pastor Hanson until the next chapel day. He knew which pew I was in, and zeroed in on me, waiting until basically every girl in the school had followed the direction of his gaze. "We here at Sacred Heart have a long history of generosity to those less fortunate," he said, outing me as a charity kid. Then he went on to say that he'd had a visitor, a concerned parent, who came to tell him that his students might be uncomfortable with being skirted. We were silent. All six hundred girls. How many had told? How many wanted to?

Then Hanson's assistant, Mrs. Bunty, marches out to the stage with her polyester A-line and buttoned-up blouse and we girls look at each other, like, okay, maybe Shelley knew what she was doing. So now Mrs. Bunty's going to do the skirting? Slightly less disgusting. But the Pastor's secretary reaches into her blazer pocket and takes out a pair of white latex gloves, which she passes to Handsy, and he stares straight at me as he slides his hands into the gloves like he's strapping on a Trojan. "Rory Miller. Let's start with your row."

The gloves made skirting worse. Just saying.

I didn't tell Jinny Hutsall that whole long story, but I did ask her if she had skirting at her old school.

"Of course," she said.

"Okay, well, then you know the whole idea of skirting is pretty objectionable."

Jinny laughed. "You're so funny. *Objectionable*. What are you, a lawyer?"

Brooky explained. "Her parents are lawyers."

"Plus, she's a writer," Fee added. "So she likes vocabulary. A lot. And talking. A lot. You'll see."

"Stop." I knew Fee was teasing. But I loved that she called me a writer.

"Rory wrote a blog about the skirting thing," Brooky said. "Comedy gold."

My post "Consider the Femur" wasn't actually funny at all. I argued that since we all have unique body types, and our skirts hang differently, and the length of our femurs differs substantially, the ruler becomes irrelevant and the practice of skirting unreliable. I didn't out Pastor Handsy or even get into the sexism. Still, I got more likes on my skirting piece than any other blog I've posted.

"Laughter's the best medicine," Jinny said. Like, what is she? The voice of the *Reader's Digest* from Gramma and Pop's bathroom?

"Be sure to wear a padded bra to school," I warned.

"Why?"

"If your nipples show through your shirt, Bunty—Hanson's secretary—makes you wear the shame poncho."

"I always wear my sweater at school," Jinny said, clearly made uncomfortable by the word *nipples*.

"It's like a thousand degrees here for half the year—you won't want a sweater. Besides, you don't wanna look like the Crusaders. We've got a lot of those types at school. Watch out, because they'll try to recruit you with all that walkwithusinthe-light shit, like, they don't actually say shit, or any other curse, and they, like, don't go on social except to Crusader sites, so they're not exactly looped into life. They have posters of Kirk Cameron in their lockers. So."

"I'm a Crusader." The way Jinny Hutsall said those words. Like a challenge. I mean, it was a challenge.

"Oh," was all I could think to say.

Jinny Hutsall didn't wait to pounce. "Are you a hater? Like, are you a Crusader Hater?"

"No." I totally was. Am.

"Rory, right?" The way she said it—it was like she already had a file on me. Now I'm thinking, did she? Fuck.

"Rory Miller."

"Doesn't my father know your father?" she said. "I think he does."

"I don't know who Sherman knows. He's a bag of tricks."

"Sherman Miller . . . right . . . Your father's on the board at my uncle's church in Orange County. I've heard about the Millers. You're mega donors. Bless." She made prayer hands at me. Ugh.

"Mega donors? Um. No. Not me. My mom and I don't go to church. Plus, I'm Jewish."

"Jewish?" She said it like she'd never heard the word before and someone needed to explain.

The pavement tilted under my feet as the Hive stood silent.

"Wait, what? Are you being serious?" Jinny said, looking around at the others. "You're Jewish? Are you girls being real?"

"Well, my dad was sort of Jewish, but atheist before his recent conversion," I said. "His parents' parents' parents were observant. And I have, like, survivors in my bloodline. So I'm Jewish. Like not in an observant or religious way, but still." Why could I not just shut the fuck up?

Jinny turned her blue eyes on my girls, a pretty little frown between her brows of threaded perfection. "Sacred Heart allows that?"

Brooky shrugged. "You know what they say about Californian Christian schools? Jesus on the walls. Jews in the halls."

"They say that?" Jinny looked muy confused.

Fee goes, "We even have Muslim girls."

I'm an asshole for saying this, but I wished Fee hadn't lumped me in with the Muslims at that particular moment. I think even Muslims would get why.

Jinny wrinkled her nose. "Jews and Muslims? At Christian school?"

Fee goes, "Anyway, Rory isn't, like, Jewish-Jewish. They totally have Christmas."

Zee added, because Zee's always been a tad edgy with me, "But then again, she's got one of those methuselahs at the front door. So Jewish enough for that."

"It's called a mezuzah, Zee, and it's a Hebrew prayer that you put at your door."

"But you just said your parents aren't religious," Jinny said.

"They're not. They just always had one growing up, so . . ."

Jinny nodded in this way superior way, and goes, "I get it. It's, like, superstition."

And I go, "Yeah. Like putting a crucifix on the wall."

"You're so funny! It's not the same at all! Anyway, why would your parents send you to Christian school if you're Jewish?"

"Like I said, I'm not Jewish . . . that way. And I don't know what it was like in Chicago, but here, like, a quarter of the student body at most Christian schools are not practicing Christians. So. I'm just one of them."

"God moves in mysterious ways," Jinny said with a shrug. "Just, aren't there other private schools you could go to?"

Bee encircled my waist. "We've known each other since we were babies. Rory wasn't gonna be the only girl in our cul-de-sac going to King Gillette, which is public school. Other than that, there's Hippie High in Topanga. No. Crest Point. Double no. Or New Jew. It's not like she was gonna learn Hebrew."

Jinny still seemed confused.

Fee explained, "Sacred Heart is progressive. So, like, Rory has every right to be there."

So tell me, how did we go from a bunch of besties hanging in my bedroom to standing in my cul-de-sac defending my right to attend my own fucking school? Scholarship kid or not?

Jinny goes, "Progressive Christian? Oxymoron? Jesus was right two thousand years ago. And He's just as right today."

"My mother says Sacred Heart got progressive because the libtards ruined the economy a long time ago and they have to take anybody now," Zara said. "No offense, Ror."

"Oh my God, you guys. I'm an atheist anyway. So what. Like, can we flip the script now?"

"We kid Rory about being our very own heathen," Brooky said. "But Rory kicks . . . it." She'd been about to say "ass," but Jinny. Already we were censoring ourselves. Already we were shape-shifting.

"We really respect everybody's beliefs." Dee was sticking up for me too. "Rory used to be a huge believer . . . but now she's not. Even Jesus doubted."

"I don't get it," Jinny dug in, coy as fuck. "You don't even believe in Jewish God?"

"No God. Godless. Deity-free zone. That's what *heathen* means."

Jinny Hutsall peeled me with her eyes. "Heathen." She rolled the word around in her mouth as if she liked the way it tasted.

Fee opened her eyes again a little while ago. I saw her watching the moon through the window. I asked her if she was feeling any better and she said she feels like she swallowed a sea urchin. I asked her if she thinks it's possible that Jinny put something in those ganache thingies at the AVB. She made a face like I'm actually crazy. Maybe I am.

I asked her what she thought was happening. The bomb. The accusations. "Jagger and Jinny obviously had something to do with this," I said.

She closed her eyes again and went back to moaning. This is the longest night of my life. Waiting for the winds . . .

It's the Shelley Hour online right now. My mother is everywhere in the news, because of us. They're showing cap 'n' gown pics of

Shelley Frumkin from her University of Toronto graduation. Unpacking clips of her speaking on abortion rights at women's conferences from years ago. Surveillance vid from a DACA march. They showed a piece in the local paper from when she was trying to persuade Hidden Oaks to harvest the fruits from our thousands of backyard trees—oranges, lemons, grapefruits, persimmons, plums and peaches, avocados and whatever else—so that the food could go to the homeless instead of the roof rats. Nothing the media's "exposed" proves anything but that my mother has a social conscience.

Her photos. Oh Shell. Her style has not evolved past her freshman year. Same long blond hair parted in the middle. Same makeup palette—mascara and ChapStick. Same untailored shirts and roomy khaki pants. She's always stood out in Calabasas. Never leaned into the Hidden Oaks vibe. She loves the other mothers in the neighborhood, and they are, well, were her friends, but there's a language barrier. Shelley doesn't speak shopping, or hair, or mani-pedis. She doesn't understand plucking and exfoliation, or Swedish massage at Four Seasons. She buys her moisturizer at the drugstore, and she never used the facial and fillers gift certificates the other mothers got her for birthdays. I love Shelley's wrinkles, but her friends don't understand why she'd let her face tell a story when there's such a thing as Botox.

It's unbearable to think my mother is in detention. What does that even mean? Is she in a room? In a cell? God. I hope Aunt Lilly's on her way. I mean, she is. She must be. She'd never let us down. She's our rock. She got here in time to witness my birth, which she has described to me in disturbing detail. She's never missed a Christmas or Thanksgiving or birthday. She even made it to my eighth-grade graduation. Sherman didn't.

My father was joining Sugar Tits on her movie shoot in Portland instead of attending my grad night. I didn't want him there, but I wanted him to want to be there. It's not like I went, Oh, well, my dad's a dick so there must not be a God. I'd been questioning my faith for a while, plus graduation day was the same day the story broke about that slave camp in West Africa and there were all these pics of bony babies covered in flies and all those chained human beings. Then at chapel, Pastor Hanson went on about how we should pray for those African people but remember that it's all part of God's glorious plan. God's will be done.

No. Just. No. And that empty seat between my mother and Aunt Lilly at the graduation ceremony? I wanted a word for how I felt. How hard I wanted to reject my father, and God's fucking will. Heathen was it.

I think the girls respected that I knew when to leave a toxic relationship. They didn't care what I thought about God. Well, Zara did. She's just more comfortable when people believe the things she believes, I guess. Mostly we played "don't ask don't tell." Like with Santa, when you know your friend still believes and you don't challenge, like, Dude, all those chimneys in one night? The truth is I don't think any of the girls, except maybe Brooky, have ever really questioned their faith. They're not evangelical types, obviously. Not Crusaders. They're more down with the loving Jesus than the eye-for-an-eye Old Testament God. They support gay marriage and LGBTQ rights. And we're, like, feminist. We all think equal pay for equal work. Not one of us ever talked about saving our virginity for our wedding night. Not even Zee. Jinny Hutsall's cast a spell on them. She's the witch, on a witch hunt. I'm living the fucking *Crucible*.

I wish Fee would wake up. Like, wake up, and sit up, and be

well enough to talk me off the ledge. I have to figure out how to find her some fluids. I keep getting up to look out the window, wondering where I could get water. There's a hose coiled up at the back of Javier's cabin, but that's not going to do us much good. When we were little kids, you could still legit drink from a hose in California, but now irrigation water's reclaimed so not potable, and you can only drink bottled or tap, but only if the tap has a filtration system, which many poor people still don't have. I can't see any water bottles on the dashboard of Javier's truck, but I wonder if he has one of those barrel-shaped water jugs strapped to the back of his flatbed. I should go look, but there are too many moving lights still up in the sky.

So I'm sitting here in this filthy shed, basically free-bleeding all over my gown because I soaked through the paper towel wad in a second. I feel disgusted with myself, and think of the blog I wrote challenging the logic in the Bible regarding women and their monthly shedding. The Bible shames menstruating women and uses words like *untouchable* and *unclean*, but I argued it's an essential bodily function that ultimately makes conception possible. Why wouldn't God tell His people to celebrate the bleeding woman, and, like, bring her some chocolate truffles and draw her a hot bath? In theory, I was so right, but I feel so wrong.

Does Shelley have a lawyer? I mean, she is a lawyer, but does she have a lawyer? I hope she has a sweater because she's always chilly and needs layers. I hope she eats something, because when her blood sugar dips, she gets snippy. She's thinking about me, I know, and feeling my pain and fear on top of her own, but I figure she's also thinking about Sherman, and how none of this would have happened if he hadn't left us. Maybe she's right, but also, maybe it doesn't matter.

The Santa Anas have arrived from the desert right on schedule. Must be gusting at thirty or forty miles an hour out there. The blue tarp on the Airstream next door is billowing like a sail. It'll be still for ten minutes, then the wind crashes in from out of nowhere and picks up whatever isn't tied down—bang, clank, crack, whomp, whoosh, whack. It's scary. Especially when big branches from the dying oak beside the shed clatter on the roof.

I can't even believe, with the trail of blood I left in the hills, that coyotes aren't circling this shed. I heard a pack howling on the ridge earlier, but they've gone silent. I hope they've moved on. The coyote population is way out of control, and with all the attacks on humans lately I'm also pretty scared to go outside with my sloughing endometrium. I wonder if the police tracker dogs will pick up on that too? I think we threw them off our scent when we crossed the creek behind the school, but who knows? And the black pit bull next door? It's only a matter of time until we are sniffed out by one canine or another.

Look at me. This bloody white Mishka. I loved this gown so much. Eggshell satin, fitted at the bodice, with tulle underlay. Sherman had gone silent on the phone after I told him how much it was gonna cost. He choked on the ridiculous expense of the whole American Virtue Ball experience—thousands and thousands of dollars—but couldn't say no without looking bad in front of the Oakwood Circle dads. He hadn't been worried about the rift with me, or Shell, but if he couldn't go to poker night at Big Mike Leon's once a month, I guessed he'd have to curl up and die. I was delighted that my participation in the AVB caused a ton of conflict between Sherman and Sugar Tits too. I heard her over speakerphone telling my father that he was nothing but a credit card to me. Ain't a lie.

When I tried on my gown, I made a promise to myself that it was the only wedding dress I'd ever wear, because I'm never getting married. I mean it. I'm not ever getting married. But I definitely wanna fall in love. And I'm gonna have sex. We girls talk about it a fair bit. We've all chosen our cherry busters. Even Zara said she'd lose it to that half-blazed Nickelodeon kid if she met him for real. For Brooky, it's Drake. He's old, but I get it. Delaney said she'd do our piano teacher's son, who is caliente, but also spectrum-y. Fee's gone back and forth from the inked-up dude at the iPhone Fix kiosk to the valet with the tight fade at Sushi Raku.

I've been thinking about losing my virginity to Chase Mason since eighth grade. He was a frosh then, and new in town. UnCalabasas without being antiCalabasas. With all the girls who came into the library to hook up with him in the empty media room, it was clear from the start he was a total joystick, which made my crush safe—if he could basically choose any girl, he'd never choose me.

Chase used to shred me about being a prim little Catholic schoolgirl until finally, like, this year, I told him I was sorta Jewish, but actually atheist, and that my Christian school isn't Catholic. He didn't seem to know there was a difference. I tried to explain that all Catholics are Christians but all Christians aren't Catholic, the main differences being confession and Virgin Mary and Holy Communion.

My glutes contracted when Chase reached out to touch the gold crucifix hanging on a thread-thin chain around my neck. "So why do you wear this?"

I have the necklace on right now. Sherman bought it for me when I was four and a half, and asked if I could have a "*t* necklace" like the other girls. I tell myself I wear it to be ironic. I don't like to think I wear it because I'm sentimental about my father.

Chase goes, "So this is just a disguise?"

I'd shuddered because, as he handled the little gold cross, the back of his hand touched a sliver of my boob, but also because he'd just nailed me. I was in disguise. I was not who I am.

I tried to think of something flirty to say back. "That's right. I'm in disguise. Witness protection. And now that you know? Your life's in danger, Chase Mason."

"I'm no stranger to danger, Rory Miller."

I snorted at his corny line. "So if I get in trouble, I should come to you?"

He reached into his pocket and gave me his card. All it said was *Lark's Head*—along with his website address.

"Your card? You have a card, yo? That's so old-school."

"Just in case," he said.

"I'll definitely be needing this, Chase. I'm, like, super gangsta. Always looking for trouble."

He was like, "Um. Okay. Well, maybe you're also looking for a bat mitzvah band? Or sweet sixteen? Or quinceañera? We do a lot of those."

Awkward. I changed the subject. "Why Lark's Head? You guys could come up with something way fresher than that." What a powerfully uncool name for a band. No wonder they can't break outta the local scene.

"I don't care about fresh." He looked hurt. "I care about meaning."

"Lark's Head has meaning?"

"Me and Miles wrote our first song at my uncle's place on Larkspur."

"The music producer uncle?"

"Yeah. He let us rehearse there for a couple of weeks."

"So you wrote 'Eat My Cheese' there?"

He was impressed. "You remember?"

"I'm very into early Lark's Head."

"You're fucking with me right now."

"'Eat My Cheese.' Hilarious lyrics about twisted sex acts that parents do not get. Catchy with a good beat."

"Too true."

"So why Lark's Head?"

"Because Miles hit his head on the garage door when we were leaving, and because Kyle Keyboard's always talking 'bout getting head. And the drummer has a huge head. And because Larkspur is a flower, genius, and we're a bunch of dudes."

I looked forward to Mondays and Fridays at the Calabasas Library as much as I looked forward to anything in my life. I don't just crush on Chase because he's so scorch—that would be shallow. I love his mind. I love that we can talk about books and music, and our friends, and whatever's crazy on our feeds. One time I was bragging about Brooky's finish times in a track event, and he said something about his older sister being an amazing athlete, and I was like, wha...? He'd told me he didn't have sibs. I knew I shouldn't ask any more questions, though, after he shook his head and said, "She died in a car crash."

Later I tried to google her obituary in Cedar Rapids, Iowa, which is where he lived before his parents moved to Calabasas. His mom's an X-ray technician at West Hills Hospital. His dad's retired, but drives Uber and has a five-star rating. Couldn't find anything else about the Masons. I hate when people don't have proper identities online. Makes them so hard to creep. I really just wanted to see a picture of the sister whose death haunts my bae.

When I was thirteen and first started my volunteer hours, Chase told me he thought the YA book he saw sticking out of my book bag was stupid, and turned me on to literature, which he pronounced *litricha* to be funny. I loved that he read books at all, let alone novels by old black women, and dead Chinese women, and people of other cultures. Not long after I told him I was Jewish, Chase fished a copy of *Diary of Anne Frank* from the shelf. I didn't tell him that was required reading at my house and I'd read it three times already, but I did tell him I knew the book, and loved Anne, and loved her writing, and how I thought if she lived in our time she'd be an influencer. He was like, "Rory, if Anne Frank lived in our time, she wouldn't have had to hide from the Nazis and her entire life would have been different. She wouldn't have been persecuted." I thought, but I didn't say, like, Chase, Jews have never stopped being persecuted.

Deep as they got, our convos never seemed to last very long. We were usually interrupted by a blonde in a tube top jiggling in the local history section, or a smokin' redhead in booty shorts, or a skinny brunette from his school waving him over. He'd just grin at me like "what can a dude do" and motion them into the media room to conversate. I died a little. Every girl. Every time. I have no claim to Chase Mason, but it still razed me. Fee says I'm too good for Chase, and that I'm only obsessed with him because of the familiarity thing—a guy who would prolly, definitely, cheat on me? Daddy issues.

I do have daddy issues. I saw a girl wearing a T-shirt with those words in the parking lot at the public school. That is such a fucked thing to announce because it's clearly a sexual invitation, yet an acknowledgement that our relationships with our fathers shape our relationships with men. Daddy issues. Does everyone have daddy issues?

Delaney hates Tom Sharpe for having an affair on her mom and then marrying the woman, who's twenty-five years younger than he is, after her mom died. Dee had to go on Wellbutrin to get through the holy shit of it all. Zara's dad owns four Pasta Gardens and he's hardly home because work. In the time they do spend together, Zee's prickly because she resents him for always being away and wants to make him pay. Brooky idolizes her dad, Big Mike, but she's so afraid of disappointing him she can't tell him she wants to quit track and field. She can't tell him that she wants to go to design school and not the Olympics. And Fee? Oh my God. Fee's got huge daddy issues. She tells people that her dad died when she was a baby. The truth is that her father went to Mexico for a relative's wedding when she was a few months old and he never came back and was never seen again. So he disappeared, which is worse than dead. Sorta my point with Sherman.

Fee's mom, Morena, has worked for Tom Sharpe for sixteen years, and two wives. When Fee's dad went away, Morena lost their apartment, and you can't be a homeless procit without risking deportation, so Mr. Sharpe and Delaney's mom, Miss Amber, let Morena and baby Fee move into the two-story guesthouse. Delaney and Fee were raised together, like sisters, which is why they're the least best friends. Everyone, including Fee, has heard the rumors that Tom Sharpe Schwarzeneggered Morena back in the day, which would make Fee and Dee actual half-sisters, and Tom Sharpe Fee's actual father, which could make a whole bunch of things make a lot more sense.

I asked Fee once if her mom was bitter about her life, 24/7 servant to Tom Sharpe. Fee rolled her eyes at the question and started listing: Mr. Tom—both Fee and her mother call him that—pays Fee's tuition at Sacred Heart High. Mr. Tom enrolled her in dance and soccer, and piano and horses, and bought her Patriot Girls dolls and iPads and phones. Mr. Tom has made sure she's had every single thing all of the other girls on Oakwood Circle had. He threw her a huge quinceañera just last year! Bitter? No. Fee was sure that Morena felt blessed. I see the lovey-dovey way Morena looks at Tom Sharpe. I have definitely searched for genetic similarities between Fee and Mr. Sharpe. The nose, I think. The rest of the Hive and I joke about it—just a little—when Fee's not around.

Daddies and daughters. Think of all the daddy issues the American Virtue Ball has stirred up.

Sherman showed up at the Hutsalls' tonight while we girls were still up in Jinny's room doing finals on our faces. His was the loudest voice on the lanai, joking and dirty-laughing about fuck knows what. When the housekeeper came up to say the limo'd arrived, we fluffed our tulle and smoothed our satin, and headed for the staircase single file.

In the foyer, in their stupid white tuxes, the dads looked like a boy band reunion. They whooped when we appeared and whipped out their phones to film our beauty parade as we began our descent. Then there was Sherm. He wasn't recording us coming down the stairs. He was texting. Sugar Tits no doubt.

While the other girls twirled for their admiring dads, I waited for Sherm to look up from his phone. He seemed to take a sec to recognize that it was me standing in front of him. "Rory!" he said. And he smiled. But it was a fake-ass smile that I wanted to smack off his face.

I was about to say something snarky when Warren Hutsall strode over. Jinny's dad clearly thinks he's a silver fox. He is not. He does have a full head of thick white hair, but he also has a potbelly and mean, ferrety eyes.

Sherman smiled for real when Warren patted him on the shoulder. "Aren't they all just lovely?"

My father nodded, then used his sincere voice. "They sure are, Warren. I'm so proud of Rory for making this choice."

Gross. Even if he believes this is a real thing for me? An actual commitment to chastity? All he's talked about since I first brought up the AVB is his wallet. Never his pride.

We were heading out the front door when Jinny grabbed my arm and asked in a baby voice if I would "be a bestie" and run up to her room to grab her white pashmina because she had to fetch her tote from the kitchen.

My father widened his eyes at me. I widened mine back. And then Warren Hutsall, who hadn't yet acknowledged my existence, gently pushed me in the direction of the stairs, going, "Of course you'll get Jinny's pashmina, won't you, darling?"

I couldn't find the shawl. I'd seen it earlier, when Jinny was trying it on in the mirror, but it wasn't in the bedroom or closet. I found it, finally, in the bathroom. By the time I made it back downstairs and out the door, the limo was gone and Sherman was standing in the empty driveway looking confused.

Jinny had accidentally booked a too-small white limo and they were way crammed in as it was, and so they'd gone on ahead. Without me. Wha...? The drive to Sacred Heart was less than fifteen minutes, but that wasn't the point. And my girls— how did they just leave me like that? They know I have abandonment issues.

Sherm had come in a car service. My Prius was parked on the street and we obviously couldn't wait for an Uber, so instead of riding with the Hive I had to drive with my freaking father. I stepped on the gas, tearing through the empty streets, daring Sherman to mention my speeding. He did. And he couldn't bite his tongue when I didn't signal a turn at no one on the road. Then he cleared his stupid throat and goes, "That dress looks a size too small. It's pulling around the waist." I flipped the radio on to stop him from saying more. He turned the volume down. I turned it back up. He turned it down. I turned it up. He shouted over the music, "Everything okay?" Nothing was okay and questions like that just pissed a person off when they were in the middle of being torn. I turned the volume up until the windows rattled. Sherman slapped my hand away from the button and turned it down. "Gosh, Rory."

"Gosh? Gosh? No more Jesus Christ?"

"Don't be offensive. You know I found the light."

"Offensive? Sherm, you said 'Jesus Christ' a thousand times while I was growing up and you said 'Jesus fucking Christ you're crazy Shell!' when my mother found out you were cheating."

He cleared his throat. "I didn't cheat."

"Really? That's your move?"

"It has nothing to do with you."

"Um. Kinda does."

"I am your father and I deserve your respect."

"I think a person has to earn respect, Sherm."

"Like the money I earned to spend on the ball? This night is setting me back nearly ten grand. Do you understand that? I deserve your respect, and your gratitude. I deserve those things."

"I guess people don't always get what they want, Dad. Isn't that what your Rolling Stones say? And Jagger Jonze?"

"Don't embarrass me in front of the Reverend tonight."

"Um. Okay."

"What has your mother done to you, Rory? How is she rais-ing you?"

"Alone."

He hissed through his teeth. "I only agreed to this thing because I thought it'd be a chance for us to bond."

I hissed back through mine. "I only asked you to come because I had to."

He made a pout face. "RorRor."

"Don't call me that."

"I want you to know my—"

"Wife? I already know her. I creep her Zipix. Actress. Wife. Spontaneous Dancer."

"Stop."

"All that dancing must be fun. My mother doesn't dance much anymore."

"What happened between me and your mother doesn't change anything between you and me."

But you're wrong, Sherman. What happened between you and my mother revealed you to me, and changed everything. What happened broke the most important person in my world. What you did changed the way I understand love. Which is not at all. I didn't say any of that, though. I just said, "Glad you're walking in the light, Sherm. Hope you don't get burned."

We didn't say anything more until we neared Sacred Heart, and that's when Sherman sighs and goes, "Jinny Hutsall seems like a real sweetie. You could learn a thing or two from her."

A sweetie? Learn a thing or two? Little did he know all the things I could learn from Jinny Hutsall. I kinda wanted to tell him what I knew about Jinny Hutsall and see if he'd still call her a sweetie. I thought if I had to listen to him breathing in the seat beside me for one more second I'd drive into a wall.

I was shaking when I pulled up beside the white limo in the parking lot beside Sacred's Grand Ballroom, but tried to act casual when I rejoined my girls. Fee was antsy even then, come to think about it.

I whispered to her, "Can you believe I had to drive with the Sherminator?"

"That was stupid, but whatever."

"Whatever for you. You weren't the one left behind."

"You weren't left behind, Ror. You're here. Don't be all like that tonight," Fee said.

"Like what?"

"You-ish."

It was only hours ago, and with all that happened afterward it should feel like a blur, but I remember every detail from the second we walked into the ballroom—the twinkling fairy lights strangling the pillars near the stage, the flames from hundreds of candles dancing on either side of the long aisle where we'd stand to take our vows, the bleached tablecloths and gleaming dinner plates, snowy roses in porcelain vases and clouds of pale gardenias on pedestals around the dance floor. Girls in gowns. Celestial. But even before anything went wrong, I could sense a vein of malice slicing through the whiteness of it all, hiding, like a razor blade in snow.

Right away Sherman noticed that the photographer had just set up in a corner of the room and there was no one yet in line. We could be first. Just the way he likes it. So he dragged me over to the booth, where the guy posed us in front of the romantic waterfall backdrop. Sherman was positioned behind me and I could feel his breath on the top of my head. The photographer told my father to get closer. Which he did. And to wrap his arms around my waist. Which he did. The photographer told me to fold my hands over Sherman's. Which I did not. The photographer told us to smile. Which Sherman did. Snap. It was over in a second. That picture is all over the Internet now. And my face says it all.

Our portrait taken, Sherman started scouting the room for Warren Hutsall. Despite what he said, I knew my father wasn't there to bond; he was there to network. He patted my arm and said he'd just be a minute and why didn't I go find the girls. Standing there, watching him walk away? I wished he were dead. It's not that I wanted him to die. It's just, it'd be a comfort to be able to grieve the loss of him officially, and get a few casseroles and some trays of coconut squares outta the deal. The father I knew is dead, for real, and I'm gonna take a pass on a relationship with the man he's become.

I wish Shelley could take a pass too, instead of trying to reel him back to who he used to be, or whatever she thinks she's doing when they fight on the phone. When this is all over, I'm gonna find a way to convince my mother that she needs to have a funeral for her marriage, find a job outside the house and put a freaking profile on Tinder.

Brooky had gone off hand in hand with Big Mike to check out a display of photographs taken by the official photographer on orientation night a few weeks earlier. Mr. Ro and Zara were making plates at the appetizer buffet. Fee and Delaney were waiting in the photo line for daddy/daughter, but Tom Sharpe wasn't with them. I couldn't see where Jinny'd gone. So I parked myself at one of the cocktail tables near the back of the room, watching, like I do.

Jagger Jonze was in a corner of the room, set apart in his T-shirt and jeans, taller than the other men. Right beside him was Tom Sharpe, his rosacea face blooming from the neck of his white tuxedo, his mouth moving a mile a minute. Figured he was prolly pitching the Reverend on the silver Maybach in the showcase at his dealership, like he'd done with Big Mike the week before.

Jinny slithered up behind me, going, "Are you watching the fashion parade?"

I didn't like what she implied. "Yeah."

"Stay here. I'll get us something from the appi table."

I figured she'd bring back a plate of cheese and crackers or something, but she came back with these three little ganache ball thingies in a paper napkin. Whatever. Jinny sunk her teeth into one and had an orgasm, but I said no thank you, because I was just so sick of following Jinny Hutsall's lead. She pushed, "You have to try one, Rory."

I did not have to try one.

Just then Fee swished over to the table looking less than ecstatic in her beautiful gown. "What's wrong?" I asked.

"Nothing." She saw the chocolate balls on the plate, grabbed one and popped it in her mouth, hardly chewing before she swallowed. Then she grabbed the other one and did the same.

I could see Jinny was annoyed that I hadn't eaten one of the stupid chocolate balls. She didn't seem to care that Fee ate two. When Dee and Zee and Brooky eventually joined us, she didn't offer to go get ganache thingies for them. I didn't think that much of it at the time. We just stood at the little table waiting for the festivities to start, watching all the virgins waltz in with their dads, listening to Jinny snark.

"Look at that one with the braids. She must know we can

totally see her huge areolas through that polyester disaster. Does she think that's sexy? Reverend Jagger hates that."

Um. No. Jagger doesn't hate that, was all I could think. Those big nips would prolly, literally, make him spoo in his jeans. I tried to catch Fee's eye, but she was staring at the floor.

Jinny looked like a goddess in her gossamer gown. Minimal makeup, soft updo. Next to Feliza Lopez—just my opinion—the most beautiful virgin there. Why couldn't Jinny just leave everyone else the fuck alone? I definitely wondered what she'd say about me if I walked away.

We daddies and daughters from Oakwood Circle were going to sit at the head table with the Reverend Jagger Jonze, which made all of the other girls hate us, which is not always a terrible feeling. I mean, if I'm being honest, when you're hated on for being rare, or having something special, it kinda makes you feel legit. When we were called to go take our seats, Jagger Jonze did not look any of us—except Jinny Hutsall—in the eye. I wanted to ask the girls if they'd noticed, but discussion about Jagger Jonze had become verboten after what happened at the Hutsalls' on orientation night.

The dads didn't know anything about that, though. As far as they were concerned, Jagger Jonze was the perfect bro. He could talk sports, music, economics, politics and God, and when a guy goes to the bathroom, Jonze will not be hitting on his daughter or wife or sister. His celibacy is part of what makes him so appealing.

Fee leaned over and whispered to me that her stomach felt weird, and I thought maybe she was sad or whatever about her real father not being there. I wondered if I should offer to drive her home, but just then Jagger Jonze grabbed his guitar and jumped up on the stage to sing "Thank God for American Girls" as throngs of virgins gathered around his designer high-tops.

The Hive hung back at the edges of the crowd, all except Jinny, who stormed the stage with the rest, singing along at the top of her lungs. The rest of us, without discussing it, kept our distance. None of us, well, except Jinny, I guess, could see the Reverend as anything more than a fraud, not to mention a freak. On orientation night—well, Gloryentation is what he called it— the rehearsal for the virtue ceremony, Jagger Jonze showed the Hive who he really is.

But I didn't know that when I first agreed to the whole AVB thing. I was jumping off the cliff just to go along with my friends. Stupid. Just like Shelley always said. I do suffer from fear of missing out, but more than that, I've been suffering from fear of losing my best friends to Jinny Hutsall. Look what happened tonight, with Brooky and Delaney and Zara. I mean, it didn't happen overnight, but it did happen over time. I'd been right to worry.

Reverend Jagger Jonze must be stopped. To save the world from his music, and from other, darker things that I will definitely be writing about. I'm done being quiet about liars and frauds.

Tonight at the ball he debuted a new song, "Marry Me, Merilee." 'Nuff said. When the screaming and applause died down, it was time to take the chastity vow. Fee was looking really pale at that point, but she gave me a thumbs-up.

We made two long lines on either side of the white-carpeted aisle—daddies on one side, daughters on the other. Baby brides and daddy grooms lit by romantic flickering candlelight. Reverend Jagger instructed our fathers to reach across the aisle and take our hands. Tom Sharpe turned so he could take Fee's hand in his left and Delaney's in his right, then whispered to my father, standing beside him, "We are favored, brother. Praise be."

My father nodded. I tried not to wince.

I couldn't really look at Sherman. The whole pledge thing made me itchy, but honestly, I thought if I looked at him, saw a hint of the daddy I used to know, the one I still kinda ache for, I might start bawling and never stop. I just wanted to get the vows done, not eat the dinner, make some mental notes for my AVB blog and go home. I kept thinking of my mother's words. My whole life feels like a lie.

Fee and I squeezed fingers before we recited the puerile—that's what Shelley called it—pledge we'd memorized in the weeks leading up to the ball:

"I vow to respect my Father in heaven. I vow to respect my father on earth. I vow to respect the body He gave me. I vow to treat ME" (this is where we covered our hearts with our palms) "like I have worth. I vow to save, till the day I'm wed, my virtue for my marriage bed. To stay chaste in my heart and pure in my soul. Father, keep me safe and whole."

At this point we stopped to embrace our fathers before we said the final lines: "You'll always be my daddy. I'll be your baby girl. One day you will share me. Until then I'll wear your pearl."

Fee looked nervous, or maybe it's just because she was sick. She blinked to hold her focus on Mr. Tom as the dads said their vows, also in unison.

"I vow to raise you with the Lord our God, and Jesus Christ His son. I vow to head a wholesome home, free from temptation. You are my light. You are my love. And I promise heaven up above, that I'll keep you pure as the driven snow, till the day I have to let you go. I'll always be your daddy. You'll be my baby girl. One day I will share you, but until then you'll wear my pearl."

Here the dads put these sweet little pearl rings on our wedding fingers. But as I said, Fee's ring wouldn't go on. It became a bit of a thing, as Jagger Jonze saw Mr. Sharpe was having trouble and paused the ceremony while he tried and failed, and finally just handed the ring to Fee, looking super-annoyed.

There's been a shit-ton of Twitter talk about the symbolism of the pearl rings. One user said our daddies should have given us pearl necklaces instead of pearl rings because we're a bunch of incestuous cunts. His tweet included a link to pearl necklace images. I didn't get the reference, so I clicked. In case, like me, you don't know either, the term *pearl necklace* describes a beaded string of jizz ejaculated onto another person's body, often the face or neck. According to the pics? Accurate description.

The Manhattan cocktails Warren Hutsall served at the house beforehand, along with the free-flowing bar at the ball, had got most of the dads pretty sentimental. Big Mike hugged Brooky, sniffling with pride. Mr. Rohanian welled up and hugged Zara too. Tom Sharpe tried to hug Delaney, but she made a face and slipped out of his arms. Fee went to hug Mr. Sharpe, but before she could, he turned to grab a fresh cocktail from a waiter with a tray. Sherman and I just looked at each other.

The ball. The gowns. My father. The pearl ring. The whole thing. I'm an asshole. I'm a Calabasshole. And just to be clear: I don't think all people in Calabasas are odious. Not at all. Not by a long stretch. It's just, when you mix wealth and privilege and religion, and isolation from the real world, I mean, when people actually believe they deserve their shit, they're gonna tend to skew dickish.

Holy shit.

Just heard something, and it wasn't the wind. There's a truck on the road, and it's coming this way.

I can barely catch my breath. This just happened . . .

The noise I heard? I jumped up and looked out the window just as this dark pickup comes swerving around the bend and pulls into the gravel drive of the trailer next door. The sound of the truck woke Fee up, and she's all feverish and confused, and like, "What the fuck, Ror?!" I had to put my hand over her mouth and remind her where we were. Ball. Bomb. Bounty. Shed. Shh.

We squeezed each other's fingers blue as the truck door creaked open and slammed shut and a man got out, cursing in Spanish. I watched his shadowy figure stumble toward the trailer. Was this the "him" Javier warned us about? The owner of the black dog? I mean, you don't own a dog like that unless you're a scary fuck yourself. The guy ripped at the blue tarp strung up over the porch and the whole thing came loose, blew away and got snagged on a dry bush near his truck.

The guy cursed some more, and fell up the stairs, and turned the knob on the door a bunch of times before finally pushing his way inside. He started calling into the trailer, mad as fuck, going— "Perro! PERRO!" Fee tried to stand up so she could look out the window too, but her legs wouldn't hold her. I told her it was just the drunk neighbor calling for his dog, who was apparently named Perro, which actually means "dog." Original.

"Perro! Perro! Te mataré! I'll kill you," the guy yelled, and I'm seriously afraid he's gonna kill that poor dog. Then the trailer door opened and he was back outside, calling, "Perro. Perro! Cabrón! Ven acá. Come here, you shit fucker!" In the moonlight, I could see his bluish form lurching toward the shed. I ducked, and Fee and I listened to the sound of his boots on the gravel, then sloshing through the tall needle grass. Fee clapped the laptop shut so he wouldn't see the light through the window. I lunged to brace the door.

The drunk guy was still shouting for Perro, and was so near I could hear the spit flying from the corners of his mouth, but before he could reach the shed, a distant crash came from inside the Airstream. Perro? The wind? The man stopped and cursed some more, then wheeled and wove his way back through the weeds.

I peeked out the window just in time to see him go inside the Airstream and slam the door behind him. Fee whispered thanks to God and meant it. I'm glad she has God. I totally support her delusion.

Our relief didn't last long, though. The man started cursing again, and there was a thumping sound and then some banging, and I could see the whole Airstream rocking. We heard more thudding, and shouting, and then this awful whimpering that stopped suddenly. This time the quiet didn't feel like a relief. Did he kill that dog? Like, kick him to death?

Fee grabbed my leg and said, "When we go, we're taking Perro with us."

The TV is still on in the Airstream, but otherwise it's been quiet over there for a while. No movement. The lights in Javier's cabin didn't come on with all the drunk guy's drama. Javier must be a deep sleeper.

Fee's passed out again. Ragged breathing. Fuck. I'm still scared, but I'm gonna go out there. I have to get her some water. Soon. I just wanna give the drunk guy time to pass out too. Guess I don't have to worry about Perro attacking me now.

Each time I go back online, which I just did, I wanna freaking scream. How can we defend ourselves against God? Apparently groups of Christian Crusaders are now mobilizing from coast to coast declining the bounty. They wanna capture us for the sole purpose of bringing light to the Cause, by which they mean Anti-Abortion—they actually believe two teenaged girls from a Calabasas Christian school are involved in the Red Market. The hard-core faction of the hard-core faction say God has spoken, and that we must die. So we're being hunted by people who hear God's voice telling them to kill us. Fucking terrifying. Same fuckers who mock the Muslim suicide bombers, who kill for their cause and the reward of seventy-two virgin angels in the sweet hereafter. Crusaders. Fuck. They gave themselves that name even though they must know history. The Crusades were all about violence and hate.

The pendulum people always talk about started swinging hard and high around the time I was in sixth grade. I'd listen to my parents' conversations at the dinner table, and the news they had on 24/7, and we girls hung on all the celebrity accusations and #MeToo confessions just like everyone else. Then came all the abortion stuff. Fetal heartbeat restrictions. Counseling restrictions. Ultrasound requirements. Near bans and outright prohibitions.

So basically, I started middle school, got my period, some gnarly pimples, started to see the world through my gender and to question my default Christianity. My hormones fucked with my faith.

I know I can be too much with all my opinions, and my cursing, and I'm aware that my friends aren't always ready for or interested in my tirades about women's rights, especially abortion, and black lives and immigrant issues, or whatever.

In seventh grade, Delaney, who's the most tranque of us all because she takes twenty milligrams of her antidepressant every morning, called me relentless. The word had been on our vocab test. *Relentless.* Too true. I never shut up. I never give up. I ask too many questions. I'm a contrarian. So I started my blog, *This Little Light.*

I had my mother's full support, though she did insist on reading everything before I posted. My first post was actually inspired by Shelley, and a conversation she had with Aunt Lilly about Tarana Burke, the black woman who launched the #MeToo hashtag a decade before Hollywood got woke. Aunt Lill and Shelley had agreed that you can't talk about the oppression of women without acknowledging the spectrum of suffering of women from other cultures and races. When I said, "So this black woman started it, but the world only listened when movie stars spoke out?" Shelley clapped her hands and said, "Maybe that can be your first blog." She helped me research, and she read it when I was done, but I wouldn't let her edit. I needed to own my words. Still do.

I wrote the blog about skirting. I wrote a satirical blog about dress codes for boys. I wrote about how, in the interest of tearing down the patriarchy, women should consider keeping their own names—even though my mother said she'd been happy to take Miller over Frumkin. (I vow, here and now, to forever be Rory Miller.)

I wrote a blog about that black teen being pulled over for driving a red Ferrari in Calabasas. When the cops found out his dad is that Hall of Famer, they turned the near arrest into a selfie-fest.

And I wrote a long blog about abortion. At this moment, I wish I'd kept that one to myself, because right now the media and social networks are dissecting everything I've ever written, saying that my blogs contain dog-whistle messages to the Red Market. Oh. My. Fucking. God.

There's all the Jewish conspiracy shit online now too. The fact of my Jewishness is trending, but the Jews don't exactly wanna claim me. Who can blame? Jewish groups are distancing themselves by arguing that my father was unobservant, as was his father. True. And that he had a lapsed-Catholic mother. True. And that my mother's father was also unobservant, and had married a shiksa. True again. My parents and I are admittedly Jew-removed. Jew-lite is what they called it, respectfully. But whatever Jewish is, I am still part of that.

Otherness. Our subtle otherness is what bound me and Fee. From the start, it was always the two of us, indivisible within the Hive. But lately Fee and I have been keeping secrets from each other. I mean, Fee kept a pretty huge secret from me about something that happened when she went to visit her abuela in Cerritos. And I didn't tell her about Jinny Hutsall. I also didn't tell her that I'm pretty sure that what I saw Jinny do is the reason we're in all this trouble. When she wakes up, I've gotta tell Fee the truth. Everything.

I mean, maybe not all at once.

So, my confession? I spied on Jinny Hutsall in her bedroom. I've been doing it since the night she arrived. From my side window, overlooking the patio, I have a clear view into her bedroom next door. I didn't just spy on her, hiding behind my curtains—I videotaped her. It was wrong, and I know that, but you have to understand, and I hope Fee understands, that I was gathering evidence, because Jinny Hutsall is the real criminal in all of this.

The reason we're here? I think—I mean, I still don't know for sure, but I think it's because she knows about the footage on my palm-cam, which is in my room, behind my big dresser, where I dropped it yesterday. And I think she told Jagger Jonze. And the two of them wanted me shut down.

Was that seriously only yesterday? It feels like a thousand years ago.

I nearly broke my stupid toe trying to move my heavy dresser to get my stupid camera. It's super-small with a super-long lens— my birthday present from Aunt Lilly. I don't know if I hope authorities have found it or hope they haven't. If they see what I recorded, Fee and I could be vindicated, or maybe they'll destroy it. If they didn't find my camera, I need someone I trust to get it from my room.

Zee, Bee, Dee—my girls? Fucking pain of betrayal.

Where are they now? Delaney, Brooklyn and Zara? Our sisters? Our hive? Well, it appears they're pulling an all-nighter with Jinny Hutsall and Reverend Jonze, still dressed in their white gowns because gorge, tweeting at us from their little command post in the cul-de-sac, begging us to turn ourselves in. They've set up tables and a coffee station for the investigators, and they've been posting selfies with hot cops, and quoting Sinner Scripture that they multi-tag with sad-angry-pukey-face emojis. Like they've ever tweeted scripture in their entire lives. Traitors.

And my father. Sherman Miller is still "helping with the investigation." Would it occur to Sherm that I might remember Javier's cabin in the woods? That we might come here? Doubtful. On the news they've shown pics of him with Sugar Tits, leaving their stunning mansion in Hancock Park. Where are they going?

Before my parents split, my mother often brought up the idea of downsizing to a small place near the old Farmers' Market or in the Hancock Park area. Sherman said he'd shoot himself in the head before he'd relocate because traffic, but I think it was more the downsizing thing, like, his ego wanted to upsize, upscale, upgrade. He wanted more, not less. Shelley never really cared for Calabasas, but Sherman loved our life, he said, plus I have to admit that I'd have pitched a holy fit and died if they'd made me leave my hive. Never. No.

"There's no place to walk to here," my mother used to say. There are actually many places to walk—clean, wide sidewalks in Hidden Oaks, beautiful hiking trails in the mountains—just no place to walk *to*. Her big-city soul never got used to the suburbs. People use that term "fish out of water" as if it's so whatever. But fish actually die when they're taken out of water. So.

I wonder what it was like for my parents when they came to America as new immigrants. California has the highest population of expat Canadians anywhere in the world, but Shelley said it was still a bit of a culture shock—the cars, the money, the swimming pools and movie stars in the Hollywood Hills where they first lived—especially for her. Shelley grew up in a humble Toronto townhouse, daughter of two hard-working parents. My beloved Gramma and Pop.

Sherman grew up rich in Winnipeg, dreaming of the SoCal life—sunshine and ocean breezes, year-round golf, and tennis. He'd tell people they left Canada because they hated the cold. Shelley would correct him: "You hated the cold, babe." I thought that was an incredibly weak reason to just up and leave your country, until we spent one magical but brutally cold Christmas with my grandparents and aunt in Toronto.

When he started law school, Sherman had aimed to become a defense attorney and make big money handling celebrity cases in Hollywood—that had been his goal. Then he met Shelley Frumkin, busty and blond, with big green eyes that look into, not at, a person. I'm sure Sherman loved her passion and her spirit and her brain, but I know what really got him sprung: Shelley Frumkin was the kind of woman who put others first. Sherman needed to be first. Match.

After my parents were selected in the immigration lottery, they headed for the coast and found jobs, together, at a firm that did a lot of work with immigrants. Long before I was born, they went out on their own to become Miller Law. Work didn't stop when they left the office. Phone calls. Field visits. Computer time. The more hours they logged, the more successful they became, the more money they made, the happier Sherman was. But Shelley never made peace with money, unless she was spending it at a discount store. Even before Sherman left us, she bought her clothes at Dress for Less. And she insisted on doing so much pro bono and charity work. I guess they never really wanted the same things.

I'm the reason they ended up in Calabasas. Shelley was nearly forty when she got pregnant with me after years of failed in vitro. Neither she nor my father believed in God, but they still called me their little miracle. When Shell was just a few months pregnant, they moved from not-kid-friendly Hollywood Hills to very kid-friendly Hidden Oaks. My parents moved for the reasons that most people do these days. First and foremost? Clean air. Shelley couldn't bear the idea of raising her child in the coral fog of pollution that hung heavy over their Hollywood home. Pollution was prohibited in Calabasas, driven out by the coastal wind currents and trapped on the other side of the valley. My parents wanted me to have the best. Best air to breathe. Best schools to attend. Proximity to the ocean. Natural environment. Huge house. Piano.

Horseback-riding lessons. The best of the best. But I truly wonder if the best is actually best. For anyone.

I ended up at Sacred Heart because that's where my parents' neighbors and friends—the Leons, and the Sharpes, and the Rohanians—were sending their kids. Five impressive buildings on fifteen hillside acres—the Grand Ballroom and chapel on the south side, the elementary, middle and high schools on the north, two Olympic-sized swimming pools, three sports fields, rigorous academics. I'd begged to go to Sacred Heart Nursery School with my little besties when I was four years old, so Sherman and Shell toured the incredible campus, and met the swarm of caring teachers, and drank the Christian freaking Kool-Aid. They didn't worry that I'd be the only non-Christian at Sacred because I'd actually be one of many non-Christians at the school. People in Calabasas send their kids to the "best" school, and it's just so whatever if Jesus goes there too.

Did my parents ever discuss that I might be sucked into the Christian vortex? Did they understand the magnitude of their experiment? Or were they just relieved—like they could cross me off their list? Rory happy with friends. Check. I mean, the cul-de-sac is a village and that village raised me while my parents were off saving the world, or whatever Sherman was doing all that time. Not to say that they were absent, especially not Shell, but they weren't always present either. And they never felt guilty about working late or business trips, because they knew I was happy with my friends. At home in their homes. Kissed good night by the neighborhood moms. The God stuff? Guess they figured that at four years old I'd be able to figure all that myself.

Guess it's no surprise I'm fucked-up. My friends and I lead such confusing lives. We write essays about Jesus's love for the

poor and disenfranchised then go shop Louis and Prada. We
laze around our pools snarking on those who have not, idolizing
those who have a shit-ton. We're jumping back and forth all day
long—spiritual double Dutch—and it makes me seriously dizzy.
I see it. Really. Clearly.

I've had a front-row seat to the grooming of Christian women.
Women must be quiet, and women must not hold authority over
men, and women should stay in the kitchen and let their husbands lead the household, and the world. I mean, it basically says
all of that in the Bible. But me and Brooky and Zara and Delaney
and Fee, we have never been down with that sexist crap. And lots
of the other girls aren't either. Honestly, bet half the virgins at the
ball tonight will be hooking up by end of senior year. And some
of them, yes, a few of those Christian girls, will hit up a Pink
Market contact for a morning-after pill, or an abortion.

I wrote my blog about abortion in freshman year when it was
all anyone was talking about. My mom told me about *Roe v. Wade*
and her opinions on a woman's right to choose years ago, when
I was prolly too young for the conversation. I watched how it all
went sideways as the Crusaders got more violent and started setting bombs at abortion clinics. Aunt Lill said the Pink Market
was born in one big push because social media. Word spread
through the ether, and girls whispered at school, and all of this
was happening as I was asking questions about God and religion
and a woman's control over her own body.

Then a guest speaker came to our school. A little leprechaun-
lookin' priest who introduced himself as Father Joe. He told us
he'd been invited by Pastor Hanson to join us that day to share his
"Love of Life." But first, he said, he was gonna show us a video,
which he did—an eight-minute montage of ultrasound images

with fetuses doing somersaults and sucking their thumbs in amniotic fluid, scored by a children's choir singing "Amazing Grace." We Sacred girls were just looking around at each other like wha...?

After the film ended, the priest took the mic to explain that the film we'd just seen of the miracle of life in the womb was taken from fifty recent mandatory ultrasounds performed in one of the states where abortion had yet to be banned outright.

"Fifty innocent lives," Father Joe said, his voice cracking. "Forty-nine angels." He motioned to the back of the room and this adorable little three-year-old boy with blue eyes and white-blond curls comes running down the aisle and up to the stage and into the priest's arms. Father Joe picked up the scared little boy and held him high for all to see. "This is David. The sole survivor."

The rest of the girls clapped loudly as little David began to cry, but I was boiling with rage. Like, first off, don't do that. Don't show fetus images to emotionally manipulate us and confuse the issue. And don't bring this terrified little sweetie onstage so we can applaud him for being unaborted. Plus, how formally stupid is it to essentially say that the mandatory ultrasound only changed the mind of one out of fifty people, who might have made a different decision anyway? Not exactly a point for your side?

After school, hanging in my room with the Hive, I went off about the whole Father Joe thing. To shut me up, or shut me down, Zara declared abortion is murder, and too upsetting to talk about. Zara'd never shared that opinion before and it pissed me off to think the priest's stunt might have swayed her. Delaney said she thought God would totally understand abortion in the case of rape or incest, but was undecided on what God might feel about abortion in other circumstances. Brooky said God gave us the right to choose, and people should stay out of other people's business. Fee didn't say she thought that abortion is murder, but she did call it selfish, saying, "What about adoption?" because no matter what, it's only nine months, and what a beautiful gift to give a couple who can't have a baby. That's so Fee.

This past year has been vile. All those celebrities being outed for having had "illegal abortions"—doesn't matter if it was yesterday or twenty years ago—and their social accounts bombed, and their careers ruined. The baby-daddies who were part of the unplanned pregnancy? Sometimes even financed the crime? They shrug and move on from the new scarlet A. Abortion. Fucking abortion. The president seems to have thought endorsing the business of purity balls would put an end to sex before marriage and cut down on illegal teen abortions. They seriously thought that putting condoms behind the counters with an ID requirement would stop teens from having sex. And that making birth control pills and morning-after pills impossible to get would create a society that would evolve past the need for Planned Parenthood or legal abortion clinics. They call the measures a way to encourage American "repopulation" and "repatriotation"? Ugh. You hear rumors about pregnant girls being sent away to these private birth houses, but what if some of those birth houses are actually run by criminals? Guess when you think of it, the government created an opening for an organization like the Red Market. Maybe it does exist.

For the Hive, the conversation about abortion is hypothetical anyway. It's not like we know any girls who have needed an abortion. Or even any girls who've actually had sex. So abortion is an abstract idea to us, really. Plus, I mean, seriously, in that position? We say the things we say, but who knows what any of us would do if we got pregnant. Even Zara. Who knows?

Since the Social Policy lady from my school creeps all our

social accounts, I was careful not to take a stand for or against abortion in my blog, but made the case that no matter personal opinions, or state laws, abortions are still going to be performed. My mother helped me research some horror stories from history when women tried to end their pregnancies by throwing themselves down the stairs or performed surgery on their own wombs with knitting needles and coat hangers. The Social Policy lady didn't say a word about it, but our health teacher, Miss Vogelvort, said she'd read it, and would pray for me.

Fee is moaning beside me. I don't know what's happening. She might just be having a bad dream? It started a couple of minutes ago and she's getting really loud. Fuck. I'm afraid someone might hear. I'm gonna try to wake her up.

I woke Fee up to stop the moaning, but she's confused and crying for water. I have no choice, I gotta go out there. At least the winds have kicked up and the sky's clear of low-flyers. Poor Fee.

I checked the dirt road that leads away from this sketchy little neighborhood. No cars. No lights. I checked the Airstream next door. The television was still on, so it was possible the drunk dude was awake, but more likely he was passed out. I also thought of Javier's words, "Don't let him see."

The Santa Anas fought back when I tried to open the shed door, and they lashed my face and bare arms as I dashed through the weeds toward Javier's truck. There was no barrel of water in the flatbed. No half-drunk bottles. A quick search of the cab turned up nothing.

I looked over at the drunk guy's truck. I had to check. So I ran toward it in a crouch, my eyes on the windows of the trailer—terrified the guy'd see me. I hid behind the truck and checked the flatbed. No water jugs or bottles. I ducked and flattened, moving closer to the cab to see if he'd left anything inside there. I couldn't believe it—a small bottle of freaking Gatorade on the floor of the passenger side. So not just water, but electrolytes and sugars and whatever to make Fee feel better from all the retching, right?

The truck door hinge screeched when I tried to open it. I stopped and held my breath, afraid that drunk guy was gonna come out with a shotgun. Plus, I'm thinking, What if he knows about the bounty? What if he recognizes me from TV?

Finally, I eased the truck door open and leaned in to snatch the Gatorade. Then I saw something moving in the trailer through a crack in the broken dog door. The drunk guy? Perro? I didn't stick around to find out. I grabbed the bottle, closed the truck door as quietly as I could and ran back to the shed. I looked out the window to see if anyone was coming out of the Airstream. No one. Nothing moved. Nothing happened. Finally, I sank down beside Fee.

She couldn't believe what I was holding in my hand. "Gatorade?"

She snatched the bottle out of my hand, uncapped it, raised it to her lips, and gulped and swallowed, and gulped and swallowed until the bottle was empty. She wiped her mouth with the back of her hand. Then she looked up at me with this face like she was gonna die. I didn't know what was happening at first. And then it hit me. Pee? Oh my freaking God, was that pee in the Gatorade bottle?

Fee took a couple of deep breaths. She was actually surprisingly calm when she finally said, "Tequila."

"Wha. . . ?"

"Rory, there was freaking tequila in the Gatorade."

I sniffed the bottle. I'd sipped from a margarita once or twice. I know what tequila smells like. Jesus. Just. Jesus.

Fee didn't throw up, which was shocking since she'd announced she was definitely gonna hurl, and I mean, tequila. She just laid her head back down and murmured, "My mom's gonna kill me."

I have no idea how much tequila was in that bottle, but I think she's passed out drunk now. Fantastic. I'm looking at Fee in the shards of moonlight streaming in from the gaps in the roof, mouth-breathing beside me. If she was already poisoned, what is alcohol gonna do? What if she's too sick to move when Javier comes back to help us? Then what?

I'm exhausted, but too afraid to sleep. Going online and reading the news and tweets is making me crazy, yet I can't stop myself. Fucking Pastor fucking Hanson is up in the middle of the night, tweeting out our school records and detention stats. He's calling me a "well-known agitator." He used that word—*agitator*. He's saying that Fee is insubordinate and points to her numerous skirting offenses. She did get a lot of skirting detentions, but that's only because she and Delaney sometimes mixed up her medium-sized skirts with Delaney's small.

Fuck. You. Pastor. Hanson. Fuck. You. Sacred. Heart. And God? Where the hell is God? Doesn't he see Fee here in pain and despair?

I honestly think I'd still believe in God if I hadn't found out how haterish He is. You really start to get that lesson when you reach middle school and start taking health class with Miss Vogelvort, whose eyes went crossed after her last botched facelift. We didn't talk about puberty or the reproductive system or nutrition in her class. No, we talked about the gays, and how much she, and God, hates them. I wanted to point out to her that Jesus is God, and if you really look at it, His profile is totally bi. He was hot for that prostitute, but then again, the Apostles? I just can't imagine that the most awesome and influential schizophrenic who possibly ever lived would hate on anyone. Not gays. Not Jews. Not Muslims. Not Hindus, and not even Mormons—well, except for the child-bride fuckers—and possibly Scientologists because cult.

Vogelvort warned us one day about the need to resist our growing "urges" when we're alone, because masturbation is a sin. She quoted a Bible verse, which isn't in the actual Bible, about "wasting seed." This, in an all-girls school.

I despise Vogelvort. We all do. Brooky does a hilarious Vortie imitation using this witchy-poo voice. "Girls. When the devil tempts you in your bed at night, think of my face and you'll get a fright. Imagine I'm watching you. With my right eye. No, my left. No, my right. Whatever. You're all going to hell!"

Brooky was right when she told Jinny Hutsall, that first day we met, that I only went to Sacred because of my friends. One day when we were in eighth, baking at Zuma Beach, I floated the idea of changing schools. The girls had laughed at the thought we'd leave Sacred, even with its stupid restrictions and bogus teachings. Even Fee thought I was joking. I mean, who leaves the best? Though I was having doubts as to whether it was the best. And I wasn't brave enough to leave the school on my own, especially since my parents had just split.

Our Sacred Heart campus sits almost directly across from the public school, King Gillette High. We girls stand behind our huge iron gates each morning, pulling at our regulation high ponytails, wilting in our woollies, watching the circus on the other side of the road. Sometimes I catch sight of Chase Mason hopping out of his Jeep, then wish I hadn't, because he's usually being molested by some Lark's Head fangirl who's, like, flopping out of her beach-wear because no dress code.

The public school kids seem like a different species—dry-humping on car hoods, French-kissing on benches, danger-ous-driving in the parking lot. Our teachers refer to them as Sodomites, and during our morning "Conversation with God" we pray for the lost children across the road. Maybe I should have been part of that tribe, instead of a secular fish swimming against the Christian current.

That's it. No more skirting. No more sexism. No more Handsy. No more Crusaders. No more God.

I'm leaving Sacred Heart High.

Keep hearing noises outside. Keep checking out the window, but no one's out there. Just the wind. There are a few copters in the sky—prolly the fire department machines that can handle the high winds—but they're far away and not a threat right now. They're concentrating their search at the beaches and all those homeless communities around the Santa Monica Pier and the tent cities in the canyons of Bel Air and the dry via-ducts downtown. There are hundreds of reports of us being seen among the homeless. People say we're handing out wads of cash so the vagrants will hide us behind their shopping carts and cardboard shelters.

I read the comments again, of course. Fuck. Me. I remember that each time I pressed Post on one of my blogs, I hoped a hundred people would read it. Now thousands of people are reading shit I've written, all the way back to middle school, and misinterpreting and misquoting. And then, also, somehow, my texts and chats on that app we girls thought was private? They—whoever they are—found it all. The thing is, I swear a lot. We all curse. But especially me. Memes of me cursing are everywhere this hour. And people are, like, freaking out that a girl who goes to Christian school swears like a normal human. One Crusader tweeted that someone should cut out my devil tongue. People are blaming Shelley for raising a potty-mouthed, baby-killing bomber. Nice. Jagger Jonze is flaming me too, tweeting about how he knew I was trouble the first time he met me, on orientation night. Hilayly. Considering what happened that night.

My mother doesn't swear. Not that she's offended by swears, it's just not her nature. But I bet even she's let a few *fuck*s fly tonight. My poor mommy. Authorities still aren't saying if, or when, they're going to release her. She doesn't know if I'm dead or alive. She doesn't believe what they're saying about us—I know that much. She's just scared for me. And for Fee. I hate so much that Shelley's alone. What about Sherman?! Why's he not making some statement that Shelley Miller's a good person and the accusations against her are false.

The old Sherm, the one who loved my mother, was an irreligious liberal who'd quote Confucius or Shakespeare when the other dads threw down their Corinthians. Where is that man now? My daddy? The one who'd scoop me up in one arm and hug my mother with the other and, just like that, make us whole?

He left three years ago and he left again tonight. But Jesus, he must have heard about the bomb exploding in the bathroom right after he left the AVB. I've searched the news footage of the bomb site for Sherman's face in the crowd behind the barricades. I guess he went home to Sugar Tits. To help with the investigation. Has it occurred to him that we didn't set the bomb—that we were actually meant to die in that explosion?

I'm so tired. And this night is so long and it's more than a little bizarre to know that thousands and thousands of people have spent these dark hours obsessing over us.

I hope Aunt Lilly's headed to California by now. I hope my mother was able to call her from jail. Come on, Aunt Lill. We need you.

Jagger Jonze just tweeted that he's going to do a two-hour special segment of his *Higher Power Hour* in the morning to talk about me and Fee and the AVB. Genius marketing. Overnight superstar. His franchise business must be exploding too. He's also announced a free concert at the Santa Monica Pier tomorrow night. Fireworks at midnight. They're expecting record crowds. Everyone's sure we'll have been apprehended by then, or shot dead. The concert will be a celebration that God's will has been done.

None of this, not any of it, would have happened if Jinny Hutsall hadn't moved to Oakwood Circle. Freaking lunachick. I can imagine her looking at herself in her mirror and going, "Mirror God, Mirror God on the wall—am I, like, the hottest, most radical Christian Crusader of them all? Amazing! I will spread your word, Mirror God, like rounds from an AK-47, and I know that you will totally, like, bless me with my own Amazon or Netflix series or recording contract or talk show. Amen."

Insta-polls say the country is split down the middle on our guilt or innocence, with the big cities being for us and the Southern states overwhelmingly against. Shouldn't actual evidence decide guilt or innocence, not freaking polls? I'm torturing myself. Each time I click on a link, I sink a little deeper into the dirty shed floor. That cognitive dissonance again. Do all people live in that state now?

The Internet is saying Zee is a twin for Khloe Kardashian. I mean, no one has ever said that Zara Rohanian looks remotely like any Kardashian ever before. Zee is Armenian, so I guess there's that. They've been showing pics of Zee's fam—Mrs. Ro with her pubey black hair and too-red lipstick and Mr. Ro with his handsome face and hairy hands.

Brooky and Delaney are getting a lot of media attention too, obviously. Everyone's saying how Brooky's family looks like they stepped out of *Cali Fashion Daily*, which is too true. Big Mike was in the NFL for a minute and he's definitely the alpha male on our cul-de-sac. Bee's mom, Verilyn, owns a Pilates studio where she trains celebrity clients. Miles is taking a gap year before college, playing bass in Lark's Head with Chase Mason. Miles is fine as fuck, but too close to crush on. He's more like the jerky big brother to all of us. Well, except Fee, who acts annoying whenever he's around.

The press is digging deep. Talking to everyone. But they've got everything wrong. For example, Delaney's mom, Amber, died when Dee was eleven, not eight—we girls had just started middle school. I was spying out my front bedroom window one night back then, and saw Tom Sharpe tonguing a skanky redhead in a blue van parked up past the Leons'. I told my mother. She told Amber. Amber died. Not just like that. But in stages.

After the affair with the redhead was out in the open, Tom asked Amber for forgiveness in front of the whole congregation at Sacred Heart. She forgave. They hugged it out and everyone cried and clapped—not that I was there, but I heard all about it.

Business at Sharpe Mercedes went up thirty percent. Lookin' Sharp! Snap. People love redemption. And public confession. I remember the dinnertime conversations between my parents around that time. Sherman was Jesus-Christing his way all over the house about what an idiot his friend was. *Jesus Christ, what was Tom thinking? Jesus Christ, poor Delaney. Jesus Christ, Amber must be humiliated. All for a piece of ass? Jesus fucking Christ.*

My mother loved my father's outrage over the affair so much I'd had to put three pillows over my AC vent to cover the sound of the headboard in their room. Ugh. The truth is I also found my father's disgust about Tom Sharpe reassuring. Sherman would never risk hurting me or humiliating his soul mate. He would never, ever, in a million years, risk everything for a piece of ass.

Tom Sharpe was repentant at church, but he actually kept up the affair with Kinga, a twenty-year-old waitress from Sagebrush Cantina, and everyone, including Dee's mom, knew it. One rainy morning Miss Amber was heading home after car pool when she got an alert on her spy app: texts between Tom and Kinga. She called her therapist for an emergency phone session and stupidly thought she could drive home in the middle of her breakdown. She lost control of her Mercedes SUV and landed in a ditch—broke both of her legs and one of her arms and hit her head hard on the dash. She was in traction for two weeks. The day before she was supposed to get out of the hospital, she died from a blood clot. Delaney blamed her dad. She doesn't know that my spying was the thing that opened the Pandora's box in the first place. I guess she will when she reads this. If she ever reads this. I'm sorry, Dee. I'm so fucking sorry.

She was pretty shattered by it all, but her prescription for Wellbutrin seemed to help. Her hatred for her father simmered, but didn't boil over the way mine did when it happened to me. Brooky and Zara had hated Tom Sharpe for breaking our friend's heart and for ruining our portrait of perfection. And then, when Sherman left Shell and me for Sugar Tits, we all blamed Mr. Sharpe for infecting my father with upgrade syndrome.

Fee never quite hated him, though. She's always been respectful and grateful to Mr. Tom in a way that none of us are to our own fathers. A few years ago she joked about getting a saliva swab and sending it off to Paternity.com so everybody would just shut the fuck up about him being her father. Sometimes I wonder if she did. And he is.

Cable news keeps replaying vid of Mr. Sharpe in his white tuxedo in the parking lot last night, throwing his hand up in front of his red face, saying, "No comment." His cheating crimes offered him a chance at redemption, but his association with the Villains in Versace has people calling for a boycott of his dealership. He must be worried. And pissed. But still—why doesn't he stand up for Fee? Biological or not, he's always called her his "other" daughter.

Being here, bloody and gross in this small, dirty shed, makes me long for the cloud of my canopied bed. I know that makes me a princessa, which is something I've obviously struggled with. On the one hand I really like my beautiful house and nice clothes and designer purses, but on the other hand I know I kinda suck for having so much shit. I talk about it with Aunt Lilly, who shakes her head a lot when she visits Calabasas, and sums her feelings up by saying, simply, "You live in a bubble. This isn't real life." My mother agrees. "It's true. Oakwood Circle is not real life."

I have dual citizenship, which makes me feel sophisticated. I

travel alone to stay with Aunt Lilly in Vancouver at least once a
year so I can experience her version of real life. She lives in a one-
bedroom apartment in a tall, round building that looks out over
the water. We walk the miles of seawall and eat at ethnic restaurants—it's our thing. And she takes me to movies, because her job
is online movie reviewer. And we always hit up the Roots store on
Robson, this oh-so-Canadian athleisure-wear company, because I
like to bring the Hive back Ts and sweaties from there. Represent.

Aunt Lill is fifteen years younger than my mother, and doesn't
have kids. We can talk for hours. About everything. Religion,
meaning her disapproval of my Christian education. Boys, meaning
Chase Mason. Love, meaning the heartbreak of the Frumkin girls.

Fee's the only one of us, besides me, who's been out of
Calabasas, if you don't count day trips, and resort vacays, or ski
week in Mammoth—and you shouldn't. Fee's seen things. For
two weeks each summer she's dragged off to stay with her father's
family, her abuela and some uncles, in Cerritos, fifty or so miles
away. She chills with her cousins and, like, runs through the sprin-
klers old-school, and hangs out at some sketch mall, and sleeps on
a cot on a screened-in porch. She doesn't talk about Cerritos all
that much, except to complain that she has to babysit the younger
kids all the time, and that her grandmother hates her because she
doesn't speak Spanish.

Well, Fee didn't say much about Cerritos until recently . . .

Los Angeles has the highest population of homeless people in
America and lots of them are undocumented or procits. Fee knows
this. The world knows this. But the rest of the Hive doesn't. I mean,
they do, but they don't. There are dozens of tent cities and homeless encampments, one of them just a few miles from us, but they
might as well be another country, or planet. One time I suggested

we could get some good community hours by going to help at one of the soup kitchens, but all the parents except Shelley put the kibosh on that idea because they believe the rumors about homeless people spreading necrotizing fasciitis.

My parents took me to sketch parts of Los Angeles to see the tent cities when I was young, and the stretch of dirt road where the hoboes beg, and they drove me down to the beach one starry August night to see the meteor shower. Instead of shooting stars, we ended up watching these little groups of vagrants sneaking past the guards to wash themselves in the sea.

We Millers served Thanksgiving meals to the homeless at City Hall every year too, until the crowds got too big and there was that riot. I was relieved when my mother told me the dinner was canceled and we were going to join the Sharpes for turkey and trimmings. To be honest, I was scared of the hoboes. Not gonna lie. Hungry and haunted, stinking of pee and cigarettes, coated with a fine layer of dust that blurred their edges like a filter app.

I've been to the homes of Sherman and Shelley's clients, the crappy trailers with no running water, and tiny shacks with cockroaches and mice, and cabins with ten mattresses on the floor, and also some sweet little places, all done up and tidy, and a few supernice places—people who'd been in America for a while and done well. Before we went in anywhere, my mother would warn me not to ask for anything but to eat a small amount of whatever was offered, and not to notice or make faces if the place smelled, and to sit if I was pointed to a chair, even if was dirty.

At one house they made me wait in the dusty yard with a wailing, tomato-faced baby in a playpen. The mother had instructed me in Spanish not to pick the baby up, before she went inside to talk business with my parents. The baby was one or two—I'm not good at baby ages—and had scabs on her little arms, dried banana in her wiry black hair, purple stains on her torn dress. This tragic baby was looking at me, crying hard with her arms outstretched, and I just couldn't ignore her. I lifted her out of the playpen and put her on my shoulder and bounced her around like a boss until she finally fell asleep. She reeked, but I didn't care. I felt like Beth March from *Little Women*, which we were reading in English at the time, kinda rare and saintly, until I remembered Beth March caught scarlet fever from the babies she cared for, and I wondered why the kid's mother had said don't pick her up, and I started wishing my parents would hurry up because shower.

I found these visits so stressful that after a while Sherman and Shelley were fine to let me wait in the car, checking my social and texting with my best friends about when we'd start our next cleanse or whatever, as they delivered cases of water and buckets of hope. I guess at some point I accepted that I'm more of a Jo March than a Beth.

I've been thinking about that stupid show we watch—*Hot'n'Homeless*. Those screechy hosts who spaff all over their makeovers, the attractive scrubbed-up homeless people—some of them are definitely mentally ill—that they pour into designer clothes, and teach how to walk in heels, or Florsheims, and do the intentionally hilarious mock job interviews with. When the cameras stop rolling, you know those people get dumped back onto the streets, where they prolly get all their swag stolen. Fuck. Why do we watch that show? Why do I watch that show? I can't help thinking of all of the ways I'm responsible for creating an appetite for actual shit.

Have to stop typing for a bit. Hands cramping.

Fee's just so pale. Even in the moonlight I can see her skin has turned gray, and she's got huge dark circles under her eyes. Question? Is it okay to describe a person's skin color in any way, shape or form when you yourself are not a person of color? Or is it better not to mention a person's skin color so as to make it irrelevant, even though we all know it's totally relevant, in hopes that society will eventually become truly color-blind? Like, last year, this new girl at school was asking us to point out Brooky on the track. Zee said, "She's the tall one." Dee said, "She's the one with the blue shorts." When the new girl still didn't see her, I said, "The black girl near the long jump pit." The way the girl looked at me? Like, racist much? But . . . wha. . . ? Is it racist to describe a black person as black? When I told Brooky what happened, she laughed. Was I supposed to say African-American? Brooky shook her head. "Too many syllables." We really do hate syllables.

The thing is, I don't wanna be a dick. The racism thing? The white privilege thing? The white feminist thing? I want to understand it all, and acknowledge it beyond the obvious, and I actually wanna get this shit right. Feels like there's a wide margin for error, though.

I've been so worried about Shelley, but Fee's mom, Morena, is in serious trouble too. The Internet says she might be deported to Guatemala. Fee will die when she finds out. Morena's procit card really had just expired and she hadn't been able to process her renewal appointment online and the phones were always busy and she'd been so swamped getting Fee ready for the chastity ball and it wasn't her fault. There are so many pitiful clips of her crying into her hands. As if her daughter's disappearance and all the Red Market shit isn't enough, now she's being sent to a place she hasn't seen in twenty-five years, where she has no family or friends. Jesus fucking Christ.

And in other breaking news? Miles, Brooky's brother, has been detained for questioning. Wha...? I mean, I get that they're questioning the Hive and the parents and the witnesses from the AVB and all—but Miles? Why him? Because he's black? Because he plays in a band? Wears his hair in dreads? What has Miles got to do with any of this?

Also? CNN did an interview with this social media expert talking about how crowdsourcing, which has been going on since cell phones, has become one of the most effective tools of law enforcement. The guy says he's created an algorithm to determine how much longer it'll take to find us, based on the dollar amount of the bounty, the estimated number of people actively searching, the number of people communicating on social, the amount of TV airtime devoted to us and the likely trajectory of our escape. He says they should have us by tomorrow night. The fuck?

He compared Fee and me to those terrorists who bombed the subway in London last year. Those guys watched the search for them unfold on their phones and taunted the authorities and responded to all the breaking news on social as it happened. The "expert" says that, wherever we are, we're watching too. And that, just like the London bombers, we will be caught—right around the time Jonze starts his free concert.

I can't stop looking at this series of pics of the Hive someone posted on InfoNow—all of us at Zee Rohanian's sixth birthday at the flagship Patriot Girls store, dressed in outfits that match our megadollar dollies, who sit beside us in wooden high chairs at the decorated table. We were all about the Patriot Girls when we were little. We wore star-spangled Patriot merch for years—so much red, white and freaking blue. For all the thousands my parents spent on them, I never really loved those dolls. They don't want mommies, or even friends, they just want to be admired for their sketch contributions to American history.

And I've been thinking of all the birthday parties and BBQs and football parties on Oakwood Circle. Somehow my half-breed Canadian Jewish family always belonged. Sherm would say he and my mom got a pass on the whole race thing because the freckled, bespectacled Millers are not the dark-eyed, hawk-nosed Friedburgs who live on the street behind us, so it was much easier for everyone to pretend we're from the same tribe.

Tom Sharpe affectionately called my parents "the Commies," and Mr. Leon teased my mother about her bleeding heart when she got passionate about immigrant issues. I'd hear my parents arguing sometimes, after parties, with Sherman claiming Tom Sharpe had a point about this and that, or that Big Mike's challenges on military spending and other economics issues had him asking himself some tough questions. Maybe it was politics that ruined them. Maybe Sherman started to lean right, and Shelley tried to yank him left, and they just tore, one thread at a time. I wish this night was over so I could stop thinking about this. We'll have to make some kind of move, sometime tomorrow. Javier will need us to get out of here. But what?

God . . . your ears really can play tricks on you when you're trapped in a shed with people hunting your ass. I keep thinking

I'm hearing my name being called in the white noise of the wind. Freaky. Keep looking out the little window but can't see anything except the moon and stars and a few tumbleweeds blowing around near Javier's truck.

Couple of minutes ago I knocked over one of the suitcases in the corner of the shed when I moved away from the window, and I have to say I was pretty relieved when the noise woke up Fee and she opened her eyes a crack. I was worried she might be in a tequila coma. Then she raised her head a little, looked around the shed and croaked out, "Water."

She's seriously dehydrated. This is bad.

"I'm gonna get some, Fee. I've been thinking about trying to break into that Airstream if the guy leaves. I just don't know how . . . with that dog . . ."

"Look in trash bags?" She pointed to the bags in the corner.

"Dude, there's no water in the trash bags."

"If we turn ourselves in, they'll give us water."

"Or kill us?"

"I'm dying of thirst."

"You're not."

"I am."

"You can go three days without water."

"Can't be true."

"I'm gonna get you water, Fee. When it's light out. In the morning. We're gonna figure out a way to get you something to drink. I'll break into Javier's if I have to."

"Promise?"

"Promise."

"Ror?"

"Yeah?"

She looked like she was gonna say something, but instead she put her head back down on the balled-up blanket and closed her eyes.

Part of me wants to piggyback her to an Urgent Care—there must be twenty of them on the Pacific Coast Highway. My mom says there was a time, not so long ago, when people were not routinely shot in the streets, in their homes and on highways. Even I remember a time when there were more coffee shops than Urgent Care Centers.

Before I left to go get ready for the ball at Jinny's, Shelley had called me into her room. She already had wine-face and it was only two in the afternoon. She patted the bed, where I plopped down beside her. "You know I think this ball is silly," she said.

"Yes."

"But I still hope you have a great time. And take lots of pics. And, you know, it's an opportunity to start a conversation with your father. It's time, Ror, I think, to figure that out for yourself."

I had figured it out for myself. I know who he is. I know what I want, and what I don't want. It was like being in the therapist's office early on, a joint session where Shelley told the guy she was concerned that her feelings about Sherman were bleeding into mine. That we were too enmeshed. Of course her feelings were bleeding into mine. And mine into hers. Unavoidable. And not the point. *Enmeshed*. I'd never heard the word before. I hated how it took my independence with one two-syllable swipe. Fuck. That. I am not enmeshed. And what I couldn't say then, or wouldn't say, was that I don't feel the way I feel about Sherman because he left Shelley, but because he left me.

Mommy. I've tried, telepathically, to let her know I'm okay. I wanna believe there's such a thing as telepathy—that you can be so connected to another human, they can feel your thoughts. I guess enmeshed isn't always bad.

This pink laptop. I've just discovered something tragically amazing about this laptop.

I opened up the contacts a few minutes ago. Looking for what? Someone who could help us? A name or e-mail I might recognize? I don't know anyone's e-mail address. Or telephone numbers. Not even Aunt Lill's. It's all in my phone. Who remembers numbers? Anyway, I didn't find any contacts I recognized, but I was nosy, so I looked at the photo files.

I'm so stupid for not connecting . . . I mean . . . This guy, Javier . . . I didn't link him with the little girl that died in Hidden Oaks, but then this photograph popped up—of a smush-face six-year-old in her white first Communion dress—on a prayer card from her funeral. Nina Fernandez.

Javier's daughter. Nina. She was riding a scooter in front of the house her mother was cleaning up the hill from us, not far from the third set of gates to the Kardashian compound, when she fell and hit her head. Another kid who saw Nina fall said she didn't even cry.

Nina got up and went into the mansion, where her mother was washing the floor, to show her the goose egg on her head, and she either tripped on the threshold or slipped on the wet floor, or her injury made her dizzy and she fainted. Either way, she cracked her skull in the foyer and bled out over the travertine.

Miller Law took on the case for Javier and his wife, suing the homeowner. But it caused a lot of controversy and conflict in Hidden Oaks. And a few weeks later, Sherman dropped it, directing

Javier to another law firm without even consulting my mother. In the end, Shelley's confusion over that decision is what uncovered my father's affair. The owner of that house where Nina bled to death? Sugar Tits. That's how my dad met her.

But before Sherman dropped Javier as a client, and before he started his affair, my parents hosted the wake for Nina at our house. I was supposed to be there for it. But I was completely stressed by the start of school and cross-country, and I didn't think I could hack all that tragedy, plus it was Brooky's birthday and she was having a sleepover and spa day. It's not like she was gonna postpone her birthday. My parents couldn't stand it when I was sad, so my mom said I should go to Brooky's but remember to stop in and pay respects.

It's possible that our parents are making a terrible mistake when they try to shield us from disappointment and pain and sadness. Maybe we're supposed to feel bad sometimes. Maybe we're supposed to feel like utter fucking shit.

I watched from behind Brooky's bedroom curtains that day— as one does—well, as I do—all the greasy gardeners' trucks jamming the cul-de-sac, the nannies and housekeepers clacking around in kitten heels, and the mow-and-blow guys in new suits from Burlington. Everybody carried plates of food in foil, even though my parents had hired a caterer.

There was this one guy, an old dude, who stood at the end of the driveway just staring at our house for a really long time. I wondered if he was too sad to go in. Then he stooped to pinch a wilted rose from the bush in front of him, palming the petals. As he headed up the path, he took the time to deadhead the roses all the way to the front door, stuffing the crisped flowers into his suit-coat pocket rather than litter our perfect green lawn. This was before Sherman left, and my mother pissed the whole cul-de-sac off, not to mention the Hidden Hills Home Owners Association, by ripping out our grass and tearing out our flowers, and replacing our landscaping with a ragged collection of drought-resistant plants adrift in a sea of crushed granite ground cover. She left the eight mature fruit trees in the backyard, though, and told our gardener to pick them clean each season and distribute the bushels of oranges and peaches and lemons among his family and friends.

I could hear sad Spanish music floating from the speakers around our pool. I knew I should grab the girls and go over to say something to our gardener and to his cousin Javier and his wife, whom I didn't know, but who'd lost their daughter. But I got this huge lump in my throat thinking about how heartbreaking it all was, and then I was so glad to see Brooky's brother pull up with the smoothies.

Fee had begged Miles to go to Jamba Juice and Miles asked what he'd get if he did. Fee said she'd do his chores for a day. Um. Static. Um. Chores? We all looked at Fee like, where are we? 1981 on a Kentucky farmstead? In Calabasas we have concierge garbage pickup. The guys get your trash from your backyard and haul it out to the trucks, rinse the bins with rose water and put the clean ones back. Gardeners rake our leaves and trim bushes, and housekeepers sweep floors and scrub toilets, and pool guys come with the scooper and chlorine and whatever. Anyway, Fee was kinda slaughtered by realizing that she was the only one of us who does actual chores. Miles got that Fee was embarrassed, so he said he'd drive to Jamba if Fee came with. For an annoying big brother, Miles can be solid.

Later, I told my mother that we forgot about the wake and that we all felt bad. She left the prayer card from the funeral on the kitchen counter so I could read Nina's school poem about all of the things she loved in her life. I opened the card and saw her little crooked printing but couldn't focus on the words.

If you're there, somewhere in the ether, Nina, if your spirit reads or otherwise intercepts this post—I'm so sorry I didn't go to your wake. I'm so sorry your life ended too soon. I wish I'd actually read your poem. Did you say you loved your mother and father? The pink laptop? I obviously hope I'm totally wrong about God, and heaven, and that you are there right now eating ice cream with your abuela and all your other dead family. Say hi to my Gramma and Pop. Tell them I love them.

Soon the sun'll rise. Then what? We sit here in this dirty shed waiting for Javier to come back with help? Like, it's all we have right now. It's gonna be an oven in here once the sun's up. And Fee may actually die from thirst. I honestly don't know if I'd find anything drinkable in Javier's cabin even if I can find a way to break in. And what about Javier? I'm putting all of my trust and faith in a stranger whose only reason for resisting the temptation of that huge bounty is that my parents were kind to him once upon a time? I mean, they did host Nina's wake and all—but two million dollars, yo?

Plus, he obviously didn't win his lawsuit against Sugar Tits. So maybe he would even wanna get revenge?

This toolshed is so freaking claustrophobic.

My period cramps are so gnarl right now I just wanna run them off, literally, like I always did in cross-country, stride after stride, just thinking, *fuck you fucking cramps*. I always feel better after a run. This is what people in jail must feel like. The urge to run. And this place, this shed, does feel like a prison.

Maybe that's why I can't stop writing. This isn't a blog any-more. It's a prison diary.

———

It's morning. After six o'clock. Didn't think I'd sleep a wink, but I guess I did. Fee's still out cold, but at least she's breathing more evenly. We survived the night.

The quiet all around us feels a little dubious, though. Calm before the storm?

Javier's truck is still in the driveway. So is the drunk guy's truck next door.

Went online already. Of course.

Interesting developments in that some trolls are now saying we are a hoax. That we do not exist and that nothing at all happened at the ball last night. In fact, they say, there was no ball. Conspiracy theorists? People are fucking crazy. I wish it were true, though. I wish none of this had ever happened. On the news, they keep playing that clip of me saying, "The American Virtue Ball is going to change my life," like it's a suicide message.

And Miles is back home. No harm no foul there, I guess. He posted a pic of Lark's Head and announced a gig next week. Like, whatever, life goes on?

The Santa Anas are trending right now, and everyone is talking about what the erratic winds will mean to the hunt for me and Fee, because copters are one of their most effective search tools. There have been a couple of near accidents since the sun came up. People are taking their machines up in a moment of calm air and then having to make emergency landings all over the place when the winds start to gust. Asshole bounty hunters are flying their GarBirds out over the ocean and the homeless encampments downtown, and at least two of them have had to make quick set-downs on freeways and golf courses when the winds start gusting. Drones can't fly at all: the winds just blow them around.

I feel more exhausted than I did before I slept. And thirsty. So thirsty. Never been so parched in my life. I can't help thinking about all those homeless people out there—how just the search for water in this desert-y climate must be . . . exhausting . . . and just piss them the fuck off. Like, they exist in one of the richest places on earth and don't have access to drinkable water? None of that is news. But when you're the one with the want. Or need. You actually, finally, get it. Water. Just . . . water . . .

And Fee. What about Fee? I gotta figure out a way to get us something to drink, but I can't leave the shed and have her wake up here alone. She'd be so scared. Plus, the winds are supposed to die down again soon. Air traffic will return.

"Fee?"

Fee opened her eyes. She sat up a little and leaned against the shed wall, and looked around the shed like, the fuck? Then you could see the memory of it all flooding back.

"Javier still here?" she asked.

I got up and looked out the window. "Yeah."

"Water?"

"I can't go out there. Hear the copters? They're over the beach right now, but they could swing this way any second."

"Please. Ror. I'm so thirsty."

"I know."

"When this is over?"

"Yeah?"

She just shrugged and shook her head. But I finally feel like she's gonna be okay. She just needs water. Right now.

Jinny Hutsall always has water. It's her thing. I guess that's why her skin is so amaze. She always has at least three bottles of water—the expensive stuff that comes in those keep-cool containers—in that big Louis tote of hers. A few weeks back we were in Beverly Hills doing a pre-shop for our AVB gowns and there was this crusty beggar—no teeth, no shoes, caked in dust and dirt, like the Santa Anas could just blow particles of him away, erode him like the hillsides. He was slumped against the marble wall of that restaurant that sells the hundred-dollar burgers, with his dirty palm out, saying, "Agua. Por favor. Agua. Por favor," over and over again as people sidestepped him and looked around for security. I don't know how he got there, because the cops usually collect the beggars

and drop them off at the encampments or jail, if they get belliger-
ent. But this guy was just sitting there looking tragic. My heart
went out to him, right, because it's a thousand degrees and dude
needs a drink. I don't have any water with me, so I ask Jinny if
she'll give him one of her bottles. She looks at me like I'm insane.
And she's trying to pull me along, but if we're not giving him
water, I'm gonna give him some money, because human. Jinny's
annoyed that I'm stopping, but I don't care. I reach into my purse,
but then I'm like holy crap because I see all I have in my wallet
is my birthday money from the week before—hundred-dollar
bills. Now my hand's in my purse and this guy's dirty palm is in my
face, and his sunken eyes are on mine, so I ask Zee if she'll loan me
a few dollars, but she says no. No? The guy's waiting and now he
looks worried like am I seriously gonna leave him hanging. Fee
and Delaney say they only have cards—no cash. So I'm obviously
gonna give the old man one of my birthday hundys then. Right? I
have to. So I did. The guy burst into tears.

Right in front of the guy, Jinny goes, "Oh my gosh, Rory, if
you give him money, why would he ever want to get a job and
earn his own?"

"Like the way we earn ours, Jinny?"

"If people don't give them money, beggars won't beg," she
says. "They're like seagulls at the beach, Rory. If you give them
food, they will never go away."

"That's straight-up unchristian, Jinny."

"You're hilarious, Rory."

"Compassion, Jinny? Like, you don't know anything about
them. You don't know what happened to put them on the street."

"Prolly illegal," Zee said, then turns to Fee and goes, "Sorry."

We were in Prada, sifting through gowns, when I saw a

security guy seize the old man and load him into the back of a van like a stray animal. Rolled him for the hundy, no doubt. Fuckers.

Wait! Oh my God! Just heard the cabin door.

Waiting.

Javier's boots on the driveway.

Waiting.

Truck engine.

He isn't gonna come check on us? Bring more water? Crackers? Hope? Instructions? Anything?

I was about to stop typing and peek out the door, but Javier shouted out, really, really loudly, "Good morning."

To whom? Not us. I didn't hear anyone respond, but maybe there's someone out there—the drunk guy or someone else—and Javier shouted as a warning to us to stay put? Maybe there are copters on the horizon or drones nearby? Haven't heard a whimper or whine or bark from the direction of the Airstream. I really hope that old dude leaves for work soon.

This just in: the Feds set up a website so people can report sightings and send in tips about us at www.CalabasasAVB.gov.org. The site crashed about five o'clock this morning as thousands of reports came in. Thousands. We've been seen at bus stations and airports and coffee shops all over the country. According to the news, a network of sympathizers has also connected over social, and they've been flooding the site with false sightings, just to send the authorities on wild-goose chases. Hundreds of pics have been sent from all over the freaking world. Women are dressing up in wedding gowns and Photoshopping pics of themselves running away from flames and smoke. There are images posted from the UK, and France, and Italy, and even freaking Brazil! People who believe in us—even if it's only by default, because they hate our accusers so much—are trying to throw the hunters off our scent. So we have sympathizers. Hope? I see you.

And thank you, Santa Anas. I usually hate the winds because hair and fire, but right now I'm, like, blow devil, blow. Keep the machines grounded. People hate sky traffic as much as they hate ground traffic. They may not have to sit in it, but it intrudes on their lives anyway. I remember thinking about that when the girls and I were lazing at the Leons' pool one day this summer, drinking virgin margs. You look up thinking a bird just flew by, but it's a drone. Did it just take a pic of us? Privacy? Is there such a thing?

The bounty. A million dollars. I mean, I get that people want that prize. That's a lot of money. So what about Javier? Will he be blowing leaves or pruning someone's bushes under the baking sun today and just go, fuck it. I mean, he might not be able to bring his little daughter back from the grave, but with a million dollars he might be able to get his wife back from Mexico. Or he could go there and live with her like royalty. There's a million things he could do with a million dollars. I wonder what I'd do, in his boots.

Brooky just posted video of men in suits taking computers and boxes of files and stuff out of my house. Did they find my little palm-cam? I don't think so—my dresser weighs a ton. Bee wrote, "Rory's mother in deep *&%#. Still being interrogated about her Red Market ties."

Brooky? Why are you hating on my mother like that? Even if she is involved in some activist stuff, you *know* it's not Red Market. Plus, I mean, your great-grandfather was a Black freaking Panther! My mother was never anything but loving and kind to you and every other girl in the Hive. How do you just turn on people like that? When this is over, I'm going to write a long-ass post about friendship, and what it means, and what you should be able to expect from a person you call a friend.

Shelley Miller is the best human I know. She's the kind who'd take off her necklace and give it to you if you said you liked it. With her friends, she was there. I mean, she doesn't really have friends anymore, but when she did, she was the type who'd be, like, dying from exhaustion, in pain from a toothache or something, but she'd never use that as an excuse if someone needed to download a problem, maybe get a little legal advice. She never minded. Not like Sherman, who got snippy when random people asked for free legal—unless he wanted to nail them, I guess. Mommy? I'm so sorry I got you mixed up in all of this.

I don't know why I still think this way, but I really do believe that justice will prevail. But, Jesus, everything the cable news and Internet is saying about what happened at the ball last night is just so wrong. The Internet also has no clue what happened on Oakwood Circle when Jinny Hutsall moved in next door. There's just so much data to unload about Jinny, and Jagger, and us, and the nights in question. So I've decided I'm gonna set it all out here. It may be a little out of order. But consider this my deposition.

That first day, when we met her in the cul-de-sac, after she iced me in front of the Hive for being the Jewy heathen I am, Jinny invited us all over to her new house—previously owned by an extremely rich older couple who sunbathed nude in their backyard (voyeurs do not discriminate), where she said there was a pitcher of lemonade and a batch of fresh brownies. It was boiling outside, and we were bored and curious. The girls were all in. Me? Fear of missing out.

We walk into this beautiful sunlit kitchen and, sure enough, there's this huge pitcher of lemonade with sparkling ice cubes and a massive plate of ridiculous frosted brownies that normally we'd only look at. But Jinny took one and ate it in three bites and we all just followed. We followed. Then I start thinking. Wait. What? Jinny literally just stepped out of the Town Car that drove her to her new house. There are no parents at home. So who put out the lemonade? And the brownies? And how could they know we'd come over?

So I say, "How did the lemonade get here?"

Jinny stared at me. "You ask a lot of questions!"

"It's just, your parents aren't here and the cubes are fresh, and—"

"Oh my gosh! What is this, interrogate the new girl?"

"It's just—the ice cubes . . ."

"Oh my gosh, you really are a scream!" Jinny said, then excused herself to go to the "loo." My gramma called the bathroom the loo and I always thought it was the cutest thing, but Jinny Hutsall saying it made me wanna hurl.

When she was gone, I whispered, "Guys. A Crusader. Seriously?"

"She's super-nice, Ror," Zee said.

"God, Rory, she's just saying you're funny!" Fee chimed in. "Seriously? That's a compliment! What is your problem?"

"Crusader. 'Nuff said."

"Yeah, but so what? We don't have to chill with her every day, but she just got here, Ror," Delaney said.

"Jesus, Rory," Zee added.

"Jesus? Did you just take His name in vain, Zee? What would Jinny Hutsall think?"

Zee shot me the finger.

Fee goes, "Just saying, be nice."

I was in dangerous territory with the Hive. They'd see everything I was gonna say about Jinny as me being jealous. "I just

feel like something seems off about her. You guys . . . you must
see it too."

But they didn't. Or didn't want to.

"Rory. You're being so judge-y," Zee said. "Like, you hate
judge-y, but you can be super-judge."

"But I'm judging the judgiest of them all. She's a Crusader.
Come on."

Bee goes, "You're just too much sometimes, Ror."

"You're okay with this too, Bee? Sincerely? Crusaders hate
the Jews, and the heathens, but they're not so fond of black people either. All those Crusaders carrying the American flag at that
rally last year? Not a lot of people of color."

Just then Jinny called out, "Girls? Come meet my brothers!"

We found her in the huge foyer. And that's when her five
brothers—one for each of us?—emerged at the top of the winding staircase, like opening night at Chippendales. Five dead-fit
college-aged guys who had no reason to be home that weekend—
I didn't think of that until just now—bounding down the stairs
with their hard bodies and fine threads, all white teeth and chis-
eled jaws.

And, like Jinny, they were so *nice*. The brothers asked all kinds
of questions about our lives at Sacred Heart, and about Calabasas,
and our families, other girls we knew in the community . . . Come
to think of it, her brother Garth asked me a lot of questions about
my mother. Why was he so interested in Shelley? Anyway, we
giggled and blushed and answered in depth, because boys. After
a bit the tallest brother, Joel, turned to Jinny and asked, "Did you
tell them about the AVB thing?"

Jinny shook her head and gave him a look like, don't, but
really she wanted to tell us about the AVB thing, very, very badly.

"You should, Jin," another brother said.

"Oh my gosh!" Jinny said, faking annoyance. "Brothers!"

"What about the AVB? Did you do an AVB?" Zee asked.

We girls all knew what AVB stood for, of course. I mean, there are so many chastity balls now, but Jagger Jonze's American Virtue Ball franchise was the most popular, but like I said, we'd always found the whole idea of it hysterical. So why did I blink my eyes at Jinny's smokin' brother and go, "One of the girls at Sacred tried to get one going last year, but we had this big fire and the school was closed for weeks. The air was so bad for so long we had to wear surgical masks the rest of the semester. Not a good look. Anyway." I implied regret about the lost AVB.

Jinny explained that she'd been about to attend a ball sponsored by her church in suburban Chicago and had everything ready—Monique Lhuillier gown, Lacroix sandals, pashmina—then her father decided to relocate the family to California. Poor princess.

Garth said, "You girls should do one here."

Zara batted her eyelashes at him. "That would be cool." Another hypocrite. Even Zee, the most Christian girl in our hive, had been totally anti–purity ball. She'd laughed about the whole idea of the chastity pledge. What are we, like, marrying our fathers?

Then Jinny goes, "Oh my gosh, you girls wanna see my dress?"

Our first glimpse of Jinny Hutsall's bedroom. I mean, I'd seen it from the side window in my own room, spied on it from behind my curtains a thousand times over the course of two previous owners. I never saw sex in that room, even though I had a clear view of the bed and the monster ceiling fan that hovered over it. Mostly I just saw old, fat people sleeping, or cleaners with vacuums, fluffing the duvet and dusting the dressers.

Jinny's furniture was oversized, fit for a queen, all of it just too big and too much, and the closet . . . ? At some point when I wasn't watching, someone had moved Jinny's whole amazing wardrobe of designer outfits into her closet. We oohed and aahed the shit out of her massive walk-in, and the floor-to-ceiling shelves of color-coded shoes and boots and purses, and then there it was, encased in plastic, hanging on the back of the door. She slid the zipper down and lifted the diaphanous gown out of the bag. A wedding dress. That's what it was. The Holy Grail. Girl crack. We wanted it. Jinny was hooking us, like a drug dealer.

Before we knew it, we were on the floor in front of the flat screen in the sitting area of her bedroom, watching this slick promo vid with these beautiful girls our age in their stunning bridal couture talking about how the American Virtue Ball changed their lives. For as long as I can remember, we'd all howled at the purity ball pics of dads and their daughters looking like messed-up mini-me child brides. But something had shifted.

Then Jinny pimped up the whole thing by telling us that her father was a personal friend of Jagger Jonze himself—and that even though Jonze almost never makes appearances at his franchise events, Jinny was pretty sure her daddy could get him to host our ball since he lived in Beverly Hills.

One of the brothers knocked on the door and asked if we wanted to go for a swim. "I have a net for water volley," he called. Dee opened the door and I think I actually saw her knees buckle. She's all about the buttoned-up types and the brothers were prep on 'roids. This one, Garth, was standing in the hallway dressed in his cute swim trunks, looking like a cross between Michelangelo's David and that rapper Diggie Dawg—all ripped and tanned and bulge-y—and every one of us wanted to get into the water with that big smokin' college boy. "Girls against guys," he said, grinning.

We all have pools. We do not swim. Never. I mean, not since elementary school. But we dove at the chance to go swimming with Jinny's fine brothers, and because Jinny didn't wanna break the spell by letting us leave, she opened a drawer filled with these designer 'kinis and tanks for us to borrow. Within ten minutes we were all in the pool playing volleyball. The thing is, it was fun. Old-time fun. Like the fun we used to have when we didn't care what our hair looked like wet or if our tummies were poochie. The brothers, sexy as they seemed, didn't flirt with us, and never said anything inappropriate. It was kind of comfortable.

After, we lay out on the teak chaises around the pool. The brothers disappeared pretty fast, which made everything way less interesting, and then this awkward thing happened. I mean . . . I guess I was staring at Jinny's tits because I was so sure implants. Jinny caught me looking, and I wanted to die because she misunderstood and started acting itchy. I thought about admiring the tiny blue bows on her halter to deflect, but figured I'd just make it worse.

In the foyer we lined up to hug our new bestie and to tell her how much we already adored her—'cause that's what chicas do. When I pressed against her, I faded a bit because her breasts are all too real.

Outside, before we split up to go into our houses, we stood in the darkening cul-de-sac. "That was awkward," I said.

"You were staring at her boobs," Zara said. "So yeah?"

"I was not," I said.

"I literally watched you," Zee said. "They're real."

"Whatever. She's weird. We're not really gonna do the AVB, are we, guys?" I said.

Brooky grinned. "We should. For a laugh. We could do it for a laugh."

"Um?"

"I mean, why not?" Zee said.

"Because we don't believe in the whole abstinence-before-marriage thing?"

"Who cares, though, Ror? In a way?" Dee said.

"Shouldn't we care?"

"I don't think it's all that serious," Brooky said. "You say what you say and then you do what you do."

Made sense. Sort of.

"Think about it," Brooky pressed. "Couture gowns and Jimmy Choos. Pics with Jagger Jonze. Think of the posts. Imagine the likes."

True. Posting pics with celebrities, even minor celebrities, does prompt a lot of likes. I really really like likes. To be honest, we're all kinda obsessed with our pics and our likes.

Fee shrugged. "Could be fun."

"I guess." I didn't think it'd be fun exactly. Also, at that point, I didn't think we'd end up going through with it.

My skin was flaking from the chlorine in Hutsalls' pool, and my hair was frizzy and tangled, and my chest heavy with the realization that this whole AVB thing, and Jinny Hutsall, was gonna be the end of my hive as I knew it. I could see, even then, I was gonna have to buckle up.

When I got home, Shelley asked me what I thought of the new girl and if she was gonna make a good addition to the Hive. Um. Fine. Um. No.

I went up to my bedroom and straight to my side bedroom window, hoping Jinny was in her room so I could spy. She was. Jinny Hutsall was lying across her beautiful bed, staring up at the ceiling fan—nekked—with her little 'kini balled up on the duvet beside her. Boring. Still, I wanted to look.

Then—and this was the weird part—she started talking. I
couldn't hear what she was saying, but I was like, who's in there
with her? All of a sudden she sits up and gets on her knees in the
middle of the bed, and she raises her eyes to the ceiling and keeps,
like, chatting in a conversational way, and waiting for a response,
and then she's saying more shit, and then waiting, and then she
starts laughing her ass off. Okay. So I was right. Jinny Hutsall is
off. She's naked, having a hilarious conversation with her ceiling
fan. Well, with God. I knew she was talking with God, which
made the whole thing seem actually dangerous.

I didn't tell anyone what I saw. How could I? They'd say I was
the whack one. They'd say, so what if Jinny was praying? And so
what if she heard God answer back? And so what if she was naked
in her own room? We all walk around naked in our rooms. Fair
enough. And they would hate me for spying. I really didn't want
to out myself as a Peeping fucking Tina, on top of everything else.
But I kept watching Jinny, that night, and most nights after, careful to hide behind my drapes, until she fell asleep, or left her room
and my pervy view.

The next day, Jinny Hutsall joined us for car pool and told us
that her father had already been in touch with Jagger Jonze and
he'd agreed to host the AVB and the orientation event. My hive
screamed like fangirls. And there it was. A seismic shift. And
rather than stand alone with my ethics and opinions, instead of
being odd Jew out, which is how Jinny made me feel, I suggested
we all head to Rodeo Drive for pre-shopping the following week.
Shelley looked at me sideways, like wha. . . ?

"You might want to check with your father first," she said.

On the way to school, the girls were excited, talking about
gowns and hairstyles and whatnot, but I was thinking about Jinny

and her ceiling fan. I noticed Fee was also quiet. Delaney saw it too, and I heard her whisper, "You know my dad'll totally buy you whatever he buys me."

Fee was like, "I know. But, like, even if he buys my dress and all, wouldn't it be too creepy for me to, like, promise my virginity to him?"

My mother kept her mouth shut but nodded. Very. Creepy.

Fee opened her eyes again, so I stopped writing about stupid freaking Jinny in this blog, prison diary, memoir, deposition or whatever it's morphed into.

So . . . not to jinx it, but Fee's sitting here with cracker crumbs all over her mouth. No puking. Her color looks better too. I think the poison—if it was that—must be mostly out of her system. The tequila too. Now she's just severely dehydrated, and scared.

She asked if I've been writing all night, and I admitted I had. She wanted to know if I'd been back online. Yep. I've been checking obsessively. She wanted to know the deets. So I told her we need to tune in to Jagger Jonze's *Higher Power Hour* later, and that Miles was detained and released, and that Jinny and the rest of the Hive have been tweeting at us all night, and that I think Brooky and Dee and Zara have been brainwashed. I told her that my mother's still being questioned, but I didn't tell her that her mother's about to be deported. I did tell her about the sympathizers sending in pics of themselves in wedding gowns, though, creating all the wild-goose chases and false leads. And the most promising development?

Journalists, and regular people, are starting to question. CNN has been looking at the uptick in violent protests and other crimes at purity balls around the country, and wondering if it's just possible that it's the Crusaders themselves doing the crimes, sending "fake" protesters, creating a picture of persecution to bring sympathy to their cause. Remember that AVB in Missouri last year? Every car in the parking lot got tagged with violent antireligious graffiti. They never found the people who did it, but the whole country heard about it. And the alt-right definitely used that event to skewer the left. At another ball in Little Rock, a bunch of people in masks threw eggs at the girls in their white gowns. There was also a bomb threat at a purity ball in Sarasota. And one in Louisiana too. Those turned out to be hoaxes, but they got a ton of press. Genius.

When I told Fee all of this, she closed her eyes. I thought, for a sec, she was going back to sleep. "Fee?"

"Shh. I'm praying."

Seriously? But then again, why not? Fee's not a heinous God person. I know a lot of Christians who aren't haters, like Miss Maureen in the front office at school, and Miss Yvonne from the lunchroom. They're sweet. And helpful. And I've never felt them look at me with anything but kind eyes. Even if I don't believe in Him, *their* God is not an asshole. I guess. I don't know. Maybe secretly I'm hoping I'm wrong, and that He's somewhere in the atmosphere, and will answer Fee's prayers.

She was still praying when we heard banging outside that sounded like it was coming from the trailer. Wind? The big black dog?

I got up and looked out the little window. The trees are bending in the wind, tumbleweeds blowing around—so many tumbleweeds at this time of year. A plastic garbage bin was rolling back and forth in Javier's driveway, and just slammed up against some paint cans stacked neatly against the side of his house.

I'm like, "When the dog-beater leaves his trailer, I'll find a way to get into Javier's cabin and get us something to drink, Fee. Or I'll break into the Airstream."

"Think Javier has a water filter, Ror?"

Highly doubtful. "Maybe there's something in his fridge."

Fee was quiet for so long I turned to look at her.

"I'm thinking we need to turn ourselves in," she finally said.

"No way. We wait for Javier. He's coming back with help."

"We can't stay here all day. I seriously think I will die if I don't get some water. I just wanna go home."

"But turning ourselves in? We won't be going home, Fee. We don't have any friends out there. Our girls? You don't seem to be getting that they've turned on us."

"They'll turn back. They're family. And Mr. Tom'll figure out the immigration stuff with my mom. She's like his sister."

We heard another noise outside. I jumped up again to look out the window and saw the blue tarp that blew off the Airstream trailer last night flapping our way like some huge drunken heron, then wrapping itself around the oak beside the shed. When that old drunk comes out of his trailer, he'll come over here to get it. I'm very afraid of that man.

"I'm worried about the dude from the trailer. Javier says we shouldn't let him see us. If he finds out we're here, it's over."

"Then it's over."

"Don't say that, Fee."

"My mouth is so dry it hurts to talk. Let's just be quiet, 'kay? Let's just sit here and think about what we're gonna do next."

Ouch. I've been so lonely here, and dying to talk to Fee, and she's just shut me down. I'm going back online.

Breaking news? Fee's purse—her little gold metal clutch—was recovered from the bombed-out bathroom. The media is making a big fucking deal of this, showing pics of Fee with the purse at her quinceañera last July (Tom Sharpe refused to buy Fee and Delaney new bags for the ball since they already had a closetful of them). Now everybody's freaked about Fee's purse and its undisclosed contents. What? Some melted lipstick? The pearl ring that was too small for her finger?

Fee is shocked that the metal clutch survived the bomb blast. I thought it was whatever, but she is so upset. Agitated. Like, I get that our purses are private, but come on. Given everything that's going on, why does the idea that people are looking in her purse make her so fucking itchy?

"Who cares, Fee? Seriously. I don't think you're seeing the big picture here."

"I am seeing the big picture. I care about my purse because it's private."

"Private? What the hell, Fee? What was in there?"

"Nothing."

"Nothing?"

"Rory . . . I don't . . . I don't understand any of what is going on. Jinny's a Crusader and all, but she's our friend. And Jagger . . ."

I said, "Jagger Jonze is a straight-up con man. And Jinny Hutsall is not our friend."

"I don't know who planted that bomb, or who put that nasty thing in your car, Ror, but is it possible Jinny and Jagger are being played too?"

Que the fuck pasa to my life? Fee is protecting Jinny Hutsall? Making excuses for Jagger Jonze? I know she's sick and tired and thirsty, but really? It's gotta be more than that. When I think about it, there's been something off about Fee for the past few days.

I think it started the day before yesterday, when she went to Cerritos to see her abuela to get some family heirloom necklace she wanted to wear to the ball. It was the first time Fee was gonna be driving out there without her mom. She was going there and coming straight back—only take a few hours—and I offered to go with. I was actually dying to go with. I wanted to meet Fee's cousin Dante, the one with the piercings and tats. But Fee hard passed.

"But what about Dante?"

"He won't be there."

"Whatever. I wanna meet your abuela too."

She was like, "No. Ror. Ugh. My relatives don't like white people."

"I can handle that."

"They're cold. They'll call you Blanca and make faces behind your back. Awkward."

"Then I'll wait in the car when you go in."

"Plus, you get carsick when you don't drive, Rory, and Mr. Tom said I could bring the convertible and I really wanna drive."

"I can take meds."

"Ror."

"I'll be fine, Fee."

"No, Rory. Stop."

I was being relentless. But, like, I've always been this way, so why didn't Fee want my company in the car? We're best friends, and we've hardly spent any time together, just the two of us, since Jinny Hutsall. I know Fee's embarrassed about the procit thing, but I had another thought—a sickening thought—that Fee was gonna take Jinny Hutsall to Cerritos instead of me. So I kept watch over the Sharpes' house from my front bedroom window Friday morning. Fee left alone. Thank God.

"The necklace?" I said, realizing that I couldn't remember Fee having a necklace on at the ball.

"What necklace?" Her face was blank.

"The one you drove out to Cerritos to get the other morning?"

"Oh. Yeah. The clasp broke, so I couldn't wear it."

Fee was obviously lying. I don't know why. Then she burst into tears, and I wrapped her up in my arms and let her heave and sob, and then I started thinking, fuck, those tears! She really needs to stop crying because dehydration.

"Fee. We're gonna get out of this. Okay? I promise."

"I'm so thirsty, Ror. It's all I can think about. Can't we just go home? I get that there's a bounty, but people aren't actually gonna kill us."

"What rock have you been living under? Remember Joyce Johnson? Leslie Givens? Those girls from New York? Remember what the Crusaders did to them? What about that Allegra Coombs? She was shot by some Crusader for wearing a My Body T-shirt, for the love of fuck!"

"Well, I'd rather be in a prison cell drinking water than here dying of thirst! Please, can we just start walking on the road and see what happens? I can't take it anymore, Ror. I can't!"

We were quiet for a long time, then Fee said, "What exactly are you writing, Ror? What all did you write about what happened?"

"Just the facts."

"You didn't tell about me crapping myself and puking all night?"

"I'm writing our defense."

"Okay."

"I'm explaining about the Hive, and our lives, and about Jinny and Jagger, and I'm gonna write about orientation night next, and all that went down at the ball, and I'm, like, writing our convos down—not verbatim, but, you know, close."

"Okay, well, I really hate that. And you can't write about orientation night. You cannot write about that, Rory."

I can. And I'm gonna, but I don't wanna fight about it with Fee.

"Wait. Can't they trace us through your posts?"

"I'm not posting. Just writing. I won't submit until we're safe. Or found. Whichever comes first."

"If they were gonna find us here, wouldn't they have by now?"

"There are a lot of people looking, Fee. We're a gold mine."

She reached for my hand. We squeezed fingers.

Now we're just sitting here as the sun rises higher and the shed becomes a pizza oven. Fee's staring straight ahead, like she's lost in fear. Maybe confusion? I used to think I could read her mind, but now I just don't know. Maybe she's so thirsty she just can't deal. I'm thirsty too, but I'm also edgy from being stuck in this shed. My period is flowing thick and sticky, and all of it just makes me wanna punch Jinny Hutsall in the head.

The winds seem pretty calm at the moment, which is not good. Fee managed to pull herself up to look out the window. I joined her and we counted the little black specks in the distance—small planes and copters flying our way from the airport in Santa Monica. Twelve of them. "The copters look like tadpoles," I said. She nodded.

You'd think, with all the fear and stress, my period would stop, but I'm a crime scene. I just opened the dusty suitcases wondering if maybe I'd find some clothes or towels or something, but they were empty. The white trash bags? Can't bring myself to open one. Looks like they're filled with leaves and shit. The smell. I mean, aside from me and Fee. Definitely mice. Or rats. What if there are rodents in the trash bags?

Then Fee asked me what I was thinking about and I said, "The fiery deaths of Jinny Hutsall and Jagger Jonze."

She took the high road again, which is really fucking annoying. "Hating on Jinny and Jagger isn't gonna change anything. Besides, we don't have the facts."

"You're doing it again. Protecting them. The fuck, Fee?"

"I'm not protecting anybody. I just said I can't see Jinny and Jagger Jonze doing this to us."

"Can't see? You saw. You were there."

"But what actually happened? We don't even know. You really think Jinny or Jagger Jonze planted that bomb? And the rest of it? Why would she set us up? We don't have any proof of anything. Aren't we doing to them what people are doing to us? You hate conspiracy theory people."

"What is even happening right now?"

"It just doesn't make sense, Ror. Why go to all that trouble to frame us? You really think Jinny wanted you to die because she hates Jews?"

"Yeah, Fee—that's never happened in the history of the world."

"And you think Jagger Jonze hates Jews so much too? I mean . . . I'm not Jewish and I'm in this too."

"It's not just that, Fee. I'm not sure what all the connections are, but something happened. The night before the ball. I did something."

"You did something?"

I know I have to tell Fee about spying on Jinny Hutsall and filming her in a very compromising situation the day before the ball. I have to tell her that I think the real reason we're here is that footage on my palm-cam, on the floor behind my dresser in my room.

Fee knew I'd asked my aunt Lilly for the little long-lens palm-cam for my birthday because I told everybody I was interested in making short films. Not true. I wanted that camera for the sole purpose of filming Jinny Hutsall. I thought if the girls saw how actually flaked she is—how fully insane she looks on her knees on her bed talking to the ceiling fan—we could push her out of the Hive. Ever since I got the camera, I've been recording Jinny's bizarro conversations—no audio—but I couldn't always get a great angle, or she didn't look as crazy through the lens as I thought she would. I needed the kind of footage that would persuade my girls to take a step back from her.

Then, the night before yesterday, I looked out my front window and noticed there were a bunch of cars at the Hutsalls'. I figured maybe one of her brothers was home and having friends over or something. I didn't really expect to find Jinny in her room when I crossed to my other window, but there she was, on her bed, naked as always. Truth? If I had a body like her, I'd be naked as much as possible too. So I grabbed my little video camera, and

I'm in position behind my curtains, and there's Jinny stretched out on her bed. She's talking, but not to her ceiling fan. She's looking toward her door. There is definitely someone in her room. Holy fuck.

My hand is shaking, but I keep filming. And then this pair of jeans walks past the bed. I can tell it's a guy. One of her brothers? I'm freaked that her brother's in her room when she's nude. I wait. Jinny stops talking. Then she kneels like she does, ready to pray, and I totally zoom in, and that's when it happens. She gets down on her hands too, and sticks her perfect ass up in the air, and she turns around to look at the person in her room, and I realize she's, like, presenting herself. I watch, and I film, and I'm trying not to tremble so my camera work isn't shaky.

I keep on filming as the guy—which fucking brother?—walks up behind her, naked too. I can't see his face because I'm in so tight, but I watch as this guy jams himself balls deep into Jinny Hutsall's butt. Then I tilted the camera up to find the guy's face. It wasn't one of her brothers.

And that's when the Reverend Jagger Jonze looks up, and I feel like he's looking right down the lens, and I freak. I dropped my camera, and it fell behind my dresser. The thing is, I don't know for sure if he saw me filming them. I just . . . But it has to be that. Right? It's the only thing that makes sense of what happened.

This news, my confession, doesn't freak Fee out the way I thought it would. The way it should. She doesn't believe me.

She actually says, "That didn't happen."

"Wow. Wow. Fee. Seriously? You think I'm making this up?"

"I think you think you saw something you didn't see."

"So I'm delusional?"

"He's abstinent. I mean, he made that pretty clear, right? That whole weird thing at orientation night, Rory. I'm sorry. I think your eyes were playing tricks."

"Fee, I filmed it. And you'll see it on my camera. Jesus, it's not like we've never heard Christians arguing that anal sex doesn't affect the virgin status. You know what they say about fucking a loophole?"

"Maybe you were at a weird angle."

"Jinny was at a weird angle."

"Okay. Well. You're a psycho for filming her. And I think you're wrong. And even if you're right, it doesn't prove anything about the bomb or that thing in your car."

"Jagger's a freak."

"Whatever, Rory."

"Fee, she's like, sixteen, and Jagger's thirty at least, and it's totally against the law, and if people found out, his whole franchise would die and his reputation would be ruined. If people saw what I filmed, he'd go to jail. It'd be over. So that makes me a threat. It happened, and they must know I know. You get it now?"

Fee shook her head then stared at the dirt for a really long time. Finally she goes, "Okay. Well, I guess after we get some water, we gotta find a way to get to Oakwood Circle without anyone seeing us, get your camera from behind your dresser and get it to someone who will believe that you filmed sodomy between a famous preacher and a Christian school girl and that they set a bomb in the bathroom to kill us so no one would find out."

"Yes!"

She stared me down. "Hello? I'm being sarcastic. Jagger's messed and all, but he wouldn't do that to me. To us. Kill us in a bomb blast? It's crazy. He just wouldn't. I don't believe Jinny would either."

"That's the thing. I don't think it was supposed to be *us* in that bathroom. It was just supposed to be me. I think, when you ate those stupid ganache thingies—the poisoned chocolate balls—I think when you ate them, and got sick, you ended up being part of it by accident."

"Oh my freaking God, Rory. Your imagination . . ."

I have to remember that Fee hasn't spent the night hoovering news reports and connecting dots and writing her whole life story. It's easier for her to choose denial.

She goes, "Okay, let's say everything you're saying is true, Detective Miller. Shouldn't we turn ourselves in before we get shot by some bounty hunter who thinks we deal dead babies on Craigslist?"

"Javier—"

"You think all Latinos are these, like, good-hearted people because they used to ass-kiss you over your parents. They aren't saints, Ror. They're just people. The bounty is a million dollars? Hello?"

"Then why hasn't he turned us in already? He could have collected the bounty last night."

"How do you know he hasn't? How do you know somebody isn't on the way here right now? I don't just blindly trust him."

"But you blindly trust Jagger fucking Jonze?"

"Holy shit, Ror. Stop! Will you just stop!"

There was another noise outside. We both heard it. Something brushing up against the wall of the shed. The blue tarp?

———

Out the window I see more tumbleweeds blowing around. Couple of squirrels chasing each other around the oak beside the shed. The blue tarp hasn't moved. The drunk guy's truck is still here.

I can't stop steaming that Fee would in any way excuse or protect Jinny Hutsall or Jagger Jonze. I wanna remind her about all the fucked-up things Jinny has done, like what happened the week after my birthday. But Fee's not speaking to me right now, so once I'm through staring out the window, I go back to my blog. I have to get this stuff down.

So this one day, we were all drinking lemonade around Jinny's pool, talking about Brooky's track event on the upcoming weekend. I'd been stoked to drive Bee's fan club—us—in my new, old Prius, which was my birthday present from Shelley. Since Bee went on the team bus, I had enough seat belts, even one for Jinny.

Jinny was, like, "I'm so sorry, but I hate the Prius. I know your parents are Canadian and whatever, and not to be offensive, but ..."

Okay, so if a person says "not to be offensive," they're about to offend. If they say "not to be racist," whatever they say next will totally be racist.

Jinny goes, "It's just that Priuses are so weak, Rory. They're just so libtard."

Offense taken.

The Hive said nothing, of course, because they kinda felt the same way about the Prius. Automobiles are everything in Calabasas. Tom Sharpe says that in California you don't own your car, your car owns you. Your success is in your whip, your tinted windows, and mag wheels, and fly rims. Some people spend more waking hours in their cars than their actual homes. A Prius? People say it's the hemp sweatpants of cars. I don't care.

I looked around and I go, "Come on, chicas—I just got my license."

Zee goes, "We can just order a van service like always."

And Jinny says, "Plus, your mom won't let you drive us because it's illegal. Right? Underage passengers and all?"

I'd already asked Shelley if I could drive the Hive. I'd done six months of driver's ed so we could save money on insurance, and even though it's not legal for a new driver to carry underage passengers, it's done all the time and Shelley was chill about stuff like that. "Shelley's cope with it."

"But the rest of the parents won't be cope, right?" Jinny said.

The girls all shrugged. Like, basically the parents around here can't wait for the kids to get their driver's license so they can stop carting them around and paying for expensive car services. So they'll find a way to be copacetic about illegal shit that benefits them, no matter how Christian and rule-following they are. Everybody here gets a car for their sixteenth. It's a thing. Already established that we're spoiled brats.

Dee goes, "Nah. Everybody's chill with it. They know we don't drink and drive and whatever. If we don't speed, we won't get caught, and anyway, Rory drives like a gramz for real."

"I do not!" I kinda do though.

Then Jinny goes, "Well, if the folksies are good with it, then why don't we take our Tahoe? We'll be sooo much more comfy."

I didn't even know she had a Tahoe. They had a four-car garage and with her brothers always coming and going I'd seen 'Rarris and Mazzis and whatever parked in the drive. Never a Tahoe.

I explained to Jinny that I had to drive because of my severe carsickness, and that if I didn't drive, I'd have to take meds and would be sleepy and feel shitty. The girls did not support me, though, since obviously they'd be more comfortable in the Tahoe. And there were chargers in all the seat belts. Huge bonus. So it was decided that Jinny would drive us to the meet.

She goes, "Where is it?"

"Pasadena."

Jinny got way too excited about Pasadena. I should have suspected an agenda.

Saturday morning, I took two honkin' non-drowsy carsick meds, which never worked anyway, and told Shelley we'd be back late afternoon depending on traffic. She asked who was driving and was fine that it was Jinny, and she kissed my forehead and went straight back to her computer. I wish I could've told my mother what was going on in my life. But then again, she would have just told me to stand up for myself. Be true to myself. Express my beliefs. And none of that applied in this scenario. I also didn't want to worry her. I was glad she was working again. I didn't want to interrupt her flow.

Even though I get way less sick riding in the front seat, and my friends are all aware of this fact, Zee shotgunned it, and I didn't ask her to move because needy and demanding. Dee and Fee climbed in the back, and Jinny looked at me like she would have been so okay if I went home. I climbed in and buckled up.

Jinny played Jagger Jonze music the whole way there, and we sang along at the top of our lungs. It wasn't awful. At first. It was actually kinda fun, doing harmonies, pretending we were a girl group. I kept checking myself about my own hypocrisy—I was being a hater, right? Judge-y. Jealous. So maybe Jinny is a little freaky with her ceiling fan God, but maybe I also just needed to lean into this new us. Plus, sometimes the screaming desire to be part of something is so loud you can't hear your gut going, *Nooooo.*

In the back of the Tahoe, even with my meds, I started feeling carsick a few miles out of Calabasas. The traffic was horrible. The traffic's always horrible. And Jinny was so irritated and she was driving so fast—well, at least trying to. We were telling her it was no problem because the track events weren't usually on time and we'd get there for Bee's first challenge, but Jinny didn't let up. She was bug-eyed, not cursing but muttering about the other drivers—procits, and illegals, geezers and gramz—weaving in and out of lanes that were not moving anyway, and I was getting sicker and sicker. I wondered if that was her plan.

And then we pull up in front of the Pasadena Courthouse and we're all like, wha. . . ? And Jinny goes, "Surprise."

That's when I realized why the road trip to Pasadena had gotten her so excited. The courthouse in Pasadena is where they take women who've been caught in illegal clinics, since the other courthouses in the area couldn't handle the traffic from the protesters. Pasadena handles all of the abortion-related crimes and built permanent barricades to keep back the Crusaders and hired a squad of goons to make sure there was relative peace.

The rest of us got quiet in the car, wondering exactly what we'd signed up for, but Jinny was on fire—flaming nervous energy and euphoria. After she parked, she got out and hefted this big green garbage bag out of the back of the Tahoe, going, "Come on. Come on. We don't wanna miss them!"

We got out and followed her over to join the other fifty or so people already there singing old-timey Christian hymns. "Onward, Christian Soldiers." "Nearer My God to Thee." Ugh. No wonder Christian rock got so popular. No wonder Jagger Jonze rose so high so fast. It was a crowd of mostly white people.

Mostly women, but a few men and children too. They all had signs but hadn't hoisted them yet. I read the stack against the wall: *Baby killer. Murderer. No Mommy No!*

I said, "Um, Jinny . . . This is one hundred percent not okay. What are we doing here?"

Jinny couldn't hear me over the roar of the crowd as a police van pulled up to the curb. She reached for the green garbage bag.

I'm like, "Jinny. I don't want to be here. You should have asked us."

That she heard. She turned on me slowly, making sure the other girls were watching. "Don't tell me you believe in abortion, Miller," she said.

"Get your religion off my body?" I replied.

Jinny turned back to the idling police van and began to shout, "No, Mommy! No!" Around us, the crowd took up the chant, including Zara, which really tore me.

I wasn't down with any of it. Plus, *No, Mommy! No!* Seriously? That was a creepy fucking thing to yell at a woman who'd recently terminated her pregnancy, or who'd been caught in the waiting room of an underground clinic.

The first woman out of the back of the van wore a pair of mud-caked faux BushBoots, pleather disasters that made my heart ache for her before I even laid eyes on her face. Her coat was what we oh so sensitive girls called Nino Kmarti, a term we applied to all clothes that poor people wear. She had blue hair twisted up into a knot at her crown. Dirty face. She looked homeless. And broken. The next woman was older, almost Shelley's age, and wellish-dressed in Ann Taylor and good shoes. What's her story? Did she already have fifty kids and a demanding job and couldn't deal? The next person out of the van wasn't a woman. She looked to be our age. A girl. She was wearing jeans and a crop top and she had frizzy hair and freckles and she was sobbing, and all I could think was, That could be me. It could be me.

The woman in bad clothes didn't look our way. None of them did, even when the protesters began to shout from behind the barricades, "Baby killer! Murderer!" An armed security guard took the elbow of the sobbing teenager after she stumbled on the long walkway toward the courthouse steps.

Jinny's face was red. Veins popping at her temple. Zara shouted along with her, taking the sign someone shoved into her hands, "No Mommy NO!"

"Oh my God. You guys. This is not us."

"Not you, maybe," Jinny said.

"Can we please go now?"

Dee and Fee were just sort of there, not joining in with the protesters but not supporting my objections either. I wished Brooky were with us.

"YOU WILL PAY FOR WHAT YOU DID! NOT OKAY TO KILL YOUR KID!" Jinny sang when the rest took up the new chant.

"Stop. Please stop this," I said.

Jinny fished in her pocket and tossed me the keys to the Tahoe. "You're welcome to wait in the car."

I looked around at my hive. "What are we doing here? Since when is this us?"

Jinny took a breath, eyes blazing. "We're here because killing innocent babies is sin. And this *is* us."

Zee backed Jinny up. "You don't have to believe the Bible to know killing is wrong."

"It's about choice. A personal choice. You don't get to decide for other people. You can't see that, Zee?"

Jinny goes, "So if I get annoyed with you and borrow my mom's pistol to shoot you in the head, it's a choice?"

"Not the same thing."

"Murder is murder, Rory." She squatted down and opened the green garbage bag. I nearly puked when I saw what was inside. A dozen or so foam rubber fetuses, fake blood–covered and real-looking. Like they could have been used on a movie set. Fucking disturbing.

Jinny grabbed one by the teeny tiny hand and hurled it in the direction of the women being marched into the courthouse. The thing hit the young girl on the side of the head.

Then Zee dipped her hand into the bag and threw the fetal abomination as hard as she could, missing all three women because Zee has no aim.

I grabbed the heavy green garbage bag before Jinny could take another of those horrible things and started marching back to the Tahoe.

Fee followed me. Rather than head for the car, we sat down in a grassy area near the parking lot, under the shade of a eucalyptus. "Fee," I said. "This is messed."

"I know."

"At the very least, she should have told us she was bringing us here."

"True."

"Did you see Zee? What was that?"

"I know. Gross. It's just . . ."

"Just . . . ?"

"Well, they have a right to their opinions, right?"

Fee? I mean, I know she was rattled by what we'd just seen,

but why was she not offended? "So it's okay to scream at those poor women and throw shit at their heads?"

"Not saying that. Just . . . I just want us all to get along."

When the protest ended, Jinny and Zara and Delaney came bounding up to find us under the tree, all chatty and friendsy like it was all no big thing. "We're twenty minutes from the field," Dee said. "We gotta fly."

In the car, Zee asked Jinny where she got the foam rubber fetuses because they looked so dead real, and Jinny said her dad imports them wholesale from China because they're made of some substance that's banned in America.

I couldn't help myself. "So on top of how formally shitty that was, now those toxic things will just sit in a landfill polluting the earth? Ugh, you guys."

"Oh my gosh. Here goes Planet Girl," Zee said. *Gosh.* She stopped saying *God*—taking His name in vain—when she noticed it made Jinny Hutsall cringe.

"I'm not Planet Girl." I couldn't let it go. "It's just, come on. Little kids make those foam thingies in sweatshops in China? So basically you exploit children as you protest to save children?"

"You worry about the Chinese people and their job benefits and I'll worry about American children who're being murdered by their own mothers," Jinny said.

"Women are still going to have abortions. You get that, right? No matter the law. No matter you Crusaders. So they gotta go to Mexico? I mean, knitting needles in the basement like in our freaking grandmothers' time? I'm glad there's a Pink Market. I'm glad there's an underground network with actual doctors and surgical instruments. Thank God." I said that last part pretty emphatically.

"So you obviously won't be coming with us to the next protest, right, Rory?" Jinny said. "The week after AVB there's a really big one in Palm Springs. We can all stay the weekend at our desert place. And I know I'm going to sound like a brat, but my dad said he'd get UberCopter for us so we don't have to sit in traffic."

I closed my eyes because I felt sick from the driving, and the demonstration, and Fee's attitude that this wasn't worth rocking the boat over, and also because I couldn't stand to see how excited my friends got about going to Jinny's place in the desert. I definitely wouldn't be joining them, but I also knew that if Fee went, I'd die.

Brooky won all of her events at the track meet except for long jump, where she took second. We celebrated her victories and took tons of pics, and I faked a smile because I didn't wanna be a bummer for her sake. I wished she could have driven home with us, but she had to take the team bus. If Jinny started up again about abortion and baby killers, at least Bee would've stood up to her in her own unconfrontational way.

I really felt sick on the way home. Turns out that I was on the first day of a really bad flu.

Jinny was slick, calling to me in the backseat, "I think I owe you an apology, Rory. I didn't know you were an anti-Life person. Just never occurred to me. Guess I should have known."

Was that an apology? Fuck. "What would Jesus do? Right, guys?" I said. "Right, Zee?"

Jinny smiled, but I could see in the rearview mirror all the microaggressions on her face. "Christ would weep, Rory. God wants us to save the babies."

I wanted to ask Jinny if she heard God talking to her through the white noise of her bedroom fan or if He was, like, riding the rotating blades, and didn't that make them both super-dizzy. Instead, I said, "Those women just looked really scared. What if they were raped? What if it was incest? Anyway, it's not for us to judge. Judge not lest ye be judged? Remember, Jesus said that."

"He did," Dee agreed.

"Jesus said a lot of things," Jinny said.

"I don't feel well," I said. "I think I might be getting the flu."

"Me either," Fee said. I don't know if she was trying to have my back or also felt carsick. "Can we turn up the air-conditioning back here?"

"Fever in the body opens a door for the devil," Jinny said.

"You're already a heathen, Rory, so watch out," Zee said, mostly joking, I think.

Jinny knew I was sick. So of course she goes, "Let's stop for fro-yo before we go home."

The drive took forever. I watched the world pass by from the window of the Tahoe, wondering about the people in the cars all around us. I spend a lot of time wondering about people—the voyeur thing again. I really wanted to know why the old couple in the Audi beside us were arguing, and who the bald guy in the Beemer was yelling at in his speakerphone, and if the kid crying in the backseat of the Honda knew his parents were assholes for not putting him in a car seat. You never have to wonder who the Crusaders are. They wear Bible verse T-shirts and put Jesus fish and sword decals on their bumpers and windows. So many of those decals around now, and more as we approached our Calabasas bubble.

On the outside patio at the fro-yo place, as the girls licked Oreo crumbs and frozen oil product off plastic spoons, I sat sweaty, shivering and silent. Jinny wouldn't give it up. "What we did before the track meet, Rory? That was God's will. You have to fight for right. You get that? Like, God is waiting for you to come back to Him. And all the stuff you're saying now and doing now against His will? He'll forgive."

"Okay."

Jinny put her spoon down and said we should all pray that I'd see the light sooner rather than later. Zara looked at me, kinda apologetic, then joined hands with Jinny as she whispered, "Please God, help our sister feel the power of Your spirit. Please lift the curtain on the darkness in her soul."

Fee and Delaney kept spooning yogurt into their mouths so they didn't have to take part in praying for my soul.

"I don't need prayers," I said. "I just really need to go home."

Jinny pretended she didn't hear. "My mother's best friend was a heathen, you know, Rory. When she was young. Like, she wasn't raised with God, and she's the best Crusader I know. There's hope for you. I'll never stop praying for you."

"Okay."

Zee asked, "So how did she find God? Was it through your mom and dad?"

That's when Jinny told this story about the best friend of her mysterious mother—who has been working at some mysterious job overseas since they moved to Hidden Oaks. Jinny said that when her mother's friend got out of college, she took the first job she could get, as a receptionist at an abortion clinic in Chicago— "back when killing babies was legal."

According to Jinny, one night the woman got home from work then realized she'd forgotten her phone, so she drove all the way back to the clinic to get it and was surprised to see some sketch strangers, not clinic employees, working in the operating room. She wondered what was going on, so she listens at the door and she hears these people laughing and she looks inside and sees these skeez guys there smoking weed and sorting the frozen bagged fetuses from that week's abortions, separating them into three bins. One of the bins was labeled *Medical.* Another was labeled *Cosmetic.* The third bin had no label.

The other girls were hanging on Jinny's words, but I couldn't let her go on. "That's not true, Jinny. None of that was ever proven."

"Abortion clinics were definitely selling dead babies to the cosmetic company for that thousand-dollar firming cream, Rory. Everyone knows that."

"My mother said all of that stuff was made up. Propaganda."

"Well, my mother's best friend saw it with her own eyes." Jinny made a screw-face.

"What was the third bin for?" Zee asked.

"Well, my mom's friend wondered about that too. So she got in her car and waited until they'd loaded the bins into this van and she followed."

"She didn't call the cops?" I said.

"No. She followed the truck for an hour to this suburban neighborhood, and this guy gets out of the van and he takes the *Cosmetic* bin to the door and this geezer answers and smiles and gives the guy a briefcase, which was obviously full of cash, and he takes the bin like it's pizza delivery and goes back inside. Well, guess what? That guy was a retired chemist who was working for that cosmetic company. My mother's friend outed him later that night. And he's in jail right now. For life."

I grabbed my phone. Ready to google. "What was his name?"

"Don't remember."

"I call bullshit."

She ignored me. "She keeps following the van and the guys take the next bin—the one labeled *Medical*—to the parking lot of a vape shop and he gives it to a guy in a black car parked outside. He gets a duffel bag in exchange, which was also, obviously, full of money."

"I can't believe you believe this stuff. There was no evidence for any of those things, Jinny."

Dee piped up. "Unproven doesn't mean untrue."

Zee goes, "So what about the bin with no label?"

"Well, she keeps following, right, and they drive and drive and she's wondering if they're going to Cleveland or something, and it's been like an hour, and she's getting tired, and then the van pulls up outside this Chinese restaurant."

I groaned, loudly.

We'd all heard the rumors. For years. Everyone had. Urban legend. People point to those disgusting rumors as part of the reason the government defunded Planned Parenthood. We girls had discussed the fact that we did not believe the old stories.

"Stop," I said. "Please stop, Jinny." I thought I might throw up at the table.

Jinny paused. "You're calling my mother's best friend a liar?"

"I'm just saying stop."

"Fertility soup." She stared at me.

"No."

Dee's chin started quivering.

"Those stories are really dangerous, Jinny. It's like people used to tell stories about Jews with horns and all. It's just too much."

Fee, who had been focused on her frozen yogurt during the whole exchange, looked up and said, "Can we agree to disagree

and talk about shoes for the ball instead? Mr. Tom said he'll buy
me the Miu Mius."

Dee clapped. "Told you he would!"

Zee tilted her head. "People used to say Jews have horns?"

"Yes. And tails. And that we smell like sulfur."

Fee put her nose in my neck and goes, "Only if sulfur smells
like Dior." Then she realized I was burning up with fever. "We
gotta get you home."

That night, I was too sick to watch Jinny from my window,
but I imagined her convo with the Jesus fan was pretty lively, as
she no doubt shared with Him, like a proud daughter, the many
righteous acts of her day.

Now I want to remind Fee about that day of the track meet,
and how Jinny was fanning the flames with that story about fertility soup. I want to make her understand that Jinny sees her acts
of aggression as a service to God, and that makes her freaking
dangerous. If she could only see how truly warped Jinny Hutsall
is, I think Fee'd join me in my fear and loathing instead of resisting me, and the truth.

But she's busy looking out the window, leaning against the
wall for support. All she's said in the past little while is, "Winds
are starting back up."

The drunk guy's truck is still in his driveway. I wonder if he'll
be mad when he finds out his Gatorade is missing.

Fee asked me to check online again. She seems relieved when I'm writing, or checking online, instead of talking. It's all too much. I get it.

Courtesy of breaking news and trend alerts on Nina's pink laptop, we now know that my DNA has been found in my Prius. Shocking. My DNA, in my own car. Some of the media is treating the discovery like proof of guilt. Hilarious, and yet not. They showed an illustration of my 2015 white Prius with the turtle decal—they keep showing the freaking turtle decal like it means something, but it was the previous owner who actually put it there, so whatever—with hundreds of red dots to indicate where my fingerprints have been found. They've matched Fee's DNA to hair samples found in the car too. Seriously? Like, it's my car and she's my friend, so, of course . . . They don't have results on the blood in the backseat yet. The blood. Oh my God. I can hardly bring myself to think about it.

What the fuck???????!!!!!!!!!!!!!! Someone just knocked at the fucking shed door!!!!!!!!!!!!!!!!!!

The knock. It was so timid. So sorry to intrude.

And even though Javier said not to open the shed door to anyone, I did. Just a crack. No one was there. So I think I'm hearing things, right? I'm, like, losing my shit because of all the trauma? But no. I look down and there's an old plastic grocery bag—hardly ever see those in Calabasas—at my feet.

I stay hidden behind the door because I can hear copters in the distance. I look around, and I can't see anyone at first, and then something catches my eye behind a nearby bush. Not the pit bull. No. It's a kid. A girl. In a red-white-and-blue dress. A skinny little shaved-head girl in a fucking Patriot Girls dress. I had that exact dress when I was seven! I thought I was seeing a ghost—Nina, maybe? This little girl is Latina, but she looks nothing like the pics of Javier's daughter, and besides—ghosts? Um. No.

We lock eyes, this little bald girl and me, and she lifts her chin to the sky to alert me to the fact that there's a drone hovering right over the shed. I don't move a muscle until the drone flies off. I look at the girl again and she kinda smiles, and nods, and dis-appears into the brush.

The drunk man's truck is still in the driveway. I wonder if she knows him. I wanna warn her she shouldn't be playing near his yard. I drag the white plastic bag she left us into the shed with my foot, and shut the door.

Fee is like, holy shit, and we open the bag, and inside— I can't even tell you what it was like to find three cans of cold soda and two squished peanut butter sandwiches. This little girl? Wha...?

The experience of drinking that freaking cola was orgiastic. When Fee finished her can, she reached for another, and I'm like, "Fee, we gotta save it for later. We don't know when we'll have anything to drink again." We hoovered the peanut butter sand-wiches, though, and afterward Fee said she felt almost like herself again, and I did too.

Then, like at the touch of some unseen button, I was taken by a crygasm. Lasted five whole minutes. First time I've cried, I mean for real bawled, in so long. I think it was partly because that little kid took such a risk for us, but also because the stupid peanut butter sandwich took me back to Sunday mornings when I was small, and the rest of the cul-de-sac was at church, and Shelley would go for a walk to nowhere, and I'd snuggle with Sherman on the sofa, eating the peanut butter toast he made us, watching *Rick and Morty*—our secret because Shell thought it was inappropriate—feeling so loved, and safe, and so close to my dad.

The last Sunday morning I spent with him? Shelley left the house so that my father could pack up his suitcases in peace. She wanted me to come with her, for a walk at the ocean, or a drive to the Grove, but I told her I was gonna laze with the girls because they'd just gotten back from church. That's not why I stayed, though.

He left the double doors to my parents' master wide open. I watched from behind my door at the end of the hall, as Sherman collected his belongings from his bedside table—his watch and phone, a couple of vials of pills, loose change and some crumpled bills, eyedrops and lip balm, most of which he stuffed into his pocket.

But the framed family portrait that he kept at his bedside—a silly photo snapped by Zara's dad at that Super Bowl party where my parents are laughing with each other as they pretend to crush me between them—the one Sherm called the best family photo ever? He left that on the table.

I crept down the hall, unseen, as my father emptied his drawers, tossing the contents into the three suitcases that lay open on the bed. It was like he was fleeing. Not just leaving. He headed into the walk-in closet off the bathroom as I reached the door. I stood there listening to the sound of hangers clicking.

In a minute my father came back into the room, struggling with an armful of suits and shirts, and jumped when he saw me.

He'd cleared out his closet of everything except the floral Hawaiians. I guess Sugar Tits didn't care for Tommy Bahama.

"I thought you were at Brook's?" he said.

I shook my head. I didn't wanna cry in front of him so didn't, couldn't, speak at all.

He folded his suits in half and stuffed them into the largest suitcase. He said nothing for a long time, and then, "This doesn't change anything between us, RorRor."

I looked at the detritus of my father's life in the suitcases on my parents' bed. Dude.

"I just need a break, Rory. Your mother's been . . . I just need a break. Some space."

I tilted my head. I remember thinking, like, maybe this will all make more sense if I look at it sideways.

"There's no villain here, Rory. Marriages go through hard times."

I noticed then that he'd taken off his wedding band. Instead of the thick gold symbol of love everlasting, there was a thick white tan line on his naked finger. He saw me looking and hid his hand in his pocket. Like, why?

"You shouldn't be here for this, Rory."

I stared.

"It's just making it harder on both of us."

I stared harder.

"Wanna have a hug and then you can head over to Brooky's?"

I didn't respond.

"Please don't, Rory. Honest to God, I've had enough from your mother."

I said nothing.

"I don't know what she's told you, but you should not be involved in any of this."

I was driving him crazy. I realized it felt good. Powerful.

"Ror, this is—"

His phone rang in his pocket. He didn't take it out. He knew who it was. So did I.

"Rory. You have to go now."

I stood my ground. His phone rang again. And again. And again.

Finally he answered, and told the person on the other end, in a whisper, that he'd have to call back. Then he turned back to me and said accusingly, "This day is hard enough."

I gave him nothing.

"Please."

I kept staring.

"Rory."

Nada.

Now he was really getting pissed. "Should I call your mother to come and get you? This isn't okay, Rory. I don't know what little game you're playing here . . ."

I wanted to scream at him about the little game *he* was playing, but bit my tongue. Sherman didn't know what the fuck to do with my silence.

He shook his head like nothing more could be done here, and headed back into the bathroom to pack up his toiletries. I listened to him opening drawers and rattling bottles, wanting to hear some sign that he was upset, but no. Hadn't shed a tear for us. Least none that I'd seen.

The family photo on his bedside table called to me. I picked it up, thinking, Who even are these people? This blond woman and middle-aged dude making love eyes at each other? The freckly teen squished between them with the big loopy grin?

These people were a lie. Before my father returned from the bathroom, I crammed the framed photo into the middle of the smallest suitcase, between his socks and underwear.

When Sherman came out of the bathroom, he seemed surprised to find me still there. I'm fucking relentless. Haven't you heard?

"I love you, Rory."

"I know," I said.

"I know you know, but I still need to tell you." Relieved that I was finally talking to him, he smiled at me.

"I know." I didn't smile back.

"I know you know." Still smiling.

"Sherman," I said, making sure he was understanding me. "I *know*."

He stopped smiling. "What do you think you know?"

"Sugar Tits," I hissed, then turned and left him there.

Tears blinded me as I careened down the hall toward my bedroom. I slammed the door shut behind me and fell onto the bed, crying out in my head: *God. Help us. Please.*

Anyway.

There is no God. Prayers are not answered.

The little bald girl bringing us soda and peanut butter sandwiches? Fee thinks that was an act of God. I think it was just human.

Stopping now. Fee asked if it's time to check in with Jagger Jonze's *Higher Power Hour.* It is.

So Fee and I watched the show. Jonze said some pretty shitty things about us under the guise of praying for our souls. Fee shrugged like it didn't hurt. But it did hurt. This does hurt. It hurts like hell to be wrongly accused and scared for your life. And then, in the finale, Jonze announced that he was raising the bounty to TWO million fucking dollars. And he was purposefully vague about whether the bounty means dead or alive.

Everyone in the audience—all the Crusader types—cheered his condemnations of me and Fee. Who cheered the loudest? Front row center in white sundresses even though it's freaking November and that's so boojie? Our girls—Zara and Delaney and Brooky, joining hands with Jinny Hutsall—whom Jagger invited up onstage to sing "Thank God for American Girls."

If words were arrows, we'd have died a thousand deaths by now. Online, the ultra Crusaders have been calling for an old-fashioned crucifixion. I am so done with violent religious people. So done.

Apparently the Feds are holding a press conference soon about the contents of the purse. I think it's hilarious that this is press conference material, but Fee is really freaked. She's like, "What if they lie, Ror? What if they say something was in it that wasn't in it?"

"Now you're getting it, Fee."

"I know people lie, Rory. I'm not stupid."

"They've already accused us of doing the most heinous shit imaginable, so what's in your purse that could make us look any worse?"

"Nothing. It's just—my purse. You know."

What is it about that purse? I'm remembering last night in the bathroom with Fee. Before the bomb. I'd gotten my period, which I only realized when I sat down to pee. Fee was still in the stall feeling the first effects of what I'm pretty sure were poisoned chocolates. I left the stall and was so pissed to find the pad dispenser empty, as usual, so I asked Fee if she had a tampon because we cycle together and she's usually prepared. Her Gucci clutch was on the counter and I go, "Fee, you got a plug in your purse?"

And she's like, "NO!"

"Okay."

"Do not go in my purse, Ror!"

"Why can't I go in your purse? I always go in your purse."

Then Fee said she was out of toilet paper and asked me to find her some, so I got distracted. But now I'm thinking—what is in her purse that I wasn't supposed to see?

Warm blood trickles down my arse and into my sopping gown as I sit here on the shed floor beside Fee. "What's happening, Fee? What was in your purse? Are you doing Addies again? I mean, don't, because I'd kill for your curves, and Adderall makes you bitchy."

"It's not Addies."

"What then? Talk to me?" I'm worried. Fee's no stranger to pills. She's used Addies, and had an unhealthy reliance on Tylenol 3s for a while there too, and told me her cousin Dante gave her Zan when she was in Cerritos.

"Nothing."

"Something."

"I just . . . There's a pic of my cousin Dante in my wallet."

"So?"

"Ror, he's illegal."

"Okay, but, I mean, they already raided your abuela's procit community and he wasn't there, so . . ."

"I just don't wanna get him in trouble."

"Sure that's all?" I obviously don't think that's all.

"Ror . . . please just . . ."

I toggled back to InfoNow, but the Feds haven't made the announcement yet. I guess I'll find out what the fuck is in my best friend's purse when the rest of the world does.

Fee goes, "What about that little girl, though? Where do you think she came from? How did she know we were here?"

"Dunno."

"Think she'll come back?"

"She must live in one of the trailers on the other side of that bunch of oaks."

"Maybe she'll bring more food. I can't stop thinking about Fatburger. And all the other stuff I didn't eat when it was in front of my face . . . all that stuff I hurled on purpose."

Remember that overloaded buffet table at Leons' Labor Day barbecue? Waste. Such an abstract concept to us. Waste was wasted on us. Abundance we understood.

Then Fee said, "I wonder if Miles is, like . . . I hope Miles doesn't believe we did this."

Brooky's brother? "Who gives a shit about Miles?" I get the feeling she's trying to distract me again.

Still nothing about Fee's purse, but guess whose face popped up on my screen on cable news? Chase Mason. That bald anchor from CNN just did an interview with him on the steps of the

Calabasas Library, where this big crowd of people has gathered to chant for our capture.

When I saw him, I wanted to weep with relief, because, like, my crush is gonna have my back, and say something like, "I believe Rory Miller is innocent." Right? But I'm watching his beautiful face—those big brown eyes—and I'm hearing these words coming out of his mouth, and I really do cry, but not from relief.

The reporter asks him, "Can you give us some insight, Mr. Mason? Who is Rory Miller?"

Chase looks straight into the camera, like he's looking straight at me. "Well, I guess she's not who she said she was. I guess she was kinda in disguise."

He used my own words—my flirty words—against me.

The reporter prods some more. "Was anything suspicious about her behavior while she was volunteering here? Did you have reason to be suspicious?"

"Do you mean did she meet people here at the library?" Chase says. "Did a lot of people come to see her here? Yes. A lot. She used to take girls into the media room. Not sure what they did in there."

What the fuck? My hive came to visit me at the library a few times. No one else. Literally no one else. My four friends. And Jinny, a few times this fall. And never once did I take anyone into the media room! That was him!

"The girls who came to see Rory Miller? Were any of them visibly pregnant?"

"I couldn't tell. I couldn't say."

"Would you say it's possible that she used the library as a base for her Red Market activities?"

"I don't know about all that. I just know she said she was looking for trouble."

You. Fucker. Throwing me under the bus. Undercover Crusader? Chase is the one in disguise.

The news showed footage of the inside of the library. Empty. It is usually empty. Hardly anyone uses the local library except a few fogies from the nearby retirement village. Then the reporter starts talking about how this quiet, empty building would make the perfect, unassuming place to meet teen girls seeking illegal abortions and Red Market payouts for the sale of fetal tissue, or girls looking for ways to sell their unwanted babies for cash.

They cut back to Chase and the crowd outside on the steps, and he's saying, "Rory Miller's smart. I wouldn't put anything past her."

"You believe that a couple of teen girls are going to outwit the Feds and all the Crusaders and bounty hunters and everyone else out there looking for them?"

And Chase says, "Actually? Yeah."

Et tu, Chase Mason?

As I'm watching this vid of Chase's interview, in the crowd behind him I spot a green Roots ball cap hiding a mop of curly, dark hair, and under the cap is this heart-faced woman in too-big sunglasses, and then I'm like, *Holy shit. That's Aunt Lill.* My Aunt Lilly is standing behind Chase Mason on the steps of the Calabasas Library, looking like she's in some kind of disguise.

Aunt Lilly would never wear a ball cap because hat-hair, and plus, she's wearing a pink T-shirt, well, actually a V-shirt, like the Crusaders wear, with Bible verse numbers—Corinthians 14:34. She hates pink—like, it's a thing. She'll wear the pink ribbons in support of breast cancer research, and maybe, like, a pink button or whatever when she marches for women's rights. But what's with the pink Bible verse shirt? Trying to blend in? I'm looking at her in her pink V-shirt and I can't help but go—those numbers? Do they mean something? Is it a telephone number? Is the other half of it on her back? Turn around! Aunt Lilly? Help?

The reporter asks Chase if he has any final words or thoughts. Well, doesn't Mr. Lead Singer just whip out his old-school card with his band name and website info and hold it up to the camera and go, "If you're looking for a band for your next event, check us out." Fuck. So that's his gig? He wants publicity for his stupid fucking crap-ass band. Crushed by my crush.

I told Fee Aunt Lilly was here, but she doesn't seem excited, because Lilly can't save us. And when I tell Fee about Chase Mason's betrayal, she is not mad for me. She is not sympathetic or bestie-ish in any way. Fee is not acting like Fee.

"Who cares, Ror? It's not like he's your boyfriend. And Lark's Head sucks anyway."

"Too true."

It just hit me that something was wrong with the business card Chase Mason held up to the camera.

I just went back online and I'm like—right—the card says *Larkspur*, not *Lark's Head*. They changed the shitty name to an even shittier name. Okay. Whatever.

Will the betrayals never end? I will never forget what Chase Mason did.

Makes me think of Montreal. My parents dragged me along to a weekend conference there when I was in seventh. We got stuck in a traffic jam on the way to our hotel and I noticed the license plates on the cars said *Je me souviens*. Shelley told me it means "I remember." Like "Lest we forget" in America. She said it was a call to keep in mind all the terrible things that have happened in history or else we're doomed to repeat them. Maybe because of the Jewish thing, or the human thing, I don't know, but it stuck with me.

Je me souviens, Chase Mason.

More noises outside. Can't see anyone or anything, but I'm really scared about that old man coming over here to get his stray tarp.

According to the news, the air surveillance and bounty hunters are concentrating their efforts on a homeless encampment near Griffith Park now, where hundreds of tipsters say we're hiding. They've shown pics of all these ATF guys—because we're packing, don't you know—and ICE guys, of course, hassling the homeless. I'm sorry to all of the humans who are enduring this bullshit because of us.

The little bald girl's nowhere in sight. I hope she doesn't come back, because what if she leads the hunters to us? What if someone in a copter wonders what a little shaved-head girl is doing playing around a random shed in the hills? Wish I could thank her, though. Well, I can. Here. Now. Thank you, little bald angel in the Patriot Girls dress.

Just occurred to me that little girl might have cancer or something. So skinny. Damn.

Also in the news just now—the Kardashians. Mama Kris has posted a pic of her and her five daughters, and all the granddaughters, in long white wedding-style gowns. So *Vogue* cover, but whatever. "Innocent until proven guilty": that was the caption. Choked me up. Seriously. Thank you. From the bottom of my shattered heart. I will KUWTK until I die. Fee too. That must have been hard for those girls, because they are God people. Like, that shout-out means everything. It gives us hope.

And hope is hard to hold on to right now. Especially since I also just read that they're going to be moving my mother to another facility because the crowds where she's currently being held are clogging up the roads and making it hard for emergency vehicles to get to a fast-moving brush fire that broke out near Bel Air this morning.

They showed the crowd gathered outside the courthouse, and I'll be fucked if it isn't Chase Mason again. Front and center of the crowd, wearing a red Larkspur T-shirt. Must have taken a copter to get there so fast.

He wasn't waving an American flag around, chanting, "Burn Shelley, burn," like some of the protesters, but he was standing with them. And Aunt Lill is there on the courthouse steps too. She's still wearing her Roots ball cap and she's still got on that gross pink T-shirt. Those numbers: 14:34. I googled the Corinthians verse—something about "women should be silent in the churches." I'm so bad at riddles. The fuck, Aunt Lill? I know she's trying to send me a message. Just? What? Go to a church and be quiet? Doubt that. Those numbers mean nothing to me. I've been adding the numbers up and moving them around. Nada.

Aunt Lilly knows about my crush on Chase Mason. Maybe she went to the library to see if he had any ideas about where we might be? Or did she think we might be hiding there? In the courthouse crowd, I saw her moving closer to Chase. Why? Is she gonna kick him in the balls for all the crap he said about me to the media?

After Chase's interview, I watched a panel discussion on CNN—one of those split-screen jobbies with multiple guests.

Jagger Jonze was streaming live from the foyer of Hutsalls' mansion, the crystal chandelier a halo of light over his head, along with three other female guests. One is this well-known feminist who was there to discuss abortion laws, and steered the conversation away from the AVB incident, which she claimed was a publicity stunt orchestrated by the alt-right. She said Fee and I, two little Christian virgins, were prolly in on the whole thing. Another guest was the evangelical adviser to the president, who made a fierce plea to the bounty hunters not to kill us. The blue-eyed former pageant queen didn't say not to kill us because killing two innocent girls would be wrong, or don't kill us because mercy. She said, "Don't kill them because they'll become martyrs." Ugh.

The other guest was a well-known child psychologist, who last night tweeted out "Another Case of Gucciosis?"—a term she just coined, which is now the title of her new book. She claims the label-whorishness of my generation, our worship of celebrity culture and the steady bombardment of images of designer goods causes a constant craving that turns into addiction, and that, like any addict, we'll do inconceivable shit for our shit.

Jonze is nodding his head over the shame of it all, tugging at his designer T-shirt in the light of the hundred-thousand-dollar chandelier. Then he tells the world they should pray for us. He says my involvement in the ball was obviously just a way to mask the truth about who I am and what I do. He even floated the idea that I brainwashed Fee! Godless people, he said, have no moral compass. If people have no God, and no book of rules and guidelines to follow, they can't be good. So they must be evil.

That is just so impressively stupid. If you don't believe in God, you have no ethics? What about remote tribes—like that one they just discovered in the Amazon when they "accidentally" clear-cut one of the last protected areas of the rain forest? Those people lived peaceably, though they had no word for God, and no word for war, and no word for hate. When the American anthropologists figured out their language, and asked them about survival, the people said, basically, "All men are my brothers. All women my sisters. All children are my children. We care for each other in the way we want to be cared for."

Reverend Jonze says the Christian God is the one true God. Dude, it's like the guys from the tribe say—the do-unto-others thing is just common sense. It doesn't need to be based on theology. Like, treat people the way you want to be treated and the world works, and we survive as a species. So fucking simple. The Golden Rule is on our hard drives as human beings! Religion is the virus that corrupts.

Oh fuck. Fee just got up to look outside. She says the little kid in the Patriot Girls dress is back.

"Where is she?"

"Over by the trailer? Are you typing what I'm saying right now? Please don't."

I can't help myself. I can't stop my fingers. "Yes, Fee. I told you, I'm writing it all down. Someone has to document this shit."

"Okay. Well, blog this—the kid is dancing in the gravel driveway. Dancing and singing."

"Got it."

"Maybe she's whack."

"Maybe."

"There's sky traffic."

"I know."

"A MiniCop coming up over the cliffs from the beach. He can see her."

"No one will mistake her for one of us."

"True. She's tiny."

"Think she's sick?"

"She's bald. And skinny. She has some big bruises on her legs, but she's a kid, so, I don't know."

"What's she doing now?"

"She's still dancing . . . Oh my God, Rory, she's doing the moves from the intro to the kids' show! She's doing the choreography. Remember how we used to do the choreography for *Dancing Dina*? Remember how we all practiced the dance and performed it for the parents in the Leons' backyard? That makes me wanna cry."

"Why isn't that dog barking or whatever with the kid kicking gravel around in his driveway?"

"Maybe he's, like, hiding somewhere, licking his wounds. Or maybe that drunk guy killed him last night."

"Does she have another plastic bag?"

"Not that I can see."

"And no one's watching her from the trailer window?"

"No."

"Is the TV still on in the trailer?"

"Ror? Ror? RORY!"

"Shh."

"Stop typing."

"I can't." I really can't. I actually can't lift my hands off the laptop. How's that for addiction?

"Rory? Seriously, stop typing right the fuck now and listen to me."

I'm listening, but my fingers keep pressing keys.

"There are three dudes with rifles coming through the brush."

I take a minute to repeat to myself what Fee just said. *There are three dudes with rifles coming through the brush.* "Tracker dogs?"

"Don't see any dogs."

"Heading this way?"

"Yes. Huge guys, with long rifles, dressed in camo like they're out to shoot deer."

"Maybe they've come to help us?"

"With rifles?"

"Maybe Javier sent them?"

"I don't think so." She turned away from the window and crouched down beside me "Is this it? Oh God, Ror. I think this is the end."

"Should I press Post?"

She's crying. "Yes."

"But what if they don't find us? What if they don't look in here?"

"What if they do, though? Ror, stop typing!"

I can't. "If they don't find us right now, and I press Post, the whole world will know where we are."

"Press it, Ror."

"But what if they're here to save us?"

Fee raised herself back up to peek out the window. "They're carrying an American flag."

"Fuck."

"Oh my God, Ror. The little girl. She's running over to them."

"Oh no. Oh no. Oh no."

"We're gonna die."

"No. Shh. We're not gonna die."

"She's talking to them. They're looking around. They're looking at the shed." Fee backed away from the window again. "I peed," she whispered.

"It's okay."

"Oh my God, did you just write that down?"

"It's all right."

Fee peeked out again.

"Are they coming?"

"They're still talking to the kid."

"What's she doing?"

"Nodding. She just keeps nodding."

"Think she knows about the bounty? She must."

"She's a kid."

"Kids know what money is. What's happening?"

"She's just nodding."

"Oh my God. Oh my freaking God."

"Ror . . . ?"

I don't know what to do. If this is the end, I need to get this blog out there, but there's so much more to tell . . . Please, God . . . I mean . . . Hey, God . . . I mean, just saying, if I've been wrong about you all this time, can you throw us a fucking bone here?

"Ror . . . ?"

"I think I just accidentally prayed."

"Well, pray for real."

"Are they coming this way?"

"They're all on their phones now. They keep looking up. They must be talking to someone in the sky. Oh my God. A big drone just showed up."

"Fuck."

"They're still talking."

"I'm pressing Post."

"NO!"

"No?"

"Stop!"

"Stop?"

"Oh my God. They're going away."

"What?"

"The kid is pointing to the road. The guys with the rifles are heading out that way. They're leaving, Ror."

"What?"

"They're walking away down that windy dirt road."

"Oh my God."

"They just went around the bend. And the drones and a bunch of copters are flying in the same direction, down the road and into the bush on the other side of the clearing!"

"Back into the bush?"

"I can't see them anymore."

"Oh my God."

"The little kid just looked over here. She gave me thumbs-up. They're gone, Ror. They're gone."

"Holy fuck." Holy fucking fuck.

"Rory Miller! I'm going to punch you in the tit if you don't stop typing right now!!!"

We're still shaking from the close call. When the men left, Fee just, like, dove at me, and we held on to each other for a really long time.

Then we heard another noise outside, and nearly died thinking the guys with rifles were back, or this time it could be a crew of Crusaders dragging a big wooden cross. I was the one who looked out the window, but there's no one out there, no sounds of clomping boots, nothing but the drone of the copters circling over the highway and beach. No sign of the bald girl either.

I stood at the window for a while, watching the wind kick up waves of dust around the tires of the trailer next door, creating an optical illusion so that the Airstream looks like it's in motion. The Calabasas temp online is ninety-six degrees. In here it must be one hundred and twenty. We have no fluid left to sweat.

Fee is still so thirsty. I really can't listen to how thirsty she is anymore, so I told her to go ahead and drink the can of soda we had left. She didn't even offer me a sip. Not that I would have taken it, but that's just not Fee.

I went online for a quick sec with Fee reading the bullet news over my shoulder. This old pink laptop, missing the %5 button, and with broken volume control, is everything. A lifeline to the real world of fake news, but also a dumping ground for my messed-up mind. Thanks again, Nina. If I wasn't writing about our situation in real time, I prolly wouldn't remember it the way it's actually happening. If I wait to tell our story until after we're saved, I'd likely try to trick it out with meaningful lines, censor my *fuck*s, and lay down a load of shit that sounds right instead of the ugly, uncensored truth. If I waited, I'd know how the story ends, and I'd be driving toward it, instead of taking the scenic route.

With Fee's chin on my shoulder, I scrolled down the InfoNow site. After the news about the fire in Bel Air and the threat to all the celebrity mansions, we're the second most trending topic in California. The hunt for us remains global news. Fair enough. The world wants to know if those demonic teens in wedding gowns have been caught yet. I hit the link to the article announcing when the Feds are gonna hold the news conference about the contents of Fee's purse. Fee read along with me and started to cry. I can't even ask her about the stupid purse anymore.

Gonna be honest. Fee's mood swings, her irritability, the way she hasn't been acting like herself? I asked her if she was doing Addies before, but now I'm wondering if it's something way worse. Like, I'm kinda scared she's been doing parfaits— those little test tubes of liquid caffeine with the cocaine cloud you snort before downing the shot. Parfaits started trending last year. Chase Mason told me about a guy he knew who died from doing two in a row. Parents all over the country have been checking their kids' trash for plastic test tubes that smell like espresso. Like, are they gonna announce that Fee is a drug addict? Further evidence of our guilt?

Fee wants it to be over. She wants us to get caught, as much as she doesn't want us to get caught. I get that. But she still doesn't seem to understand, or accept, that over could mean dead. Maybe I feel so different because I'm Jewish. Like, when you're even the slightest bit Jewish, your reality is that there are people in the world who want to eradicate you from the face of the earth because of the blood that runs in your veins. I remember Sherman telling me that, before he died, his dad gave him a map, a crayon map (his dad had dementia) with an escape route from his house in Winnipeg to the Israeli embassy in Toronto. It was the 1970s. Sherman's father wasn't observant in any way, but that kind of fear is passed down through generations. It has a name: epigenetic trauma. We learned about that in our psych class, but in relation to the Christians, not the Jews, or black people, or the homeless.

My father continues to escape scrutiny for the most part, which I really don't understand. No comments from him. No accusations about him. Maybe it has something to do with his generous contributions to the box church in Orange County. According to the news, Sherman's hired some big attorney to "protect his interests." What does that mean?

What I said before about how I wished my father were dead? I don't. I really don't. To be honest, for the past three years, I just wished that Sherman would ditch Sugar Tits and come home. That he'd fall on his knees and beg for forgiveness and tell his soul mate he was gonna spend the rest of his life making it up to her, to us, and just, like, be my daddy again. Stupid. I know. Fuck happy fucking endings.

Happy. I hate that word. I want to stab that word. That word offends me the way curses offend people who don't swear. The way taking the Lord's name in vain offends the Christians even though half of them do it anyway. *Happy*. It's a bullshit word. *Happy* is the word equivalent of Valentine's Day—Aunt Lilly said that. She told me about how her ex would say, "People choose happy." And that would make her crazy, because it's a fundamental lie. Christian people talk about happiness a lot, but that word does not appear in the Bible one time. Not once.

Aunt Lilly's barometer for all things? First World versus

Third World. So people can choose happy? People can find a hundred keys to happiness? Twenty tips for happy? All those stupid books. Like, there are seriously more books about how people can find personal satisfaction and happiness than there are books about how people can help other people find water and food. So basically, the "ingredients" in that idiot book *Recipe for a Happier You*? If you can't apply them to the starving mother cradling her fly-covered baby in the slave camp in West Africa, then it's bullshit. Period. If all of humanity can't use the same formula for this thing called happiness, it's a big fat North American lie.

I get that I'm an asshole for calling bullshit on happiness. I live in paradise. But I'm not happy. I have everything, but I feel confused, and empty. I don't wanna find happiness so much as I wanna find purpose. And love. I've been thinking—being a prisoner in a sweltering shed really makes you think—about how I can help the world when I grow up. Like, how I can be an activist, a volunteer, an influential blogger or lobbyist or something. Purpose. I get that. But happy? Aunt Lill says happy is like a rush of propofol—that drug they put you out with before surgery. It's just so much anesthetic.

Joy, though? I believe in joy, and not because that word is in the Bible. It's because joy is fleeting and real, and comes without a recipe. That orgasmic feeling of celebration and communion with something outside yourself? I've felt that. Never because of my fab clothes, or my big house, or anything material. Once upon a time, when I believed in God, I felt joy when I sang that song about how much Jesus loved me. And that other one about letting my light shine. I've felt joy with Shelley, because even at half-mast my mother's still boss. With Sherman, when he used to be Sherman. And I've felt joy with Fee. And the Hive.

Not a lot of joy in this shitty fucking shed right now.

It's sooo hot in here. *Caliente.* People say that's how our state got its name. *Caliente Fornia*—hot oven.

Come on, Javier. Come back already.

Fee moved to sit against the wall across from me. Says she's hot, and that I reek. It is. I do. She says she's not pissed at me, but she obviously is. She says she doesn't blame me for any of this, but she does. I mean, it is my fault we're here.

She's just sitting there, rubbing her poor tummy, staring into space, prolly hoping whatever embarrassing or incriminating thing that was in her purse melted in the blast and all this angst is for nothing. Damn. In this moment, I feel like I don't know her at all. Just sitting here looking at her and—

Oh. Fuck. There's a freaking lizard in the shed! Just saw him slink under the suitcases in the corner. Little green alligator lizard about the size of my palm, with a very long tail that I can see poking out from where he's hiding, less than a foot from Fee's bare leg. Fee is petrified of lizards. Like, how many times a day does she screech because there's a little blue skink on the path at school, or a harmless gecko resting on the Pebble Tec under the chaise by one of our pools. Even if we're in the car, she screams if she sees a freaking salamander in one of the flowering bushes in the medians. I love lizards. I think they are my spirit animal. In fact, if not for Fee, I'd see this little guy as some kind of good omen. If Fee sees it, she will scream.

Too late.

Oh. Fuck.

Just heard the trailer door creak open.

So, people, this happened. Fee saw the lizard and screamed like I knew she would. I'm looking at her going like, NOOOOooo.

Then we hear the neighbor's trailer door screech open, and boots pounding down the metal stairs, and I look out the shed window and there's the mean freaking drunk standing in the gravel beside his truck, stock-still, one arm in the air, one crooked finger pointing straight at the shed. My girls and I used to play Freeze Frame. He looked like that. Like scared that if he moves a muscle he'll get tagged out. I whisper to Fee, "Holy shit, the guy from last night is out there." We're dead. There's no place to hide in this freaking shed.

The wind is gusting hard. A big, spiky tumbleweed rolls toward the dude and stops at his feet, but he doesn't look down. Doesn't move at all, just stands there, still pointing, his eyes on the shed. There are no copters or drones overhead, at least none that I can see, and I'm just thinking, the fuck?

Fee comes to look out the window with me, careful, so he doesn't spot us. We can see that he's not as large as he'd seemed in the moonlight. We keep watching. Dude's not moving. Doesn't even blink.

Then the lizard skitters out from under the suitcases and winds his way to the greasy lawn mower near the door. Fee sees him from out of the corner of her eye. I don't have a chance to cover her mouth before she screams again. *Fuuuuccckkk.*

I nudge the lizard toward a gap in the wall with my toe. Fee's scream hangs in the air.

Out the window, dude's on the move, goose-stepping through the weeds toward us. But the little shaved-head girl appears from out of nowhere, sneaking up behind the guy. Where did she come from?

She calls out to him. We can't hear what she says, but he stops, and makes a six-point turn to face her, like it's all happening in slow motion. She moves a little closer.

We watch the dude raise his arm and swat at the little girl. She dodges his hand, and starts to back away. Then he reaches out with both arms and starts after her, like a zombie. That's when Fee and I bust out of the shed.

We didn't talk about it. Didn't check for copters and drones and bounty hunters. We ran straight out into the stinking, dusty wind, screaming, "Hey! Hey! Leave her alone!"

The guy turns around, and we see his face. He totally looks like the undead—unblinking eyes, just no one home. He starts taking uneven steps toward us, and the little girl seems scared.

Fee and I step to the guy, calling out to the little girl to run away, but she doesn't. And the dude—it's like he "comes to" for a sec, and he starts blinking, and I can see he recognizes us. He breaks out into this huge, ugly grin, and turns around and starts back for his Airstream—no doubt to get his phone. The little girl tries to stop him, but he pushes her into the trash cans beside the front porch.

Fee grabs his arm, saying, "Please. Stop." He throws her off, then shakes his finger at us, saying things in Spanish that I do not understand. Sounded like he was stroking out.

The little girl gets up and dodges the dude as she runs into the Airstream. The man stumbles after her. And that's when we hear the sound of a chopper coming up over one of the hills. We can't

run back to the shed across the open yard without being seen—
and we gotta stop this guy from hurting this little girl, and calling
the cops. So we run for the trailer too.

Hoarder. Piles of crap everywhere in a space already too tight.
Stuff he must've taken from people's trash—broken chairs and
old computers, bulb-less lamps, and stacks and stacks of hard-
cover English books. I nearly gagged from the smell—cream of
sewage soup.

The old TV is on—pictures of us flashing on the screen. He
points to the screen and back at us, and he nods 'cause he knows
he just won the lottery. Then he's muttering, stumbling over crap
on the floor as he's looking for his phone in the mess. We can't see
the little girl, but we hear her moving around in a curtained-off
room at the back.

Fee's trying to talk to the dude, telling him that we are innocent, that we didn't detonada the bomb, and please don't turn us
in, kinda like the way I'd pleaded with Javier when we got here.
But he just keeps looking for his phone. On the counter I see a
line of black ants marching toward a peanut butter–covered knife,
so I nab it and hold it behind my back. My hands are shaking bad.

Thought dude was looking for his phone, but when he turns
around, he has a gun. He gestures us toward a couple of broken
chairs. He wants us to sit. Never imagined it would end this way.
I think of my mother. And I think of my blog, and how I won't
have a chance to tell the whole story. That I'll never press Post.
Maybe I should have started at the end instead of the beginning.

Through the window we can see the helicopter banking in a
circle over the clearing. The guy with the gun turns his attention
to the copter too. I wonder if we could overpower him and take
the gun. He's got the shakes, which is terrifying. When he turns

back to us, I'm really afraid he's gonna pull the trigger by accident. He stuffs his free hand into his pocket to get his phone, laughing. Like, this guy is definitely not all there.

He's staring at the numbers and he can't seem to press them, or his phone's not working. He's getting frustrated and he's all over the place with the gun, and he starts calling out, "Ven acá! Ven acá!"

The little girl appears from the other side of the curtain. She doesn't meet our eyes. She starts talking to the dude in Spanish—so fast I can't catch a word. He sneers at her, and says something about her dress, and pauses to spit on the floor. Disgusting. But the kid keeps talking to him and he starts nodding.

The old dude starts looking around again and the little girl reaches for his coffee mug, resting on a stack of ancient mags on the table. When she hands it to the guy, I can smell that it's not coffee but whiskey, and I wanna tell the kid that's a bad idea.

Dude shoves his phone into his pocket and takes the mug, waving the gun at us shakily. I've still got the peanut butter–covered knife behind my back, but what am I really gonna do with it? Against a gun?

We can hear the stuttering blades from the copter making circles overhead. The dude lurches over to look out the window then turns toward the door, like maybe he's gonna go outside and alert the copter, but the little girl shouts at him, and I can pick out the Spanish words. *Tell. Share. Bounty.*

Fee and I reach for each other's hands, because that's what we do. When the dude sees this, he starts yelling again, no idea what he's saying, but I wonder if he thinks we're gay and there's a whole other level of hate he's about to deploy.

The little shaved-head girl whispers to us in English, "It's okay. He not gonna hurt you."

Um?

The guy drains the mug, sets it down and takes his phone back out of his pocket. He starts pounding on it with his index finger, still holding the freaking gun. Then he starts to lose his balance, like he thinks he's leaning against the wall or something, but he's not, and he sinks down into this nasty old chair near the TV.

Fee whispers, "His phone."

Now I get why he can't make a call. His phone is screen-side down. Okay.

Now the dude starts to nod. He's still trying to use his phone, but he can't keep his eyes open. Then the phone drops to his lap and the gun drops to the floor. Fee and I look at each other and don't even know what to say.

The little girl kicks the gun under the chair, snatches the phone and repeats, "He's not gonna hurt you." She has a thin, scratchy voice to match her scarred little body.

"Is he dead?"

She shakes her head.

"What the heck?"

"Pills," she said softly.

"Pills?"

"I give to him for to make him sleep."

"Jesus."

We're silent for a sec, looking back and forth from the girl to the drugged dude. Then the kid says, "Villains in Versace."

"So you know who we are?"

"I see you come in the dark."

"You saw us with Javier?"

"Yes. I watch the TV. I see the bomb. I see you come in the night."

"We didn't plant that bomb."

"Everyone are looking for you."

"You know about the bounty? I mean, you obviously know."

"Yes."

"So why didn't you . . . ?"

Fee interrupted. "Why didn't you let him call the police? Why didn't you call the police? It's two million dollars."

"I don't believe."

"You don't believe we're guilty?"

She shook her head. "I don't believe."

"Why?"

"My mother . . . she tells me Reverend Jagger is a bad man."

"Your mother? How does your mother know about Jagger Jonze?"

"Her cousin work for him in the Beverly Hills. She clean his house. She know."

"Wow. Wow. Okay." We looked down at the curtained-off room. "Where is she? Your mother?"

"My mother has the cancer. She with God."

Poor kid. Poor bald, bruised, red-white-and-blue Patriot Girl. "I'm sorry. I'm so sorry," I tell her. "Sure your father won't wake up?" I ask. He looks like he might never wake up.

She nods. "Not for long time. Is not my father. Is my father father. Mi abuelo."

"What's your name?" I ask.

The little girl lights up, like it's the best question she's ever been asked, and she takes a big breath before she says, "Paula. My name is Paula."

"Paula. That's a beautiful name," Fee said.

"Yes. A good name."

"I'm Feliza, but everybody calls me Fee. And this is Rory."

"Yes."

"You know you saved our lives?" I said.

Fee goes, "You are so brave."

"I am just Paula."

"Are you sick too?"

"I don't have the cancer."

"But your head . . ."

"I have the lice. Mi abuelo shave me."

I feel relieved to hear this. Fee does too.

All of a sudden I remember. "Wait. Your dog? Where's your dog?"

"Dog?"

"Perro? The black pit bull?" I say.

"He is dead. Abuelo kick him very hard."

"Fuck. I mean, sorry. That's awful. That's so awful."

"It's better. His life is bad. I bury him in the woods where we play."

"You buried him already?"

"I bury him in the summer. When he die." She looks at us, confused.

"The summer? But last night? We heard your abuelo beat the shit out of him."

"No."

"But we heard him calling for Perro, and then there was all the crashing around."

"My dog is called Blackie." She drops her eyes.

So she is Perro. Her grandfather beats her and calls her Dog. That's her life. Choose happy. Right.

"So, do you, like, drug your abuelo a lot?"

"Yes. I give to him the pills mucho times."

"Sleeping pills?"

"In his whiskey." She counted off on her little fingers. "Vicodin. Percocet. Tramadol."

Fee looks appalled. I'm frankly impressed. Paula's an angel, but her halo's pretty warped.

"So many pills left from my mother. I give to him the pills so I can play with my dolls. And for when he is too drunk and too mad."

"Right. You like the Patriot Girls," I say. "But why do you have to drug him to play with your dolls?"

She doesn't answer. Instead, she runs back into the curtained-off part of the trailer and returns with a big black backpack. She presses it into my hands and says, "I put clothes. His clothes. They small. Is better for you to go in the shed now. Sometimes his friend comes here."

I realize I'm still holding the peanut butter knife and put it back down on the counter. We take the backpack, gratefully, and head for the door.

Fee stops. "Come with us. Come to the shed with us."

"Paula come?" It's like we're inviting her to Disneyland, she gets that excited.

I go, "It's not really safe, Fee. I mean, Paula, you understand people are hunting us?"

Paula's abuelo let out a long, low fart. Safe? It's all relative? Right?

Paula goes first, acting casual, trying not to be blown away by the winds that've kicked up pretty hard during the time we've been in the trailer. The chopper has flown off, because of the wind, or because he thought the area was clear. I'm afraid he will come back around for another look.

When we're sure the sky's clear, and no humans are lurking in the bushes, we run, the three of us, back to the relative safety of the metal shed. Paula heads straight for the corner, and digs into one of the white plastic garbage bags I was so afraid to open, and unearths a Patriot Girls doll and a matching outfit from the dry leaves and lawn clippings.

Paula goes, "Yesterday I be Maggie Martin. Today I be Hannah Good!"

"Cool," I say. "We used to love Patriot Girls too, right, Fee?"

"Yeah, but Paula, why do you keep your dolls here?"

"It's Nina's dolls. She is dead. Hurt in her head. I never know her. Mr. Javier give to me the dolls and tell me hide them here."

"I still don't get it. Why do you have to hide your dolls in the shed?"

Paula shakes her head. "Abuelo."

"Nina had Patriot Girls dolls? They cost a fortune," I say.

"The people give to Nina when they daughters don't want to play no more."

Oh. My. God. Shelley packed up my Patriot Girls dolls years ago, along with the matching outfits that I'd outgrown too, and told me she was gonna give them to her clients' kids. That's actually my doll. I know it. My fucking Hannah Good doll.

"Your abuelo's gonna wake up eventually," Fee says.

"Yes."

"He beats you. A lot?"

"Yes."

"Fucking asshole. Sorry. But."

"I know those words. I have the cable. And the Twitter."

"What are you, like, seven?"

"I am ten. I am small."

"So, fourth grade? Fifth?"

"No school. I am illegal."

"Oh, Jesus. Paula . . . like, my mother's an immigration lawyer and she's gonna help you. We'll figure something out. I promise."

"Okay."

Paula digs into her backpack and takes out two half-frozen gas station burritos. "The microwave don't work. I don't have no more soda. No water. Abuelo don't have the filter."

"Thanks, Paula. It's okay—Javier's said he'd come back with help. When does he usually get home?"

"When the sun go down, Mr. Javier is coming home."

Paula digs deeper into the backpack and starts pulling out the old work pants and sweatshirts, baseball caps and T-shirts she stole from her grandfather.

I couldn't wait to get out of my cursed fucking Mishka. Fee couldn't wait to ditch her Prada. We start peeling off the gowns—thousands and thousands of dollars shredded and puked on and bled over. I'm so grateful for the dingy T-shirt and the brown work pants and even the ball cap that keeps my dirty hair off my face. I fold up one of the other shirts to use as a makeshift pad. Feels like a diaper, but better than free bleeding.

Paula changes into the Hannah Good Patriot Girls dress over by the window, her back to us, keeping a lookout for hunters and drones. I don't mean to look—I wasn't being my usual creepy voyeur self—but both Fee and I turn when the little girl knocks over one of the suitcases. And that's when we notice that Paula is wearing little boys' undies, and inside those undies is a little boy's penis.

Paula doesn't see us see her penis. Fee and I just looked at each other. Everything is illuminated. Why the old man hates the kid, and won't tolerate her playing with dolls and wearing her Patriot Girls dresses. That old man beats this little kid because she is an aberration to him. A dog. Perro. He calls her freaking Perro. When she told us her name was Paula, maybe it was the first time she ever said the name she's given herself. Her real name. Javier knows about her, though. He must know. Javier's protected her. Well, as best he could.

Paula took her grandfather's phone from the side pocket of the backpack and showed us. "Abuelo have the VIV tracker app."

"VIV tracker app?"

"For you."

"There's a freaking app?"

"Yes. There is a freaking app. Also, Abuelo have the app for the police. He is procit. Don't have a driver card. Too much DWI."

"Makes sense."

"I get blue alert if police are nearby."

"Oh my God. That's amazing."

"I can stay here with you?"

"Yes, Paula. Stay with us," Fee says.

"And I come after?"

"Come after?"

"To where Mr. Javier take you? Rory? I come?"

Fee and I look at each other like, um . . .

"We don't know where he's taking us or how soon we'll be, like, safe . . ."

"Me too." The way she says it, like, yeah, every day she's in danger, so leaving with us doesn't exactly feel risky.

Fee hugs Paula. "You can come with us, Paula. Wherever we go."

Paula reaches into the black backpack and pulls out this old electronic game—merch from *The Dancing Dina Show*. That's probably mine from when I was little too. Paula goes, "You play *Dancing Dina* with me, Fee?"

Fee laughs and nods. Life is bizarre. An hour ago I thought we were dead; now Paula and Fee are curled up with each other, passing the game back and forth, giggling like kindies, and this, I think, is what joy looks like. It's not happiness. It's a moment of connection.

I think we have at least a couple of hours before Paula's abuelo wakes up from his tramadol dreams. Javier should be home by then. I still can't believe that Paula is here. And that she brought us burritos, which are still half-frozen, and which I'm ridiculously excited to eat.

The last time I felt joy was orientation night. Which is ironic. We were driving to the school, me and my hive, in my Prius. The dads were meeting us there. Jinny wasn't with us because she was riding with her father and Jagger Jonze. It was like old times, me and my girls, music cranked, singing at the top of our lungs, and there it was . . . joy. Seems like a thousand years, but it was just a little over a month ago.

Orientation night. We were pretty fueled for that. Even me. In spite of what I knew about Jinny's Jesus-freakishness, and in spite of the shifting vibe of the Hive, I was pretty eager to get dressed up and go fangirl over the preacher man. I figured Sherman'd be hanging with the dads, so I wouldn't have to deal with that, and meeting Jonze—like I said—I thought it was gonna be oh so cool to take selfies with him. How many likes and fresh follows would we get from that, right? A lot. Plus, because he was a personal friend of Jinny's dad, he was gonna hang out with us at Hutsalls' after the official thing at the school. When the other girls heard about that, we were the object of some powerful envy.

I think, for the good Reverend, orientation night was all about the promo pieces he makes—the commercials like the ones they've been showing of us on cable news. Plus, we paid—well, our fathers paid—a premium for having Jonze host the whole shitty fucking thing, and that night we got to hear his personal story—not like we didn't know most of it because Internet, but still.

Tables and chairs had been set up in the ballroom on the far side of our massive school campus, but the rehearsal was pretty casual. No flowers or fairy lights. No candles. Chick-fil-A for dinner, though the AVB charged a grand a head for the orientation part. Quite a markup.

The night was one disappointment after another. We'd already picked out cute dresses and shoes and then we get this AVB bulletin telling us we gotta wear our school uniforms. Seriously? We all felt ugly in our tartans.

But when I laid eyes on Jonze from across the room, in his tight white Armani T-shirt under a blue cashmere blazer and Cavalli jeans that totally showcased his package? As hot as he was, my vadge clenched and my nips inversed and my whole body just went, *No*.

When Jinny dragged him over to meet us, I was already holding back. A "specimen" is what Brook called him. And he was. But you could see, or I could see, something feral about him. He didn't even look at us as Jinny introduced Feliza, and Brook, and Zara, and Delaney, because his eyes were darting around the room, like he was scanning for prey. He only turned his attention to our little group when Jinny said, "And this is Rory Miller."

I knew by the way he looked at me that he'd been told I was a Jew. Or a heathen. Or both. I could smell his distaste.

"Shalom," he said, making prayer hands at me.

What the actual fuck?

"I told the Reverend about all my new friends," Jinny explained, staring up at him with reverence—and what I realized later was actual lust.

The other girls stood knock-kneed and watched as he put a hand on my shoulder. "All are welcome," he said with his mouth, but not his eyes. Definitely not with his eyes.

Nothing about orientation night went the way I thought it

would. I'd been looking forward to taking some celebrity selfies, but after meeting him there was no chance I was gonna promote that anti-Semitic miscreant. When Zara asked to take a pic and he sternly reminded us that phones had to be checked at the door, I didn't even care.

Before he moved on, the Reverend told us he was really looking forward to getting to know us later at the Hutsalls', where he promised we'd have a great rap sesh—that's what he called it—about the pledge and all. He also said we should go get in line for our filmed AVB interviews. I nodded enthusiastically, along with my friends, afraid he'd hear my thoughts. When Jonze walked away, the girls circled me, crying no-fair that I'd gotten special attention. Oh my God.

After we did the brief on-camera interviews, the dads segregated themselves at tables on one side of the room and we girls sat in our cliques on the other as the Reverend took the stage. First he sent the younger girls, eighth grade and below, out of the room to watch a movie with Mrs. Piggott. Then he said, into the microphone, "Dads. Papas. Fathers. Daddies. And young ladies. This is my story. It's real. It's uncensored. It's the story of what brought me to Jesus and how I came to stand before you today. It's a cautionary tale, and an important one for you and your daughters to hear. May the Lord Our God be our guide tonight."

I bet half the dads there were going, Wait? What?

"Amen," we all said.

We knew his story. I mean, everyone knows his redemption story—reprobate from the streets of Chicago finds Jesus blah blah—but hearing it from him was still pretty powerful. He could sell anything to anyone with that million-dollar mouth.

"My mother was a homeless teen drug addict who left me in a bar called Jonze's Joint in Cabrini Green when I was barely a week old." A pretty good opener.

"The only thing anyone could ever tell me about her was that she looked to be about fifteen years old and was wearing a Rolling Stones T-shirt when she said she needed to use the bathroom, passed me over to a waitress and disappeared forever."

I couldn't help but tear up. Mother loss is my worst fear.

"I grew up in an orphanage, then foster homes, angry, violent, without love, without human contact—at least none that I wanted. I changed the name they gave me—John Jonze—to Jagger Jonze when I was ten years old. It was a way to feel close to my mother, and a way to never forget where I came from. I had a hard heart. A lot of hatred. I had love for my mother, though. I forgave my mother for abandoning me. I respected my mother for not murdering me in her womb. This was back in the days when women had easy access to abortion, but she made a choice not to kill me. I saw what she did as an act of love. Can I get an Amen?"

The rest of the crowd gave him his Amen. I couldn't.

He went on. "Trust me here, dads. I'm telling you the truth. I never had God in my life. Never went to a church. Never heard a sermon, or sang a song of praise. I didn't know God from the drug dealer down the street. I didn't understand the wages of sin. You beautiful girls here today are already blessed to have the Lord Jesus God in your life and in your heart. But I was hollow. An empty vessel. My only friend was an old guitar I found in the trash. I learned to play the Rolling Stones, by ear. 'You Can't Always Get What You Want' was my anthem."

As he spoke, Fee noticed his tattoos peering out from beneath his collar and cuffs and elbowed me to look. The Hive is hot for ink.

"By the time I got to middle school, I was doing drugs. By the time I got to the middle of freshman year, I was kicked out of my foster home for selling drugs. I was on the street when I was fifteen. There were ways to get money fast. It was easier if you were wasted. I used my body to make money to buy drugs so that I could endure the shame I felt because I used my body to make money to buy drugs . . . vicious cycle. Horrible godless life. Men. Women. Young. Old. I went with anybody who'd pay me for it." He hung his head here.

The dads were uncomfortable. Lot of throat clearing. I don't think they were primed for this degree of confession.

"I woke one morning naked in a stranger's bed. It wasn't the first time. I had no idea when I looked at the body draped in the sheet beside me if it was a man or a woman."

Zee's dad, only Zee's dad, shouted, "Amen." Um.

"I lifted the sheet, pretty relieved to find the most striking woman, the smallest and most delicately beautiful woman I'd ever seen. Her hair was the color of sunshine and fell over her face and shoulders as she slept. She was so still I couldn't tell if she was dead or alive. I was afraid to touch her, so I leaned in close to see if I could feel her breath. She opened her eyes. That startled me. And then she opened her pretty mouth and said, 'Did you rape me last night?'"

Rape? There was no mention of rape in his online story. The dads were looking around at each other, but no one said a word.

"The truth is, I didn't know if I *had* raped this woman. She looked so scared, and she said, 'You roofied me, right? My coffee last night? Did your friend rape me too?' The dealer I'd been sitting with at a coffee shop the night before wasn't exactly my friend. I didn't need to roofie women to get them to sleep with me, so I was confused. I asked the woman her name and she said, 'Merilee Magee.' Then she said, 'I'm so sorry.'"

I looked around at the girls and their daddies. Were any of them wondering if his story was true, like I was?

Jagger kept rolling. "Why was she apologizing? I felt her pain, like nothing I'd ever experienced before. It was terrible—and beautiful—and I knew I was in love with her. Just like that.

"Then she asked my name, and she smiled when I told her it was Jagger Jonze. She said she loved Mick Jagger. I told her about my life, the evil I'd done, and that I was afraid, and sorry, because maybe I had raped her. I begged her forgiveness, and this woman, this stranger, who for some reason seemed to know me better than I knew myself, reached up to touch my face and said, 'I forgive you. And God does too.' I felt this surge of warmth from her touch. This feeling of purity, and goodness. I never thought of God before, never in my life, except maybe as a joke, a punch line, a curse, but I felt Him in that moment. The power of His forgiveness through Merilee Magee."

The audience was in deep, totally invested in this romance—this ménage à trois of Jagger, Merilee and God.

He went on. "We talked for a while, about nothing and everything. Merilee's pretty hair fell into her eyes, and when I brushed it back, I saw, on her forehead, a large purple blemish. I noticed another one on the side of her neck. She saw me see the spots. 'Kaposi's sarcoma,' she said.

"I realized in that moment that Merilee Magee was dying. I didn't want to die too. I couldn't get out of there fast enough.

"Beneath her apartment there was a small greengrocer called Valetti's. I walked inside to buy some smokes and found a man threatening the little Italian woman behind the counter. It was the dealer I'd been with the night before. I was hit with the memory of the two of us carrying unconscious Merilee Magee up the stairs to her apartment. I stood there looking at this guy as flashes from the night before hit me like machine-gun fire. As the dealer was leaving the store, he bumped my shoulder. He disappeared down the alley before I could say anything—before I could remind him about the night before, and before I could tell him that the woman he'd drugged was HIV positive. That haunted me. And you understand, girls, this is a cautionary tale—another reason to rely on abstinence to keep yourself safe. You are sleeping with every person your partner has slept with before you. And everyone all those other people slept with. HIV. Venereal disease. Condoms aren't enough. And they aren't reliable. The only way to be safe is to abstain."

The fathers whistled and applauded loudly. Jagger let the noise die down before he went on.

"I thought about following that dealer, figuring my life was over anyway since I probably caught Merilee's horrible disease. I wanted to get high more than anything. But I heard a voice whispering my name, but the only person inside the grocer was the old Italian lady.

"I heard the voice again—*Jagger Jonze*—and realized it was coming from the direction of the crucifix hanging behind the cash register. And even though I hadn't believed in His glorious existence prior to this day, I knew in my heart and soul that it was Jesus Christ the Lord Our God. He had a message for me, and it was simple: 'Take care of her.' It was like He whispered the words right into my ear. And the urge to follow His word—which is the very definition of a calling—was so strong that instead of going after the dealer, I told the Italian lady, Mrs. Valetti, about what I'd just experienced. She crossed herself, and never doubted for one

single second. Then I told her about Merilee Magee, dying in the
apartment upstairs."

Now the dads were wiping tears from the corners of their
eyes. I checked my hive. They couldn't look away from Reverend
Jonze. Ugh.

"Mrs. Valetti and I climbed the dark stairs up to her apartment
with some soup for Merilee Magee. I stayed, and hardly left her
side again. That's when I started writing songs about love, God's
love for us, my love for Merilee. I would sing Merilee to sleep every
night, strumming on an old guitar I found in her closet. Mrs. Valetti
built a shrine around the crucifix in her little store downstairs. Soon
the neighbors got wind of the story of me and Merilee Magee. The
women from the church fed us, and paid Merilee's rent, and kept
me strong with scripture and love. Through it all, Merilee never
expressed her pain or suffering, just her gratitude, and her abiding
love for God, and this unworthy man."

His voice cracked.

"On her deathbed, I made Merilee my wife. And I promised
her that I would honor her always, and never touch booze or drugs
or have intercourse again. Sobriety and abstinence were my path to
God. And Mrs. Merilee Jonze? We never consummated our marriage. Our love was pure and deeper than any love I've ever known,
except for my love for God. Merilee showed me that sex isn't
love, and that love comes straight from God and Jesus Christ His
Son, and is the most beautiful thing in His world. Merilee's last
words, before she left my hands for His, were 'God's will be done.'"

The Reverend needed a minute.

"The morning after Merilee's funeral, I went to help Mrs.
Valetti in the store. The door opened as I was stacking the shelves
and my heart leapt because, with the sunlight in my eyes, I thought

I was seeing Merilee. But it was a beautiful young girl who had walked in. She was maybe sixteen years old, like some of you, wearing a sundress. By the way she stood in the morning light, I could see that underneath she had thong underwear and a lace bra—she was practically naked. And she saw that I was looking at her. And she liked it."

The dads murmured uncomfortably.

"She came over to the counter, and I heard Jesus Christ speak to me from the crucifix, as He has many times since—that crucifix hangs in my house to this day. You know what Jesus told me to do? 'Take care of her.' That's what He said. And I realized then that Merilee hadn't needed my help. I'd needed hers in order to know God, and to know the virtue of true love, and to hear my calling and find my purpose. That's when I understood that God wanted me to take all I'd learned from loving Merilee Magee to help young girls."

Jagger paused for applause before he went on. He got it.

"So I brought that girl upstairs to the apartment and I told her Merilee Magee's story. My story. And by the end of it, that wanton little teenaged girl was covering herself up with one of Merilee's old sweaters, and vowing to lead a godly life through abstinence. That's when the idea of the American Virtue Ball was born. And so, as my beautiful Merilee said?"

We all got the cue and shouted—well, all accept me, because I just couldn't—"God's will be done!"

The Santa Anas have launched a full-out assault on the dying oak beside the shed. The tree is groaning like its limbs are being amputated, and they are, one twisted black branch at a time.

Paula just looked out the window and let us know it's all clear. Her abuelo, near as she can tell, is still sleeping in the trailer. I asked how many pills she gave him.

"Four."

"Jesus," I said.

"Abuelo's gun. Should I go get?"

Fee goes, "YES," at the same time I go, "NO."

Freaking guns. I hate guns. I'm afraid of guns. Every home on the cul-de-sac, except mine, has a gun. For protection. Behind double gates. In crime-free Hidden Oaks. I mean, even Fee's mom has a gun. My parents, because Canadian, but also because statistics, hated guns, and brought me up to fear and loathe them too. The Shooter On Campus drills we do once a month never made our neighbors question their stance on gun control. Didn't even make them wonder where the disturbed teens are getting the weapons, because they knew: from the racks in the den, and the bedside tables of their parents' freaking rooms. And the hundreds of stories in the paper about domestic homicide didn't have them asking, like, if the husband, or sometimes wife, didn't have access to a firearm, maybe one of them wouldn't be dead. Besides. What would we do with a gun? Really? Are we gonna shoot a bounty hunter? Do we really want to play into the media's hands? We aren't killers. That's the point.

We're counting down the hours until Javier gets home. His workday is over when the sun starts to go down, and we keep telling each other, soon, soon.

Fee and Paula just asked me what I was writing. I told them that I'd just gone on a tirade about guns, and that before that I was describing the story Reverend Jagger told us on orientation night.

Fee looked at me accusingly. "You promised you wouldn't write about that. What has all that got to do with anything?"

"It's got everything to do with everything," I said. "How do you not see that?"

"Oh my God, Rory. It's embarrassing."

"To Jagger Jonze?"

"To all of us."

"I'm not gonna stay quiet about him anymore, Fee. I'm telling. Everything."

"We'll look like hos."

"We won't."

"And you can't write about what you think you saw happen between Jinny and Jagger because—Jesus, Rory—Jinny? Never."

"Well, I already wrote about that. Especially that."

"Oh my God."

"It's the truth."

"No one will believe it," she said.

"Not gonna let that stop me."

"Ror?"

"What?"

"Please don't say anything about the stuff I told that night. Please don't write about Dante."

Hope. There's hope. People in the media are seriously investigating Jagger Jonze now. They're examining his past—and his present—asking, Who the fuck is this guy? He's only been on the scene for a couple of years. His rise has been fast, and last night meteoric, but aside from the personal redemption story he's put out there, he's one big mystery. No social accounts until he started recording songs. No credit rating before he hit the charts. No vehicle ownership in his past. Hmm.

One news station spent an hour on fact-checking the Reverend's personal story. They found no record of any person named Merilee Magee in Chicago, and no one called Valetti ever owned a grocery store on the street Jonze described. They found no one from the neighborhood he named—not one person—who could remember Jonze himself. His story's been out there for nearly two years as he's been climbing the Christian charts, and then getting his own TV show, but people are only asking questions now. This is good for us.

I'm hot and thirsty and crampy and still scared, but Paula's here, and Fee's feeling better, even if she is kinda pissed at me about my blogging, and finally people out there are starting to figure some things out.

Just got a news alert that the police chief at last is gonna make an announcement about the metal Gucci purse found in the ruins of the bathroom. I just told Fee and she put her head in her hands. Please God don't let it be drugs.

———

It wasn't drugs.

It wasn't melted lipstick.

They found a pregnancy test in Fee's Gucci clutch. A positive pregnancy test.

The police say DNA tests have confirmed that it belonged to Fee. Our enemies are saying that the pregnancy is obviously evidence of our Red Market involvement. Clearly, not only are we runners, but one of us had been paid to have a baby for the mafia's international baby trafficking ring. Of course, everyone is speculating about what this means. I stared at the headline for a long time: CALABASAS BOMB SUSPECT FELIZA MARIA LOPEZ PREGNANT.

When I looked up, Fee knew from my face what the news headline said. And I could tell from her face it was true.

Definitely did not see that coming.

Fee and I just stared at each other.

Paula looked back and forth from me to Fee, then finally asked, "They find something bad in your purse?"

Fee took a long breath then said, "I wanted to tell you, Ror. I was gonna."

Paula goes, "To tell what?"

Fee widened her eyes, begging me not to say it out loud, but I couldn't help myself. "They found a pee stick, Paula. Fee's gonna have a baby."

"Embarazada?" Paula said, using the Spanish word for pregnant. "You don't look like you have a baby."

Fee glared at me before she turned to Paula. "It's true, though."

I'm thinking, how could this have happened? And why did she keep it from me? How did she not tell me about having sex in the first place? And when she thought she might be pregnant, why didn't she share her secret? I blurted out, "Who's the father?"

"It doesn't matter."

"Um. It matters."

"I don't wanna get him in trouble."

"Well, you're a minor, so . . ."

"Exactly."

"Is he a minor?"

"No. That's the point, Rory."

"I agree, Fee. That's the point."

"Stop it. This is why I didn't tell you."

"So who is he?"

"You don't need to know."

I do though. "Fee?"

"Rory."

"Fee?"

"I'm not talking about it."

"Have I met him?"

"Stop."

"Who are you, Fee? Yesterday you were my best friend and today you're a pregnant teen with a secret boyfriend?"

"We're still best friends. And he's not my boyfriend. It's not like that."

"What's it like?"

"Stop."

"It's just that . . . I know you. I know your life. You're either at school or you're with me and the Hive. So in your pie chart of time, there's a pretty slim freaking slice for meeting guys, let alone having sex with them. It must be someone I know."

"I'm not telling you, Rory. I'm sorry. I can't. I just can't."

Paula stroked Fee's arm, deliberately shifting the conversation. "You can still go to school when you have a baby?"

"I'm not leaving high school."

"Your mamá can raise?" Paula asked.

"My mother!" Fee covered her face with her hands. "Oh my God! She must be dying. Maybe she doesn't know. Think she knows?"

I hadn't told Fee that Morena was facing deportation. I couldn't tell her now. But I also couldn't lie. Of course her mother would've heard what the Feds just announced. "She'll understand."

"She won't."

"But she like the babies?" Paula said hopefully.

"Not really," Fee said.

"How you gonna raise a baby by yourself, Fee?" I asked.

"I can't raise a baby by myself."

"You give to adoption?" Paula said.

Fee shook her head.

Even Paula, at ten years old, knew what Fee meant.

"I'm gonna take care of it," Fee said quietly.

Paula slumped back against the shed wall and returned the *Dancing Dina* game to the backpack. The fun—if you can call it that—was over.

"Are you saying . . . ?" I asked.

"Yes."

"Yes?"

"Yes."

I know I was grasping at straws. I just didn't wanna believe this was happening. I mean, on top of everything else? So I said, "Some of those tests are sketch, Fee. Where'd you get it? You need ID to get a pregnancy test. Is that why you went to Cerritos?"

"Yes."

"So?"

"I'm pregnant, Ror."

"And you waited? I mean, you waited until Friday to get a test? You waited until yesterday to pee on the freaking stick?"

She shrugged by way of explanation. "I was gonna keep pretending. I was gonna do it next week, after the ball and everything. But I was looking in the mirror yesterday. I've gotten so puffy. And I decided I had to know."

"Why did you bring the freaking test in your freaking purse?"

"I did it right before we went to Jinny's. I didn't wanna leave it in the trash 'cause I was worried my mother'd find it, and my purse was right there, and I didn't exactly expect any of this to happen."

"Oh my God, Fee. I wish you'd told me."

"I didn't wanna tell anybody. Ever," she said, tears falling now. "I prayed to have a miscarriage. Is that evil?"

Paula grabbed one of the extra T-shirts from the backpack so she could blow her nose.

"It's okay," I said. "I get it."

Paula nodded like she did too.

"Does the father know? I mean, he knows now, but did you call him after you took the test?"

Fee's chin started to quiver.

"What did he say?"

"Well, he wasn't happy."

Happy. "Guess not."

"He's actually pretty mad."

"Mad at you?"

"Mad at the situation."

"Right. So you didn't use protection? Sorry, but . . . ?"

"Please don't do that. Please don't judge."

"You found out about all this yesterday and you've already made up your mind about . . . ?" I couldn't even say it.

She looked up. "I've made up my mind. So what?"

"Nothing."

"I mean, you wouldn't be against it. I read your blog. Remember?"

"Did you tell the father what you were gonna do?"

"We agreed," she said.

"Okay then."

Paula stood up to look out the window. She didn't wanna talk about Fee's pregnancy anymore. "The wind is strong," she said.

Fee got frantic all of a sudden. "The DNA? Will they be able to tell who the father is from that test?"

"I don't know. But I don't think so."

Thoughts of every male we'd ever come in contact with flashed through my mind. Hidden Oaks neighbors. School staff. The guy with the tats from iPhone Fix? Nah. No one made sense. Who the fuck knocked up my best friend? The only person I could cross off the list for sure was Dante—Fee's cousin. First because cousin, and second because, not counting Friday's trip, Fee hadn't been to Cerritos since early July, which would make her five months pregnant, and she's not.

"I didn't ever want anyone to find out. And now the whole country knows."

"Yeah."

"And if I . . . you know . . . when I . . . they'll know about that too."

"Yeah."

"I guess I could say I lost it."

"Lost it?" Paula was confused.

"Fee?"

"The whole country knows about me, but if they find out about him . . . Oh, God," Fee said. "If anything happens to him, I'll die."

"You won't die. And whoever he is, I mean, he will get what he deserves."

"He doesn't deserve to lose everything he's built, Rory. He doesn't."

Lose everything he's built. And then it hit me. Jagger Jonze. Yes. That could explain why she's been defending him, disbelieving that Jinny or Jagger could be involved in framing us, let alone involved with each other. The Reverend totally eye-fucked Fee that night of orientation. Oh my God. Could he be the father?

"You're protecting a guy who clearly is not protecting you, Fee. You get that, right?"

"I don't wanna talk about it anymore."

"Fee . . . ?" I took a stab. "Is it Jagger Jonze?"

"What?"

"Is Jagger Jonze the father of your baby?"

"That's crazy." She hid her face.

"It's crazy. But is it true?"

"Stop."

"You can tell me, Fee."

"Leave me alone, Rory. Please."

I did. And now I'm sitting here, sad, and angry, and confused. Fee is sobbing, and I can't tell her she's being too loud because pregnant and abortion. Paula is comforting her and I just don't have it in me right now to go join that tableau. Paula is sweet, petting Fee's head, almost maternal, no, definitely maternal, telling her it's all gonna be okay.

Paula is ten years old. I love this little kid. For real.

Jagger Jonze. I've turned it over and over in my head. Could the father of Fee's baby be the same evil fuck whom I filmed nailing Jinny Hutsall—the same evil skeez who staged that whole scene in the parking lot, and put the bomb in the bathroom, and was so fucking freaky on orientation night?

I've been thinking this whole time that Jagger and Jinny wanted me dead because of what I saw them doing in Jinny's bedroom. Maybe that's not it at all. It's possible they don't even know. Maybe it's not about me at all. Maybe Jinny's just Jagger's puppet. Protecting him. Maybe Jagger needed Jinny's help to get rid of Fee and her zygote. Maybe I'm the collateral damage.

Back to orientation night? Buckle up, because a lot happened. After Jagger's emotional talk, we were completely down to ditch our daddies and go back to Jinny's for the promised rap sesh. We all wanted to go home and change into something cute before we reconvened, but the Reverend told us, specifically, not to change out of our school uniforms, and to leave our cell phones in the basket by the Hutsalls' front door. Okay. I mean, not okay, but okay.

At Jinny's, we lounged on the sectional in the den where we always did, drinking the lemonade she always served, waiting for him to come down from upstairs, where he was having a long, loud meeting with Mr. Hutsall. I don't know what that was all about, but with all the questions in the news about Jonze's financial ties to Jinny's dad, it must have been about money.

Finally, the Reverend came into the room, looking less rock star-y than he did onstage. I didn't like the way he looked at me, or any of us really, now that he was the only adult in the room.

And I didn't want to blog about Jagger's story. I guess, even then, I didn't actually believe it. I should've left, but I didn't. I'm realizing that asking questions of yourself isn't enough. Like, you need to actually answer yourself. Dig deeper. That's gonna be my motto when all this is over.

Jonze joined us on the sectional. At first he seemed fine to listen to Jinny and the girls serenade him with praise about his awesome story of redemption and how they cried buckets when he sang "Thank God for American Girls." But Jagger noticed I was quiet and kept glancing at me, not in a clearly lustful way, like he did with Fee and the others, but kinda threatening. And he kept checking a spot on the bookshelf. It occurs to me now he must've put a camera there to record the whole thing. Of course he did.

"Reverend Jagger?" I said. "There must be so many flowers on Merilee Magee's grave. People must be putting them there, like, all the time."

"What's that?" he said.

"Oh my gosh, you guys!" Dee said. "Is the grave in Chicago? We should go there! We should, like, drive there, road-trip it, and lay a huge wreath."

"It'd take, like, a week to drive to Chicago," I pointed out.

The girls, all but Jinny, seemed pretty excited about the idea anyway. Zee goes, "I would love to pay my respects, Reverend Jagger. I feel her. I feel her spirit here with us right now."

Jagger Jonze cleared his throat, ignoring the question of Merilee Magee's grave. "You girls can call me Jagger when we're here in this safe place. I just want you to feel comfortable opening up, and sometimes the Reverend part gets in the way. I'm just a man. Just a man."

Too true. Apparently.

Then he quoted some Bible verses about women, which I didn't listen to because I'm not Christian or a 1930s housewife and I've heard enough of it at Sacred. Plus, it was dead boring after Jagger's tale of drugs and rape. He noticed Delaney scratching her legs. She's allergic to wool and she has to, like, take Benadryl every day to endure her uniform, and he goes, "What's wrong, Delaney?"

Delaney could barely talk to him or look at him, so hard was her crush. She told him about the Benadryl and how she'd forgotten to take it that day because it was the weekend.

He goes, "I'm sorry about that, but I asked you to wear your uniforms because they are the great equalizer. Do you girls understand that?"

We did not. I mean, we did, but we hate our uniforms and truly didn't get why we had to wear them to orientation.

Then he looks at me—right at me—and says, "Pastor Hanson told me you girls object to the skirting practice. He said your mother lodged a complaint."

"That was in freshman year. And it wasn't a complaint exactly." Why was I downplaying it?

Jinny goes, "You complained to your mother and that's why the Pastor has to humiliate himself now, wearing those plastic gloves."

Busted. "Well, yeah, I mean. I think the skirting thing is gross, actually, and sexist." I started to talk about the femur, but Jagger stopped me.

"I read your blog."

"You read my blog?" I was kinda scared by that.

"Pastor Hanson sent me the link. You know what Timothy says about women dressing modestly. You've read that passage?"

I nodded. "But who decides what's modest?"

Zara got a tone. "Don't be all heathen-y tonight. I mean, maybe you shouldn't have come—you shouldn't even do the AVB if you just want to fight about everything."

Jagger goes, "No, Zara. I like a challenge. And I love the heathens. I do. They force me to reexamine and recommit to our Lord Jesus Christ. With every blasphemer, I become stronger in my faith."

Then he started ragging on women who wear yoga pants and miniskirts and thigh-high boots and tank tops and tight T-shirts—otherwise known as clothes—which is hilarious, because he was wearing the tightest T-shirt that you could totally see his nips through. And tight jeans that showcased his package. He hangs left. 'Nuff said.

Again, I prolly should've just gone home, or shut up, but he opened the door, so I questioned his position that women who don't dress modestly are asking to be disrespected with catcalls or worse violations.

"I just don't see why we girls are responsible for what happens in a guy's pants," I said. "It's just, like, we're feminist, Reverend Jagger, and we believe that boys need to learn how to control their reactions to our bodies."

Jinny laughed like that was the silliest thing she'd ever heard.

None of the other girls piped up, so I went on. "We aren't whores just because we want to express our sexuality through our clothes, or the music we listen to, the things we read or the things we write."

Jagger said, "You have a lot of opinions. Tell me more."

Brooky could see I was gonna be torched and tried to throw down some flame retardant. "Rory's just saying, like, we don't walk around trying to tease anybody. We're just doing us, you know?"

"I do know, Brooklyn," he said.

Mr. Hutsall stuck his head in the room for half a sec and interrupted to say he was heading to the airport, some emergency biz trip. Whatever. No brothers home. Just the Hive and Reverend Jagger Jonze.

My temper was coming to a slow boil, but I tried to explain. "We shouldn't feel guilty or whorish or unclean for growing into our sexual selves."

"Feliza, right?" Jagger Jonze said, ignoring me and turning on Fee suddenly. "Do you understand why modesty is so important to God?"

Fee widened her eyes. "Does it have to be a Bible quote?"

Jagger chuckled, charming and smarmy at the same time. "Feminine modesty is important to God because ..."

Fee opened her beautiful lips and gave this lame answer: "Because we are His children?"

"Yes, and ...?"

Zara had given this some thought. "I think God has given us our bodies and, like, the power of, like, sex, and everything, and just to, like, squander it is so wrong and disrespectful. To God. So modesty. I think."

Jagger Jonze grinned at her. "Well said, Zee!"

First—well said—really? Plus, I'm thinking, did he just call her Zee? Like he's one of us?

Jinny finally piped up. "I've been trying to explain to Rory why God wants us to be modest. Last week she wore short shorts and riding boots to the Commons. Not joking."

I'd been at the stables riding with Brook. She was the only real equestrian among us, but we all knew our way around a horse. It's a rich-people thing. (I know that's gross.)

"If I wear my boots to the mall, I'm telling men what?" I asked.

"That you want a ride," Jonze said. We all laughed.

"What if I'm not selling tickets?"

"Your clothes say the ride's free."

"You're giving too much power to my clothes," I said. "Besides, why do men get to decide what my clothes are saying?"

"Men are visual. Does anyone else think that's true? Show of hands." He smiled in his smarming way.

We all raised our hands.

"So what's your endgame? You dress in suggestive ways. A man is gonna get the suggestion."

"That's the point. All I'm doing is suggesting that I'm a sexual person. I'm not issuing an invitation," I said.

"Why are you making the suggestion? Rory, really think about it. Don't be knee-jerk in your response. It's like going up to a boy and asking if he wants to have sex with you and then—psych—just a suggestion. You wouldn't do that, right?"

"That would be assholish."

"But you let your clothes do that."

"My clothes are assholes?"

Zee goes, "Gosh, Ror."

"No. It's okay, Zara. That's what we're here for. Real talk. Rory, I'm just saying, if you dress like a whore, men are going to treat you like a whore."

"I wouldn't say I was dressed like a whore. I was in shorts because it was a hundred and six, and riding boots since we'd just been at the stables. Plus, what about respect for whores? Even Jesus had respect for whores."

"Can we not say *whores*?" Dee asked.

"It's false advertising," Jagger Jonze said.

"If you want to dress like a whore so much, why are you even here?" Jinny challenged me.

"Can we please stop saying *whore*?" Delaney asked. "No one here is a whore. Like, that's a joke word to us. This feels serious."

"Who decides where the line is drawn?" I was getting pissed. "Who decides when I look like a 'whore'?" I used air quotes.

"You do, Rory. And you know you do. Stop playing dumb," Jagger Jonze said.

Brook apologized for me. "Her parents are Canadian."

Zee chimed in, "You know those skirts we got from H&M were actually super-slutty, Ror. We all said they were. We know what we looked like in them."

Brook: "I think Jagger's saying, like, we just need to tone it down, Ror. No big deal."

"You're committing to chastity, Rory, right? That's why you're here?" he asked.

I squirmed. "Yeah." He knew I was a fraud. But come on, I wasn't the only faker in the room.

Jinny got a call then—even though we were all supposed to leave our cell phones in the basket—and said she had to go run some mysterious errand for her mysterious brother.

She had to go? Wha. . . ? And just like that, she was gone, leaving the original hive alone with this guy.

At that point, Jonze promised that what we talked about wouldn't leave the room, and encouraged us to be honest and uncensored. He said that we were there to teach him, because the better he understood us, the more successful he'd be at spreading Jesus's message of abstinence. I could be wrong, but I don't remember Jesus actually saying anything about abstinence in the Bible.

Plus, there are rumors he was banging Mary Magdalene without puttin' a ring on it. So.

"You have to know that what we're doing with the AVB is about being accountable, to God and to yourself." He paused to look each one of us in the eye. "You can be honest. The AVB is a ritual of commitment. You can be re-virginized with your pledge. So? Virgins? Show of hands."

We all raised our hands.

"What did we say about truth?" He was trying not to sound irritated. "We're here to be honest. Who here is a virgin?"

All five of us assured him that we were pure.

"Not one of you has a boyfriend?" He looked straight at Fee.

We all shook our heads.

"Five hot high school girls?"

It seemed weird that he would refer to us as hot.

Brooky said, "Sacred Heart High. It's the chastity belt of schools."

"We're at school all day, then music or sports and homework, and same on weekends and church on Sunday and we have our girl time. Even if we knew many boys, we wouldn't have time for them," Zara said.

"We only really know my brother and a few of his friends," Brook added. "Chase and Kyle and the guys in Miles' band. And anyway, I'm too busy with school and track."

"Don't tell our dads, though. They'll think we're only into the AVB for the dresses," Dee said.

"Are you?"

We all shook our heads. Lying liars.

"You're lucky," Jagger Jonze said. "This won't be as hard for you as it is for girls who face more temptation in their lives. Some of the schools I've been to . . . God tests them by the hour."

"My parents are totally on board with AVB, no matter how much it costs," Zara said. "They're afraid I'll come home pregnant. That happened to my mother's older sister, and the family shunned her."

"What's your experience been, Zee?" Jagger Jonze asked. "Your sexual experience?"

Zara, who always has something to say, just shook her head.

"You can't pass. No passes," he said.

"What about that guy you made out with on the Disney Cruise in frosh year, Zee?" Dee reminded. "Huston?"

Zee's been talking about Huston Hardon—that's what the Hive nicknamed him—from the Disney Cruise for two years. Texts so private she'd never share—just grin at her phone and go, "Oh my gosh, Huston is such a perv." Or, "Huston is asking for pics again."

Brooky chimed in. "Yeah. Tell about Huston."

Zee took a breath. "He doesn't exist."

We could not believe it. Zara wouldn't look at us as she told Jagger, "I was thinking of what you said about God loving honesty. So I wanna be honest. I made up Huston from the Disney Cruise. It never happened."

Jagger nodded, and Zara went on. "I made up Huston because that guy stuck his tongue in your ear in Maui, Dee, and Brook, you French-kissed the keyboard player from Lark's Head! I just . . . I didn't want to be left behind."

"I appreciate your honesty, Zara," Jagger Jonze said. "God loves your truth."

Zara batted her eyes and folded her hands in her lap.

Jagger leaned over and squeezed her arm, then turned to Brook. "French-kissed the keyboard player, Bee?"

"They dared me. And there was no tongue. I was scared my dad or my brother might see."

Delaney goes, "Did we dare you, Brooky? Or did you say, 'Dare me to French-kiss Kyle'?"

Jagger Jonze turned to Fee next. "Fee?"

"Nothing really."

I was getting bored. Okay. Fee's got nothing. I've got nothing. Rap sesh over. But Jagger wasn't buying Fee's answer.

"You love God, Feliza," Jagger said.

"Yes."

He smiled and winked at me as he said, "Not a heathen like your friend here?"

She shook her head.

"So you love God. And I'm a man of God. And you know what God loves more than anything? Truth."

"Truth?" Fee took a look around at the other girls but wouldn't meet my eye. She took a deep breath. "I fooled around with my cousin Dante last summer when I was at my abuela's."

The fuck? Jagger Jonze sat forward on the sofa. "Your cousin?"

"He's not really my cousin, but my abuela raised him. It's not incest."

"How old is Dante?" Jagger asked.

I was shocked. Not that it happened. That she didn't tell us. That she didn't tell me.

"Nineteen."

"Did he force you?" Jagger Jonze was laser focused.

"It wasn't like that."

"He didn't force you in any way?" There was no judgment in Jagger's pudding-smooth voice. It felt safe to talk. To tell.

"We sleep on the cots on the back screen porch. He thought I was asleep . . ." Fee suddenly turned shy.

"He thought you were asleep and . . . ?"

"And he started . . . um . . ."

"He started what, Fee?" Jagger asked, though you could see he already knew.

Thank God Jinny Hutsall was not here. Fee wouldn't have confessed with Judging Jinny in the room. But why did Jinny leave? I mean, really? She suddenly had to pick her brother up? Car trouble? Like, why couldn't he call a garage or order a MiniCop or car service? I guess I was too preoccupied with what was happening to wonder about that at the time, but now?

Did Jinny know he was filming us? To blackmail us, or our parents? Was Jinny in on it? Did Jagger think one of us might confess a pregnancy, or an abortion, or did he think he might get a lead on some other nefarious story to stir up more Red Market conspiracies? Or were our tender little secrets enough to hold over our heads?

He was filming us. I'm sure of that now. Glancing up at the bookshelf to make sure the red light on his cam was on. Yes. Jinny left because she knew the girls would never open up with her in the room. And open up we did. Like flowers.

Jagger moved closer to Fee on the sofa. "He was touching himself?" It was like a TV show, watching the good cop interrogate a witness, but being all kind and gentle and understanding. "You can tell me the truth, Fee. That's what we're here for. And nothing will shock me. Nothing. He forgives all."

Fee was ready to blow her truth wad. "I could see his shadow against the screen."

"Did you go to him?"

She nodded.

"And then?"

"I sat down on the bed."

"Did he keep touching himself?"

"He . . . took my hand. He showed me what to do."

Holy fuck. Just, holy fuck. I was shaking.

"And while you were touching him? Did you kiss him?"

"Yes."

"Did you let him touch you?"

"Yes."

"Where?"

"I shouldn't have."

"Where did you let him touch you?"

"Under my pajama top." Fee bursts into tears. "It's not incest, right?"

"God respects your honesty, and God thinks it's brave that you risked your friends' judgment." Jagger patted Fee's knee, but he was as thirsty for the rest of the story as we were. "Then what happened?"

"We heard my abuela opening the door to her room. I jumped back into my cot, but she must've suspected something, because she made me come sleep with her. And she gave me the evil eye for the rest of the time I was there."

Fee's been holding back, pretending to be inexperienced and naive like the rest of us. My bestie stroked a dick and didn't tell. I wanted to spit.

"What else, Fee? What other experiences have you had?"

I braced myself, sure she was gonna tell about the two of us practice-kissing when we were twelve. Or about how we lifted our shirts for the security guard at the drugstore. Malibu Sunset. Those were our secrets. Ours.

"Do you preach abstinence to boys too, Jagger Jonze?" I blurted.

"I would preach chastity to boys, Rory," Jagger said, "but teen-aged boys won't attend a Virtue Ball with their mothers—no incentive whatsoever—so God seeks to move through you."

Fee asked shakily, "Does our virginity really mean that much to our future husbands?"

"It'll mean a lot to your husbands, I promise, Fee. It means everything to God."

I go for it. "Is it true what you said tonight at orientation—that you don't . . . at all . . . ever?"

"I am abstinent. Celibate. That's the God's honest truth."

"Does that include self pleasure?" I asked. Bold. I was bold.

"I don't," he promised, "touch myself."

"Never?" Brooky sounded skeptical.

He could see by our faces that not one of us believed him. We aren't stupid. We have Internet. We know that guys jerk off a hundred times a day. Even Christians.

Delaney asked, "Don't you ever feel . . . you know . . . ?"

"The urge? Of course I feel the urge, Dee. I feel the urge many times a day. It's called temptation."

"Do you feel the urge right now?" I asked. Did I really want to know? I was playing with fire, drunk on this real talk. It occurs to me now, and did occur to me when I woke up the next day with a wicked headache, that Jinny Hutsall, or someone, had spiked the lemonade.

"I felt the urge five times on my way here tonight," Jagger said with a laugh. There were five of us—six with Jinny. I was pretty sure I was the one who didn't make the cut.

I poked the bear. "Just . . . I guess you're, like, made of wood? No pun intended."

The girls busted out laughing. They weren't mad because it was funny.

Jagger snapped his head in my direction. "I am made of steel. In fact. My strength comes from my Maker."

"But you never polish the steel?" I asked, setting the girls off again.

"Callin' me a liar?" The way he said it. Like a punk.

We all stopped laughing.

Zara goes, "Rory, seriously, if Jagger says he doesn't, then he doesn't."

"It's just, if you get a . . . you know . . . don't you have to, like, do something about it?" I asked.

Dee was curious too. "I mean, doesn't it hurt? If you don't . . . you know . . . let the air out?"

Jagger twisted his neck this way and that, and you could see he was pissed, really pissed. He goes, "I don't have to touch myself to get release. I don't have to do anything. It just . . . happens. It's an act of God."

"Are you saying God, like, jerks you off?" I asked.

The girls exploded with nervous laughter again, but I hadn't actually meant to be funny. I was fascinated. God always seemed so against sex for all but procreation. Jagger Jonze was suggesting He was all in. And that—what?—God brought him to orgasm through prayer? Okay then.

"Oh my God, Ror," Brooklyn, still laughing, said. "He doesn't mean it that way. Or do you?"

We all pretended we had conversations about God and sex with a celebrity Reverend every Saturday night.

"I do," he said.

"So you just sit there and do nothing, absolutely nothing, and it, like, happens?" Brooklyn said.

"I let Jesus take the wheel," Jagger Jonze said.

The wheel in this case is his dick, so we laughed pretty hard about that. But I could see Jagger Jonze thought he was being laughed at, and disbelieved, and whatever mask he'd been wearing came off and he was suddenly a hard-ass street rat. He wasn't who he appeared to be. Not at all.

"Feliza," he said, "stand here."

Fee did as he asked.

"Turn away from me."

She did.

"Bend down. No. Not like that. Not like a whore." The way he said it. "A little. Just bend a little."

Fee did as she was told.

We were silent, our eyes locked on the zipper of his jeans, wondering when he was gonna whip it out. But he didn't.

Then he told Fee to bend just a little more, and she did, and the merest glimpse of her white satin panties peeking out from under her tartan skirt triggered Jagger Jonze's lump to swell.

We girls didn't look at each other. No one called foul. No one said we shouldn't be doing this and what the fuck's happening here anyway? We wanted to see what would happen. Even if it was weird and gross. It felt something like our collective obsession with pimple-popping vids. We just had to see.

We watched Jagger, the slackening of his jaw, the loosening of his lips and the stiffening under his tight Cavalli jeans as he studied our friend. To be honest, I checked his hand to see if he had some pumping device because of the way he grew so big so fast, and the way it moved around—like a ferret under a denim blanket.

He concentrated on Fee's sliver of white pantie, as we concentrated on the crotch of his pants, and then Fee turned, because she was missing the whole thing, and when she saw the bulge, she looked pretty surprised.

Then, without touching himself or grinding against his jeans, or moving a muscle, he let out a long, low moan, and a wet spot appeared and spread—like a miracle—on his jeans. He shuddered. And so did we.

When it was done, he didn't look euphoric, or relieved of his load. His face went hard. He didn't meet Fee's eyes. He didn't look at any of us. He got up from the couch and went straight into the nearest bathroom.

We sat there in stunned silence. Frozen, the way people act after cataclysmic events. You see it all the time on TV—people sitting in the smoky aftermath of hurricanes and exploding bombs. And weird sex. Cock-shocked. That's what we must have looked like. Not because of what had been done to us. It was that, but we also felt shaken and confused by what we'd done to him.

Shame—that's what it was—ingrained by centuries of religion and patriarchy? Epigenetics again? Maybe shame resides in the DNA of all females? Maybe, even for all of our intellectualizing and marching and certainty, we haven't found a way to release the idea that we're responsible for a man's sexual responses. Or maybe the shame comes because we secretly desire that power?

We were waiting for Jagger to come back, forming apologies for challenging him, and for tempting him, when Jinny came home without her brother, who she said was at an all-night garage dealing with his car. Okay. Well, that didn't sound right, but after bringing Reverend Jagger Jonze to his humiliating climax, the fact that Jinny's story didn't track was just another drop in the bucket of what-the-fuckedness.

When we told Jinny that Jagger was in the bathroom, she knocked on the door. He didn't answer and he didn't come out. She didn't seem to find that odd, which was odd. She called through the door, "The girls are leaving now. Thanks for everything."

"Thanks, Reverend Jagger," we shouted in the direction of the bathroom, as Jinny escorted us to the front door. Just. Weird.

Weird also? She didn't ask what we'd talked about while she was gone. Didn't ask why Jagger was in the bathroom. She just said she was really tired and going to bed.

We girls left the Hutsalls' together, although *fled* is the better word. I wanted the Hive to come back to my house and do a post-mortem on the bizarre episode. So much to analyze. What he said. What he did. What we said. What we did. The pond in his pants. Ugh. But Brook said she felt sick, and Delaney was really tired, and Zara's cheeks were pink with shame, or arousal, and she just wanted to go home too.

We hugged good night, and Delaney and Brook and Zee split off toward their houses, but Fee hung back. Thank God, I thought. When we were alone, I grabbed her hands and said, "Malibu Sunset or what?"

She nodded, but seemed distracted. "I left my phone in the basket at Jinny's front door," she said.

"We can't go back. What if he's out of the bathroom?"

"He'll prolly go right back in. That was gnarl. He must feel like such a dick."

"Ya think?"

"I'm going to get my phone."

As she started running back toward Jinny's house, I called out, "Wait, I'll come with!" But she didn't hear, or acted like she hadn't. I could have run after her. Truth is, I didn't wanna see Jagger Jonze again. I'd had enough religion for one night.

My texts to Fee went unanswered. **U coming? 'Sup over there?** I waited in my driveway, imagining that Jinny was talking Fee's ear off about plans for the upcoming ball, feeling jealous but not overly concerned.

After ten minutes, when Fee still hadn't come out or answered my texts, I went inside to go spy on Jinny from my bedroom window to make sure Fee wasn't there bestie-ing up to the Crusader.

My mother was waiting up. "How was it, Ror?"

"Fine."

"Fine? Not appalling?"

"I'm keeping an open mind."

"And your father?"

"Fine."

"Fine?"

"Dads mostly hung out with the dads."

She seemed relieved, but said, "That's too bad."

"I'm really tired."

"And Jagger Jonze? What's he like?"

"Tall."

"I mean what's he like?"

"I don't know. He's whatever. He's a celebrity. So he's kinda weird."

"How so?"

It did not once occur to me to share with my mother that

Reverend Jagger had creamed in his jeans. I headed for the stairs. "I'm so tired. Going up to bed. Love you, Shell."

"Love you, Ror."

In my room, I slipped behind my curtains, in position for my stakeout of Jinny's room. She was there. Alone. She must've been too tired to pray that night, because she just lay on her bed for a long time. I waited and waited to see if Fee might appear in the room, then realized Jinny'd fallen asleep. I looked out the front window. Only Jinny's Tahoe was in the driveway. The lights were off on the main floor. So Fee must have gotten her phone and left in the time I was talking to my mother?

It's possible that Fee didn't forget her phone at all, just used that as an excuse to go back to see Jagger. Or maybe she did forget her phone and when she went to get it, he forced himself on her. Or didn't force himself. Maybe I'm wrong about Jagger. But I'm not.

We didn't talk about it. We should have. We should have dissected every word and intention of his, and ours, and disavowed ourselves of responsibility. But we didn't. We should have screamed about the grossness of his magical spoo. But we didn't.

Did we think of Jagger as dangerous? Not really. Not exactly. I think we just thought he was muy messed up. And the AVB? Our dresses were on order. Hutsalls had already booked StyleMeNow. We'd bought our strappy sandals and pretty evening bags. We couldn't pull out now. So, without discussing it, we decided not to talk about Jagger Jonze, and got distracted by pretty things.

Why don't girls tell? Not just girls, but boys? If you have to wonder, I guess it's because nothing even close to that has ever happened to you. The decision to stay quiet feels like a decision by default. In our case? Jagger is famous and powerful and beloved.

He's a REVEREND, for the love of fuck. We're a bunch of spoiled, naive Calabasas virgins. There was no evidence to prove what happened at the Hutsalls'. At least, none that we possessed. Plus—what would we say? He didn't touch us, didn't say anything criminally inappropriate if you got down to it. I mean, we were there to have a real talk about sex. Of course the whole thing was fucked—but on paper? You can't really talk about chastity without discussing what you're abstaining from.

And if we told, we'd lose too. It wouldn't have just been the end of the AVB. It'd be the end of us. As we were. We'd be soiled. Sullied. Talked about in hushed tones. Plus, the shame thing. So powerful. Why don't girls tell? Shame, big-time, and modesty too—like, you don't want other people to picture you in the sexual situations you're forced to describe, to wonder about your complicity. You don't wanna create a visual. So we buried the night together, in a shallow-ass grave.

We should have told.

The sun is setting on this horrible day, bands of orange and red streaking out over the ocean. Actual Malibu sunset, which is nothing like the lipstick shade.

Fee's curled up like a cat beside Paula, fast asleep. I can't help but think about what that media expert said about the algorithm and how it's only a matter of time before they find us. When I looked out the window the last time, I could see the distant plume of smoke from a new fire—they're calling it the Charmlee blaze— that started seconds after a reported power outage in a densely forested area east of El Matador Beach. The news is saying that if the wind shifts, as they expect it to, Malibu will be in the direct path. Jesus.

On the positive front? Paula's abuelo is still passed out.

Not so positive? My best friend is pregnant. She wants to get an abortion and she won't talk about it. And I'm pretty damn sure the ratfuck who set us up is her baby's father. Still, I shouldn't have reacted the way I did. I should've just listened and not judged, and been empathetic. I'm supposed to be her safe place to land. I'm supposed to support her choice. Choice. I believe in it. I do. And yet this random binding of sperm and egg to make life? *Miracle* is a stupid word to use when you don't believe in God, but life is awe-inspiring. Right? And when that choice is growing in the womb of your best friend, it's confusing. I mean ... Fuck. Get your laws off my body. My body, my right. But Jesus fucking Christ. This is Fee.

And now, I realize, there are four of us in the shed. Four innocent lives in this stinky little prison/haven, flies buzzing inside,
copters buzzing out.

Paula put her Patriot Girl on her lap so she can change the doll's
clothes to match her own. She wipes a little soot from the plastic
mouth and fusses with her wiry hair, and looks up to say, "So much
typing. Your hands hurt?"

"They do, Paula. Everything hurts."

I keep going back to the news, but each time I read something
that gives me hope—like about Warren Hutsall being investigated, and how Jagger's connection to him is being scrutinized,
and the AVB tax exemption is being questioned—I think, okay,
well, we're on the right track. Then the next breaking news item is
something sick, like that the roads in and out of the valley are
being clogged by Crusaders coming to join the protest at the pier
at Santa Monica, where Jagger Jonze promised to give his free
concert tonight. They showed it on the news. Thousands and
thousands of people surrounding the pier, waving American flags,
holding up their cell phones with screensavers of Jesus Christ.

Paula's head isn't filled with news and information the way
mine is. She's got different worries. She's looking out the window.
Her abuelo will stumble out from under the influence of the whiskey and pills soon enough and he'll come looking for her here in
the shed where he knows she plays with dolls. I hope he doesn't
find his gun under the chair.

"Mr. Javier will come soon," Paula promised, whispering so as
not to wake Fee.

Paula and I checked the Villains in Versace app on her abuelo's phone a few times, but nothing so far. We checked the police
alert app too. A little worrying because there are, like, a hundred

emergency vehicles heading out to the fire up the coast to control traffic and force evacuations. But Paula said the tracker won't sound off unless they're within three miles of us.

I look at Fee. Differently. Her tummy, usually flat, is a little poochy. But then again, so is mine. I prolly noticed and thought nothing of it because Fee does drive-thru Del Taco a fair bit when she's stressed. She failed that math test a couple of weeks ago and she was worried Mr. Tom'd be mad. A quesarito or two always helps. Jesus. Her baby can't be bigger than a pea at this point, though. Fuck. I'm sorry. I can't even go there. And I can't even think about Jagger Jonze without feeling like I might spontaneously combust.

Oh. My. God. My mother has escaped!!! En route to the Valley State Prison, Shelley Miller eluded the guards—they think someone was working on the inside to help her—and has vanished. Shelley freaking Miller.

How is it possible that the weepy, tired, unmoored mommy I've lived with for three years was able to escape cuffs and shackles and evade armed guards? Holy. Shit. What a freaking warrior. I can just imagine her going ninja on the motherfuckers. It's like when I was little, in the parking lot at ballet, and that big Escalade starting backing up and nearly hit me. Shelley was the Flash, shoving me out of harm's way and holding up her hand to stop the car with the force of her motherly love. At least, that's how it felt at the time.

Aunt Lill had to have helped Shelley escape—of this I feel fairly sure. They showed footage of my mother in the cuffs and shackles as she was being led from the courthouse to the prison

van. Aunt Lill was in the deep background. I spotted the pink
T-shirt in the crowd as reporters circled, asking for a comment,
snapping Shelley's pic and filming her stumble into the back of
the van. Before the doors were shut on her, my mother looked
right down the lens of the CNN camera and said, "My daughter
and her friend are innocent. Many people believe in them. Keep
fighting, Ror."

I woke Fee to tell her about my mother escaping and sending
the message to keep fighting. And that people believe in us.

Fee perked up a little with the news. "Shelley escaped?"

"Shelley escaped."

Paula misunderstands. "Your mamá is coming now?"

"Not exactly. I don't know, Paula. I just know she'll figure
something out. And Javier will be able to reach her. Won't he?
He'll hear about it and he'll be able to call her. Maybe he already
has. Maybe he helped break her out?"

"Or maybe he had nothing to do with her escape and he's
waiting out another increase in the bounty," Fee said.

Does pregnancy make women cynical?

Paula turns back to the window. She's our lookout and
happy for the job, scanning the road for Javier's truck, keeping
watch on the Airstream door. She tells us there's some air traffic
headed our way.

"You know Javier, Paula," I said.

"Yes."

"I mean, he wouldn't be keeping us here, waiting for the bounty
to go up. He's a good man, right?"

"Yes," Paula said. "But also, a poor man."

Fee stood up and joined Paula at the window. She glanced at
me. "What should we do?"

"I don't know." I really don't. "If Javier's a good guy, and I think he is, he'll get in touch with my mother."

"But if he's a human thinking about how two million dollars could change his life, then he might be on his way here right now with a van and some armed friends. Or he could just call the hotline and keep his hands clean," Fee said.

I didn't respond. I don't wanna think about that.

"We can go to my abuelo's trailer?" Paula said. "I can give to him more pills?"

Fee and I said together, "Nooo."

So many fucking betrayals already. "I don't know who to trust. My father? Our friends? Chase Mason? I just don't think I wanna live if Javier fucks us over too."

"Who is Chase Mason?" Paula asked.

"No one," I said. "But when this is all over, I'm gonna write a blog calling him out."

Fee goes, "For what?"

I didn't know, until I said, "For breaking my heart."

Fee looked at me funny. "You're not his girlfriend."

"What?"

"I'm just saying Chase Mason isn't your bf, so I don't get why you feel so hurt, plus he didn't really say anything that bad?"

Cold. That's cold. I got a lump in my throat. Fee might as well have smacked me.

Paula looked sad for me. "You want Chase Mason to be your boyfriend?"

I cleared my throat. "He's been my crush for a really long time."

"No more?"

"No more."

"He have another girl?"

"He has lots of other girls." I pictured Chase Mason at the library. "He did this interview with the press, Paula, and he totally lied about stuff that happened at the library and basically said I did things that he did."

"What things he did?"

"He always had girls coming to the library to see him, and he took them into the media room to hook up, but he said I was the one who took girls in the media room, which never happened. He made it look like I was using the library as a place to meet girls who wanted to have abortions. To, like, pass them notes and deal birth control and morning-after pills and whatever."

It hit me like a brick.

"It's Chase. Oh my God, Fee. It's Chase."

"What?"

"Chase. Chase Mason. He's the one. It's him."

"What are you saying?"

"I'm saying Chase Mason is not a traitor. He's a fucking . . . I don't know what to call him . . . an operative? A sympathizer. He's on our side."

"You're not making sense."

"All those girls I told you about always coming into the library? The card he gave me—telling me I should get in touch with him if I ever got in trouble? He changed his band name to Larkspur. He changed the name of his band overnight and announced it to the media because he's been trying to send a message to me. And Aunt Lill? The shirt she was wearing with the Bible verse? They're working together to help us."

"What?"

I knew I was on to something and did a quick Google search.

"Oh my fucking God, Fee. Paula. You guys. 14:34 on the Bible verse shirt Aunt Lill's been wearing? It's an address. On Larkspur Road. Larkspur. That's why he changed the band name. The message. 1434 Larkspur is owned by Blake Mason—Chase's uncle. It's a fucking address in Malibu, a few miles away. We need to go there. Oh. My. God."

Fee comes to look at the screen.

Paula turned away from the window, clapping and squealing. "He's coming now. To take us to the Larkspur! It's Mr. Javier truck. He is coming. He is coming now!"

Oh FUCK. The VIV tracker is blowing up Paula's abuelo's phone and the police alert just went off.

Fee screamed. "Police cars are coming! Police! It's the police!"

It's over.

We're dead.

Um. It's not over.

We're not dead.

The news is reporting that four people are, though. Four people who, if not for us, would be alive right now, watching politics on cable news. I feel totally sick about that.

We three, well, four are safe at Chase's uncle's beach house on Larkspur Road. We've been here for nearly an hour.

Where did I leave off?

I think I wrote about how the sun had set, and Javier's truck speeding up to the cabin with Paula yelling about the cop cars and the apps going off? When we looked out the little window and there were six police vehicles rounding the bend on the dirt road right behind Javier's truck. That's when Paula ripped the pink laptop out of my hands and stuffed it in the backpack along with her Hannah Good doll and said, "Come. Now."

Fee seized up like a broken machine. Paralyzed by fear. You don't think that can happen, but I witnessed it. She froze at the window, and wouldn't, couldn't, take a step. She didn't scream. Or cry. She just stood there, rooted to the shed floor. I had to drag her. Paula tried to help.

We finally busted out of the shed, and that's when we heard a voice from the sky over what sounded like an old-school megaphone. "Stop. Right. There."

We look up, and thirty feet overhead there's a guy in one of those GarBirds, with duct tape in a couple of spots and a big hand-painted American flag decal on the length of the tail. The guy flying the Bird was huge, with a big furry beard. He had one hand on the controls and was aiming an assault rifle at us with the other, screaming into his headset, "I got 'em! I got 'em."

Javier tore into the yard and jammed on his brakes, sending up a cloud of gravel, and his face, behind the veil of dust, was . . . it was horror that I saw there, because he knew, in that moment, that one of two things was gonna happen: either the guy in the Bird was gonna gun us down in front of his eyes or the police were gonna surround us, and take us away to God knows where.

Then the guy in the sky stops paying attention to his controls, or to the airspace around him, because he sees the cops coming up the road and he's realizing that the two million dollars he's got in his crosshairs is gonna get snagged by the authorities before he has a chance to claim the bounty. He brings his machine down a little, and just then a MiniCop—a legal one, a two-seater with a girl and a guy at the controls—comes chopping over the hill, and the girl, who looks about our age, has a rifle too, and she aims it at us and we can hear her yelling, "Should I kill 'em? Now? Now?"

We put our hands in the air like you see on TV, and I was pretty sure we were gonna die right there in the needle grass in the hills overlooking Malibu. My life didn't flash before my eyes— maybe because I'd already written half of it down. I thought about my mother. And then, honestly, I just thought, *So this is how I die.*

The bearded guy is pissed to see another copter there, encroaching on his prize, and the approaching cops are yelling over their speakers for the guy to withdraw, but instead he's getting ready to shoot. Fee and Paula and I grab each other's hands as the wind starts gusting hard, and we look up and see the tail of the MiniCop get twisted around by an updraft then hit the whirring blades of the GarBird, which shred it like paper. Slices of it fly at the couple at the controls, and they start screaming, and the guy with the rifle starts screaming as his GarBird starts to spin and falls out of the sky, directly on the silver Airstream, crushing it like a soda can, along with Paula's abuelo passed out inside. The contraption instantly explodes into a fireball. A large piece of burning debris hits the shed behind us, which also bursts into flames. We can hear the bearded man screaming from somewhere inside the chaos.

The other copter crashes on the road, right in the path of the cop cars, exploding too, and lighting up the dry brush all around. The flames rose so high so fast. The smoke was glowing red, pulsing with the lights on the police cars.

Paula screamed, "Run!"

We ran.

I glanced back to see if Javier was still in his truck, and if he was okay, but I couldn't see anything through the smoke. We ran for our motherfucking lives. Brook couldn't have caught us, even Fee, shaken out of her fog by the explosion, and shot up with adrenaline.

Paula knew the brush and the hills and where to hide. She's been doing it her whole life in one way or another. She didn't complain—not even when we tumbled down into the crevasse a mile or so from the shed, where the sagebrush disguised a drop. Stoic. That's the word.

Paula actually said it was a good thing we fell—"a blessing." And she was right. A few minutes later we saw the silhouette of two men with rifles appear at the top of the ridge, but they couldn't see us where we'd landed, in a thicket of scrub oak under a rocky ledge.

When, later, some nearby coyotes started yelping and yipping the way they do, Paula said it was okay, because they'd just killed an animal, a deer or a raccoon or whatever, and so they wouldn't be hungry for us. And when we climbed to the top of a hill and saw the only way down was to slip and slide in the dark, Paula said the people looking for us would never think we'd be brave or strong enough to attempt that descent. She just kept moving forward, leading us through the thickets and over the ridges and up and down the rock walls.

I keep thinking about that scene at the clearing. I didn't want anyone to die. Not even the people who wanted to kill us. Not Paula's abuelo. The bearded guy? Javier? They haven't released the names online yet. The cops were focused on the action in the sky and I don't know if they got a good look at us before we disappeared into the brush. There've been no reports that we have a little girl with us. Or that we've changed out of our "Versace" gowns.

After we made it down the hill, the three of us walked a couple of miles on the side of the Pacific Coast Highway with our heads down, disguised in our gray gardeners' clothes, hair under ball caps, backpack on my shoulders. I held Paula's little hand. A thousand cars whizzed by. Fire engines, cop cars, bounty hunters, Crusaders. No one seemed to notice. Just a couple of smallish Mexican housekeepers with their little Patriot Girl on the way home from a long day cleaning someone's mansion.

We have flash burns on our faces and some nicks and cuts from the debris. Paula has some small shrapnel wounds on her neck. Our hands are torn from all the thorny sagebrush and dry mesquite we had to rip away so we could get up the hill after we fell. We're exhausted, bruised and battered, but okay.

Here. The safe place. 1434 Larkspur Road. Chase's uncle's stunning beach house in Malibu, on the far edge of this neighborhood near Paradise Cove.

The door on the iron gate was unlocked. We cringed when it groaned open and again when it rattled shut behind us. The moon lit the grassy yard and tall hedges on either side of the driveway. All was quiet, then we heard a branch crack in a big dying oak and we looked up to see this fat raccoon, who immediately started hissing at us. Fee screamed. Paula put her hands over her mouth. Jesus, Fee.

Within seconds we heard a sliding glass door open, and footsteps shuffling through crisp leaves in the yard next door. We held our breath as an old lady's voice floated up and over the hedges. "Who's there?"

We looked at each other but didn't speak, didn't move a muscle, waiting for the old lady to shuffle back to her sliding door.

She called out again. "Who's there?"

The raccoon shifted attention and hissed in her direction.

"Shoo!" she called out, as Paula and Fee and I stood frozen.

"Monty?" the old lady called. "Monty? Come out here! Bring the broom!"

We heard the door slide open again, and more shuffling through the leaves, and after a moment watched the white handle of a broom poke up over the tall hedge to rap at the oak tree, which the raccoon was not gonna leave without a fight. The flailing broom got nowhere near the thing, but it did piss him off, and he hissed again, and that made Monty mad. "Bastard," the old man growled.

Feet crunched back through the leaves, and we knew it was Monty because the old lady was still on the other side of the hedge going, "Shoo!" Then we heard the clatter of a ladder, and we realized the old guy was gonna climb up to get closer to the raccoon, and he would be able to see us over the hedge.

He fussed with the ladder, as his wife called out over and over again, "Shoo," because that's working? I mean, Jesus. And I was thinking, why shoo the poor thing anyway? He's a raccoon in a tree.

The ladder got settled into place, and we heard old Monty stepping on the rungs, and as he did, the raccoon climbed higher. Monty was ready to give up. Then his wife said, "That's fine, Monty. Leave him there. And when he gets into that trash again, you can damn well clean it up."

Monty said, "I'll get the hose."

The old lady goes, "The hose has a tear, remember? You were going to Home Depot for a new one then didn't. Go over to the Masons' and borrow theirs. They always leave that front gate open."

Fee and Paula and I looked at each other like, actually? Is this happening? After everything we've been through, we're gonna be foiled by a fucking raccoon and some old dude named Monty?

But before I could make up a believable story about why we three were in Blake Mason's yard, a motorcade of screaming cop cars came from nowhere—flashing lights and blaring sirens tearing down the PCH on the other side of the gates.

The raccoon, maybe flustered by the noise, leapt down from a high branch to a low one, and then onto the top of the privet hedge, and then he was gone. Along with the cop cars, who headed north up the coast.

Monty and the old woman shuffled back through the leaves. The sliding doors opened, and shut. We made a beeline to the porch of the beach house.

The door was open. We basically walked right in, like, Honey, I'm home. The house was silent except for the humming air units and the crashing waves outside.

We could see the black ocean from the foyer, the stretch of moonlit beach in front of it, a coast guard boat out there skimming the surf, throwing searchlights over the sand. The beach front of the property had a tall Plexiglas security screen for unobstructed ocean vistas, and smooth ten-foot concrete walls for privacy from the neighbors on either side. A winding concrete path bisected the yard, with a rectangle of turf, which I realized was a putting green, on one side and, on the other, a collection of citrus trees, bare with the exception of the grapefruit tree, where a few fat fruits still clung to high branches. We stood there for I don't know how long, just breathing, and looking out at the sea.

Light from the full moon streamed in through the wall of windows, and blazed off the white Carrara marble floor so that it looked like an ice rink, like we'd slip and slide if we tried to walk. When we moved, grit from our shoes scattered over the marble. Because my mother raised me, I told myself I would locate a broom to clean it up later.

We could see the kitchen to the left, which was open to the great room, both huge rooms looking out over the ocean. I set the big backpack down on the kitchen counter and noticed that there was a note on the stove, under a dim light—the only light in the house. It said: *Sit tight. No lights. No calls. In or out.*

We looked around for the fridge, desperate for water, and finally found it, behind a door—a walk-in fridge like you see in a restaurant, with a fully stocked dairy section and meat department, the freezer crowded with frosty boxes, and cases upon cases of water, and juices and sodas. I was struck by the bounty of it all, so I can only imagine what Paula was thinking.

We drained a couple of bottles of water each as we continued to explore. Another door opened to a walk-in pantry, with more food, boxes and containers and cans. Our kitchens on Oakwood Circle are well stocked, but this place was like a mini–Whole Foods. We didn't touch any of it. We're too fragged to have an appetite.

Fee noticed a calendar tacked onto the pantry door. Paula used her phone flashlight so we could see it better. Dates blocked off in late November—now—for Maui. So Chase's uncle and his family are away, and their Malibu beach house is our refuge from people who want to kill us for a crime we did not commit. That would be among the ten top things I thought I'd never write.

We crept through the first floor of the house just taking everything in. Down one hall, a screening room with plush theater seats and popcorn machine. Down another, the den, with another huge screen and more comfy seating. Paula's face said it all. She might as well have been walking on the moon.

We opened a door at the end of the hall to find a sound-proofed room filled with band equipment and a big professional mixing board—the recording studio. There were pics all over the walls of old-school singers and gold records in frames. One picture I lingered on. It's of Chase Mason—pimpled and twelve-ish, at a Grand Canyon lookout with his family, his mom and dad and his dead sister, who shared his same long-haired, brown-eyed, tragic beauty. Lady Jesus.

We headed back into the main area of the house, and had a closer look around the great room. Above the travertine fireplace there's a portrait of the uncle's family. Chase Mason bears no resemblance to his bald, stocky uncle. The guy's wife is tall and blond and looks like a model, prolly is a model, and their little girl is stunning too.

Paula wanted to see the second floor, but Fee said she was too tired to climb the stairs, and settled down on the white leather sectional to stare out at the ocean.

I took Paula's hand and we went up to find the bedrooms, including a huge master suite with a double-wide king and miles of knotty reclaimed oak. On a table by the window there was an old washbasin, and on the table beside the bed an old-school phone— one of those big black jobbies with the round dial from the time before real phones. Paula gestured to the nightstand and whispered, like, in case I didn't know, "It's a telephone. I see this in the movie."

You don't see many of these dial phones anymore. Plus, people don't really have landlines much. Then again, cell reception is bad at the ocean, so maybe Chase's uncle needs a landline in case of tsunami or whatever. The note had said no calls in or out, so when Paula put a finger in one of the holes, I told her to be careful not to pick up the receiver just in case it was connected.

I looked into the washbasin on the table. It was filled with lavender. Lavender. This whole house smells of lavender. Aromatherapy unit in the venting system, I figure. I love the smell of lavender. Reminds me of the romance candles Shelley and Sherman used to burn in their bedroom. And my Gramma and Pop kept lavender sachets in their drawers. I always connected the scent of lavender to love. I guess I still do.

In the master bathroom, I asked Paula to shine her phone flashlight on the cupboards as I rooted through the drawers to find some period pads. At some point the T-shirt I'd wadded up and stuffed in my undies had fallen down the leg of my pants and been lost. I just about cried when I found a package of nighttime maxis under the sink. So grateful. Paula didn't seem embarrassed to see me clutching the box to my chest.

She shone the light inside the massive shower—all white tile and stippled glass. "Is bigger than Abuelo's whole living room."

We stepped inside the shower. There would have been room for Fee too. And the rest of the Hive, for that matter.

"They got all the Sun products—soap, body wash. Oh my God, this shampoo costs a hundred bucks a tube," I said.

I took the bar of Sun soap from its crèche and held it to Paula's nose—oranges and apples and eucalyptus and lavender—and noticed the control panel. On. Warm. Pulse. Very user-friendly. I pressed. The water shot out of the four large heads at the far end and the steam rose up from the floor. I smiled at Paula and started to take off my filthy clothes—but Paula hung back. I knew why.

"I go get Fee," Paula said.

"She can shower after, Paula. We'll be quick."

Paula just stood there watching the water pelt the tiles.

"You wanna wait? It's okay."

Paula paused, then, unable to resist, said, "I'm coming in the water."

She turned away to pull off her dirty, torn Patriot Girl dress and tossed it into the trash, where I'd put my clothes too. I was careful to look straight ahead when she stepped into the shower and moved forward under the raining showerheads. I wanted to tell her I knew her truth, and that I understood. But Paula's the one who should start that conversation, when she's ready. One day we'll talk about it. I know that for sure. One day we'll talk about every detail of this day and this night and whatever comes next. We'll never forget.

That shower. I've never actually appreciated my access to a shower. I'm obviously looking at my whole life in a different way—all the things I've taken for granted. The sense of entitlement I only saw in others, not myself. My house. My en suite bathroom. My filtered water. Agua. Not just clean water to drink and cook with, but clean water to wash myself with. Some people can't take a shower every day, or even every week. Paula? I wonder if she even had a working bathroom in that trailer. I wonder if the closest she got to a shower was splashing a little polluted water on herself at the kitchen sink. God.

We stood under the warm, pulsing spray, washing away the dirt and blood. Even though she doesn't have hair, I put a little of the Sun shampoo on Paula's prickly scalp and massaged it in. She purred like a kitten because of the way it smells, but also because I don't think she's been touched in a kind way for a long time. I thought of Paula's mother, and called out to her in my thoughts: *I got her. I'll take care of her.* When we were done, we used the huge white towels stacked on the shelf to wrap ourselves, and stood there for a sec, looking at our dim reflections in the darkened bathroom. "My hair will come back," Paula said.

My period blood stained the white towel. Fuck.

In the master bedroom closet, I found a drawer with some expensive lingerie from that place on Rodeo, matching bras and panty sets and camis, and some naughty stuff, then I opened another drawer and found a stash of period panties—granny-style, but tight-ish—that would keep the pad in place. In the section of the closet devoted to athletic clothes, I chose some sweatpants and a plain black hoodie. Thank you, Mrs. Mason, for the clothes, and the period panties and the shower and the pad.

We couldn't find any clothes to fit Paula in Mrs. Mason's closet, so we went to look for the little girl's room. When we opened the double doors at the far end of the hall, we got quite the scare when Paula shone the flashlight against the wall. Dolls—shelves and shelves filled with dead-eyed Patriot Girls, trussed up in their red, white and blue, looking like a horror movie. On the shelves of another wall was all their swag—every item—the tree house and the schoolroom, all the cars, the kitchen set and the playground set.

Paula was confused. "It's a Patriot Girls shop?"

"No. It's just the little girl's room."

"All for one girl?"

"Yeah."

"But how she can play with so much dolls?"

"She can't."

Paula took them in. "Katie May and Nancy Pool and Grace Chapman . . . every doll."

"Spoiled, huh?"

She looked at me like I was crazy. "Lucky," she said.

We found a black tracksuit hanging in the little girl's walk-in, and a matching ball cap decorated with little red hearts. The price tags were all still attached and Paula didn't feel right wearing something new, but I said we'd pay this family back for everything we ate or drank or borrowed—even the Sun products—when all of this was over, so not to worry about it. I found some underwear in the little girl's drawer. And a little training bra from that store for girls under ten—who actually don't need bras but love to look like mommy. Paula smiled when I gave her the bra and panties, and I left so she could dress without feeling she had to hide.

We went back downstairs to find Fee still on the sectional staring out at the ocean with her hand on her stomach. We told her about the shower, but she just nodded and shrugged. Paula sat beside her and reached out to pet her hair but stopped, because Fee is filthy and her hair is matted and Paula is clean and smells like Sun. Paula goes, "Soon Rory's mamá will come."

Fee turned to look at Paula. "I'm sorry about what happened to your abuelo."

Paula nodded. Was she sad? Not exactly. But something.

"You look good in that outfit, Paula."

Paula smiled, looking at her reflection in the window.

I combed out my hair and stared out at the ocean. I wanted to tell Fee to go up and have a shower because smell, and because it will make her feel better, and I need her right now, but I'm trying not to be relentless.

Poor little Paula. I can see she's exhausted. I wanna pick her up and carry her to the king-sized bed in the little girl's room and pull the huge duvet up to her chin, and tickle her neck and kiss her cheek and say nighty-nite, boo, like my mother did with me. But I think we need to stay together. And the truth is, we have no idea what happens next, or how fast we'll have to leave. Or even when.

I'm exhausted too. But I know I couldn't sleep. My head is too filled with fear, and worry, and hope.

Jagger Jonze and Jinny Hutsall have vanished into thin air. The media's reporting that their social accounts have gone silent. Gone. Just gone. Jonze never showed up for the free concert at the pier. Jinny's house on Oakwood Circle is dark and vacant. The papz got pics of all these dark vehicles leaving Hidden Oaks, but you couldn't tell who was inside. No one knows where they are. They're just gone. Just. Gone. I have to tell Fee.

"What are you saying? Did they go together?" Fee asked when I told her the news.

"No one knows."

"Why would they leave?"

"Because they're guilty, Fee. Because it's exactly what I said. They orchestrated this whole thing."

"But why would they do that?"

"Are you kidding? The entire country's talking about the Red Market. Crusaders are everywhere on the news. And Jagger Jonze is famous as fuck. Plus, look at all the sympathy this has brought to the Cause."

"So they sacrificed us?"

"If we'd been killed in that bomb blast, no one'd be asking questions about Jagger Jonze. Or Warren Hutsall either. The story would be that a couple of teen "anti-life" agitators planted a bomb at the AVB and got killed in the process. Maybe they'd say we were suicide bombers. Maybe they'd say we were idiots and accidentally blew ourselves up."

"I don't know, Rory."

She's fighting the logic of the illogical—religious fervor.

"They didn't count on us getting away, Fee. They didn't count on all the questions and the investigations and the hunt."

"I guess."

"Fee, if we'd been killed in that blast, it would've taken care of Jagger's other problem too. The evidence would have been destroyed. Right?"

Fee started blinking, like, processing the idea that Jagger Jonze was ruthless enough, and cold enough, to find a way to kill the teenager he'd impregnated, and catapult himself to superstardom in the bargain. Tears welled up in her eyes.

"I'm sorry, Fee."

"Maybe they had death threats against them. Jagger and Jinny? And they're hiding, like us?"

Wow. She still can't see it. "Maybe."

"Maybe Jagger thought he'd get shot if he showed up at the pier."

"Yeah. Maybe, Fee."

I wanted to keep trying to persuade her to see what's in front of her freaking nose, but Fee's done. Her heart must be in splinters. I could see she was still holding back tears when she asked, "What about your mother? Any news on her?"

The whereabouts of my mother is still unknown, but I feel sure Shelley's okay, and that she, along with Lilly and Chase, was part of this plan to get us here. I'm gonna see her. Soon. I feel that like a premonition. Like, I can totally see her face. Smell her Chanel. Feel her arms around me.

Sherman? The media followed him to some prayer circle at his church in the OC, where he and Sugar Tits and some other Hollywood types are praying for our souls. Um. Thanks?

The Hive? They've gone quiet too. No more tweeting at us. No more accusations and taunting and Bible verses. I think of them, my best friends, alone in their bedrooms with their laptops and phones, obsessively checking their feeds. Or maybe they're watching the news with their quiet, frightened parents. I imagine how they must have felt seeing the footage of the fire near Javier's cabin, and the crashed copters. Smoke. Death. Real shit. And all the investigation into Jagger Jonze and Warren Hutsall? At some point in these past few hours my friends and their families, and thousands more, have to have realized that the people they sided with are frauds. Is the spell finally broken? Zara? Delaney? Brook?

So we're sitting tight, as instructed, here in this lavender-scented home. Waiting. Again. For help. For someone to come and take us away. Chase? If I crushed on Chase before, what do I feel for him now? I don't know the word for it, but I keep picturing him at the library with all those girls, how it hurt, and how, if I'd known . . . I wouldn't have just crushed on him, I mighta worshipped him.

The Charmlee fire is still raging up the coast. That one in Bel Air has burned two hundred acres, five structures, and is only twenty percent contained. The local news toggles back and forth from interviews with angry Crusaders to interviews with numb families inside berms of black dirt and ash where only hours before their houses stood. In the blink of a fucking eye, through no fault of their own, the flames took everything. I feel that.

Cable news is ticking down the time from when the bomb exploded at Sacred, so I don't have to wonder how many hours and minutes and seconds we've been on the run.

Thank God I still have Nina's pink laptop. This house has a dozen charge stations, of course, so the computer's juiced and I can keep writing all night. And if no one comes, I will. Because if I couldn't write all of this down, I really don't know what I'd do. Has writing about what's happening helped me make sense of it? Definitely. If I couldn't write, I'd curl up beside Fee right now and completely lose my shit.

I don't know who all will read this blog when I press Post. Maybe by the time I submit, we'll be old news. Eventually the Crusaders will leave the Pier, and go home to their jobs and families. The other bounty hunters will move on to the next outlaw on *America's Most Wanted*. With Jagger Jonze incommunicado, how would anyone expect him to honor the bounty? It could all die down. Or it could ratchet back up.

One day, a long, long time from now, I'll give this blog to my children. I'll tell them that this crazy thing happened to me, and my best friend, and this other kid, but we survived it, and here's the whole story minute by minute, written down for posterity. Maybe the world will still be fucked-up when I have kids. Even more reason to teach them about resistance. I wanna raise the kind of people who speak up, and ask questions, and call themselves out as well as others, and dig deeper. I hope, in my future, I'll be a good example of all those things. I guess I'll have to tell my kids it's okay to swear, since their mother clearly had a mouth on her.

Every now and then I take a break from the laptop. I talk to Paula. Rub Fee's back. Feel like a coach, giving my little team pep talks, like, we're in the home stretch, and we gotta stay positive, and we can do this. I've been catching them up on the breaking news, but all they really wanna know now is when Shelley will get here. I wanna know that too.

The latest news is that Warren Hutsall's gone off the grid along with his absent, mysterious wife. The last known location of his private jet is Aruba. He's being investigated for securities fraud, and illegal trading, including human trafficking, among other things. So running away looks guilty. Right? Isn't that what they said about me and Fee? He is definitely guilty of something. Is Jinny with him? And Jagger Jonze? No point in telling Fee about Warren Hutsall. Looks like she's going to delude herself about Jagger Jonze until the bitter end.

Will all the emerging info, you'd think the Crusaders would put their rifles down and rethink the hunt? Not happening. People believe what they want to believe, plug their ears with their fingers and sing lalala when the other side talks. I mean, no one, including me, knows exactly what went down at the AVB, but shouldn't the fact that our accusers have disappeared put it all on pause? Nope. They say they're even more determined to find us. If I stood right now at the ocean's edge, I'd be able to see the Crusaders gathered on the Santa Monica Pier a few miles away. I wonder if they're still gonna do fireworks at midnight. I feel like Paula would love that.

Paula's fussing over the ribbons on her Patriot Girl doll's blouse. She tells me she's been praying since the day her abuelo brought her back to his trailer that God would send someone to rescue her. Deliver her from evil.

I thought of Javier. I hope he's not dead.

"I prayed for Mr. Javier," Paula said, like she knew what I was thinking.

"You don't think he sold us out?"

Paula shrugged. "Still I pray."

"Did your mother take you to church?" I asked.

"No church. Just pray."

"And your mother taught you to read?"

"Yes. And a little to write. And she teach to me English, but mostly I learn from TV."

"*Dancing Dina*. I loved that show when I was little too. Me and Fee and our friends used to do the choreography."

Paula laughed. "My mother dances with me too. She is good dancer. She is good singer. She is smart. She is working in the house to clean, but she have a dream to be the nurse. She pray for that. She want to care for the people."

"So her cancer—she couldn't get treatment?"

"No money. No insure. No citizen. No help. She pray."

"But God didn't answer her prayers?"

Paula made a face. "He do answer her prayers."

I wondered if Paula's mother knew about Paula—but of course she did. And Paula "has the cable and the Twitter," so Paula knows what transgender is. She's ten. Maybe she even googled about it. Maybe she's seen the KUWTK reruns with Caitlyn Jenner. And if Paula knows what transgender is, then she also knows about the hate. The Crusaders, especially, have tons to say about LGBTQ people and the thousand ways they should die. The word *abomination* comes up a lot. I don't understand how Paula can be a believer when so many of God's people say God hates her fucking guts.

"I hope God answers your prayers, Paula."

"He always do."

"God always answers your prayers?" I kinda wanted to shake her. How can she say this? Look at her fucking life? "Like, how . . . Paula? What prayers has He answered?"

"When I am in the truck to come to my mother in America, I pray the guards don't look in the suitcase."

"You were smuggled in a suitcase?"

"I am small. I am seven years old then." Paula shows me how she curled up into a fetal position. "I do this."

"Oh my God. For how long?"

"Maybe one hour? I sleep a little. Across the border I pray to have more air. He gives. The zipper breaks. I don't die."

"So you came in a truck?"

"Yes. From my village."

"Alone?"

"My father give the man money. When we get near America, he put me in the suitcase. I pray the man don't take the money and kill me."

"And he didn't."

"Yes. And when my mother get the cancer, I pray God to cure, then to take, for no more suffer."

"And after your mother . . . Someone brought you to your abuelo after your mother died? Even though he's the way he is. Was."

"There is no one else."

"Didn't you ever wanna run away?"

"Yes. Many nights I go to the hills. I think I will go to the ocean, but I come back. I am scared in the dark. I am scared of coyote and mountain lion and what will happen if Abuelo catch me. Every day I pray to God, please bring me help."

"And we came," I said.

"Yes. Always He answer my prayer."

"Right."

"He take my Blackie, my dog, when I pray for Blackie not to suffer."

"Right."

"And He give to me Mr. Javier."

"Why didn't Mr. Javier help you get somewhere safe?"

"He ask Abuelo can I come and live with him in Nina's room. Abuelo say no and get the gun."

"Right."

"God see. God care."

"Right."

"God see you too, Rory."

"Okay. It's just, Paula, I'm not down with the Bible. Like, I respect that you believe in God and all, but . . ."

Paula touched my hand. She could see my face in the moonlight pouring in through the windows, and she must have seen the tears in my eyes, because she goes, "God love you."

"But I don't believe."

"God love all the people. Even who don't know Him. And He want us to love each other. He is the way, and the truth and the light. Like a ball make of love and light."

I needed a minute with that. Paula's not stupid. Maybe that's the way to go—to think of God as a big ol' ball of light and love you can tap into. Like the way I feel about my mother. Aunt Lill. My Gramma and Pop. I don't hate that.

Paula went back to fussing with her doll. I wonder if the family who live in this beautiful house prayed for all of their good fortune and feel blessed by it. I wonder if they are God people. No crucifix on the wall. No Bibles on the shelves. Plus, they know we're here, so unless we're being set up—and I can't even go there—the Masons are just good-ass humans trying to help the wrongly accused.

On the one hand I get that people shouldn't be made to feel like assholes, and are not assholes, just because they worked hard and have more shit than others. Or even because their parents are rich and they inherited a lifestyle. I mean, I get that. It's just the disparity. When some people in our country, and in the rest of the world, don't have shelter, or food, or water, the excess of lives like mine just feels fucking foul. And I know that sounds like some Commie bullshit. It's just, not everybody starts life with the same degree of privilege. Shelley says some people were born on third base and some people were born outside the ballpark, and the journey to home plate ain't the same for all. Wouldn't it be better for everyone to, like, find a way to get everybody in the game?

Fee's just sitting here with Paula's head on her shoulder now, quiet, and stroking her stomach. She did that yesterday—rubbed her stomach in concentric circles. I thought it was because she was sick. Now I wonder if some instinct kicked in, some maternal urge to nurture and protect. Maybe I just want that to be true. And maybe thinking that way makes me judge-y.

Paula asks me where I think we might go after here. Where my mother, or whoever is coming to help us, might take us.

I have no idea. I guess that's true of all people. No one has a clue what happens next.

But I tell Paula about Vancouver. I tell her that I wouldn't be surprised if we ended up there, at least for a while. Lilly will give us all a place to stay. We'd be safe in Canada. And away from all the press. Paula smiles when I tell her that we can walk the seawall together, and shop on Robson, and see movies, and eat in ethnic restaurants. Also, there's the Aquarium.

"And then we come back home?"

"Yes."

"You have room for Paula?"

We have room for twenty Paulas at our house on Oakwood Circle. But home isn't home anymore. And never will be again.

I can never go back to Oakwood Circle. The bubble has popped. Thank God. In a way. No, actually, thank God.

"Abortion is legal in Canada," Fee said.

"Yes."

"Then I hope we do go there."

"Yeah."

"They might offer us asylum or whatever it's called," Fee said. "And maybe somehow your mom could help my mom get there too."

"She will. She'll figure everything out. Apparently my mother's a superhero."

Fee shook her head a few times. "It feels like a dream. Doesn't it? I mean, we're here, which is better than the shed, but we're still nowhere, and I'm still pregnant, Rory. And I'm afraid. I'm really afraid."

"Me too," I said.

"Me too," Paula added, and got up to go stand at the window.

"Fee? I know you don't wanna talk about it, just, you should talk to my mom, and yours, before you make any decisions."

Paula stepped back from where she was standing at the window just now and said, "It's people out there."

I got up to look, but I don't see anyone. We're all a little tense. Fleeing for your life'll do that to a person.

But wait. Holy shit.

There are people on the beach. I just saw them. Fuck.

Fuck fuck fuck fuck fuck. I fucked up.

I mean, if we're found here, because of what I just did, I won't ever forgive myself.

So those people on the beach? There were two shadowy figures trudging through the sand parallel to the row of beachfront homes. So we watched, thinking maybe they're bounty hunters, or cops, maybe coast guards—we couldn't really see them well. Then two little figures come scampering up behind them. As they got closer, we saw that it was a family of homeless, a mother and father who looked not that much older than us, and two little girls, barefoot, but dressed in layers of coats and ragged sweatpants. They were all, even the little ones, carrying backpacks and empty trash bags, their eyes on the ground, scavenging, the way they do. The mother had a plush beach towel slung around her neck, no doubt snatched after it was left to dry on a fence or forgotten at the surf. The father was tall and pin thin. They stopped on the other side of the Plexiglas, staring into the Masons' yard. We stepped back from the windows.

Fee goes, "Why are they stopping here?"

I saw one of the little girls pointing to the big grapefruits left hanging on the tree. The father picked her up and lifted her as high as he could as she strained her little arm, trying to reach the fruit. Just as she was about to grab the grapefruit, the wind shook the branch and her prize dropped to the ground behind the Plexiglas wall.

The father set the little girl down. She took her younger sister by the hand and the two pressed their faces against the glass wall, staring at the fallen grapefruit like candy in a case.

"That is so sad," Fee said.

The little girl started crying. A high-pitched wail that carried through the windows. I wondered if old Monty'd shuffle out to his back deck and try to shoo them away with the broom.

Maybe it was that—the thought of the neighbors shooing these people away . . . Don't know what made me do it. Didn't give it much thought, I guess. I ran to the pantry, stuffed some boxes of cereal and granola bars into a bag I found on the back of the door, then grabbed an armful of cold waters from the fridge and put them in another bag.

Paula and Fee were going, "What are you doing? Where are you going?"

I didn't answer.

When I opened the sliding door to the sea breeze, the little girl stopped crying and the family froze. When I took a step off the deck, they started to skitter through the sand toward the ocean. I called out in a whisper, "Wait! Don't go!"

I held up the grocery bags. They stopped.

The father started back first, cautious, followed by the mother and the scared little girls. They waited on the other side of the glass as I checked the sky. There was a copter heading our way, but I thought I had a sec, so I picked a fat, oily fruit from a low hanging branch on the grapefruit tree and tossed it to the little girl, who caught it and smiled, and immediately handed it to her little sister. I picked another fruit, which she also caught, and immediately began to peel with hungry hands. Then I hoisted the bags with water and food over to the mother and the father.

The guy looked at me weird, and I wondered if he'd recognized me as one of the fugitive girls from TV, but then I realized it wasn't that. To them I was just the rich girl who lived in this fab house and gave them food—a curious and verboten act, because, like Jinny Hutsall says, everyone knows if you feed them they'll never go away.

I hear the copter getting closer, the heartbeat of the blades, but I don't run, because the littlest girl starts screaming and hopping on one bare foot because she just stepped on something sharp. I can't help. I can't do anything. And now I'm afraid to run because the copter is about to fly overhead. I flatten against the glass security wall, trying to blend, and all of a sudden a siren starts blaring from the speaker on the deck and thousand-watt security lights flood the property. Exposed.

I look up, but the copter has banked left, heading for the valley, and couldn't have seen me. Then I thought of Monty and the old woman next door. Would they think the raccoon set off the alarm? Would they call the police? Then I thought of the armed guards from the home security service who'd likely be storming the house any sec.

The whole thing lasted less than five seconds. The lights snapped off and the alarm went silent. When I turned to look, the little family of vagrants were gone. Disappeared. I ran back to the house.

When I got inside, Paula just looked at me. Fee sighed, and almost sounded relieved when she said, "The security people are gonna respond to that. Or the cops, because some alarms go straight to the station. We're busted, Ror."

Paula had the idea to put our dirty clothes back on and hide out on the beach near the surf. This seemed like a bad idea

to me. No shelter at all? Plus, the copters? Plus, the coast guard?
I thought of Anne Frank, and wondered if the beach house had
an attic. Couldn't remember seeing any small ceiling doors, but
I did remember that Mrs. Mason's walk-in closet was huge, and
her clothes were crushed together on felt hangers, pressed
together like the layers of sediment that mesmerize me on
mountain drives.

I felt pretty sure we could hide in there, behind her color-
coded wardrobe, like when I was little and hid behind the racks
at Target, so we hurried upstairs to the walk-in and found a
spot behind the lavender-scented blouses. We stayed there for
what felt like forever. It was dark, and hot, and tight, and after
a while Fee said, "Wouldn't they have come by now? If they're
gonna come?"

Just a delayed response to a security alert at a Malibu beach
house? Or maybe they weren't coming at all? The media has
been reporting that law enforcement's spread thin because of the
crowds gathered over at the Pier and all the highway closures
around the fires. Is that why they're not here yet?

Chase's uncle definitely got an intruder alert, and a phone
call. Maybe he told them everything was fine and no need to
investigate. Or maybe he's got shitty reception on some yacht off
the Hawaiian coast. Or maybe he left his phone at the hotel and
doesn't know what just happened at the home where he's hiding
fugitives.

Then again, what the fuck about the alarm anyway? Someone
obviously disabled the alarm on the interior of the house. At this
point I have no idea why the backyard alarm went off, who shut it
off, or if the cops will come.

At this point, on top of everything else, I can't stop worrying that the sharp thing the little vagrant girl stepped on was a dirty needle. Fuck.

We decided to leave the closet and come back to the white leather sectional and the ocean view. No sign of Monty or his wife from next door. The cops haven't busted down the gates, but that doesn't mean they won't. We're all still on high alert, listening for sirens and the thud of footsteps and the clatter of rifles.

I'm back online, of course. Paula looks at the news with me, but Fee's just sitting here staring at the sea.

Kimmy K, my girl, gave a quote to TMZ as she was coming out of Nobu tonight. First she told the world that the sushi there is bullets, and then, when the dude asked what she thought about the Villains in Versace, she said, "Um. They weren't wearing Versace." Then, when the dude said he meant did she believe we're guilty, she got real. She said she's felt persecuted her whole life, flamed and trolled for just doing Kim. She said she understands how we must feel, wherever we are, but urged us to turn ourselves in. She believes the truth will prevail. And that no matter what, God is on the side of the truth.

Paula watched the interview with me. "She is beautiful," she said.

"You're beautiful too, Paula."

"Mi mamá say too."

"You're mamá's right."

"But I like to have long eyelashes."

I laughed. "Totally feel that."

"And pretty feets."

I wish I could take Paula to the ocean to put her big, unpretty feets in the water. But then again, what if we stepped on a stingray? Or a sharp like that little girl? God, I hope it wasn't a syringe. I mean, there's so much litter on the beaches these days.

I'm looking out right now watching the sky traffic. There are breaks—moments when the ocean is clear and the sky is clean. Just like with the cops, so many copters and planes had to be diverted to the fires, and a ton of them are hovering over the demonstrations at the Pier. That would actually be a good place to hide. In plain sight.

Sacred Heart does a beach day each year. It's a charity thing where we invite a bunch of procit kids, or homeless kids, to come hang with us at Zuma. We have a nice catered lunch under a tent and we tsk the shit out of the fact that all these kids live only miles away from the ocean but have never been to the beach. It seems impossible. Yet it's true. The homeless and procit kids our age hate our fucking guts, for obvious reasons, so we give our attention to the little ones, splash in the surf, Boogieboarding and all. Then we wrap them up like burritos in the huge Sacred Heart High beach towels they're allowed to take home—even though they'd prolly never get to the ocean again. We pat ourselves on the back pretty hard for our efforts. Pastor Hanson is totally in it for the pics, gathering little brown kids onto his knees and making sure the mommies who volunteered to help that day snapped tons of pics for Sacred's Insta.

I'm so freaking tired. Yet can't stop going online.

Authorities have finally released footage of the scene at the school and parking lot from all the security cams. It doesn't prove or disprove our innocence. Just shows the rest of the world the insanity of yesterday night. Now I understand why we were asked to check our cell phones at the door. Why our purses were searched—I mean, that's pretty common now because guns. And bombs.

It wasn't just Jagger controlling his image. It was Jagger controlling the whole show, making sure that two hundred phones couldn't document what happened. Warren Hutsall is definitely involved. They're saying that Hutsall is Jonze's "de facto agent," taking commission on his earnings as an entertainer and through his AVB franchise. And all of it for what? Money? The righteousness of his cause? Both?

Seems like Mr. Hutsall has been pimping Jinny out, having her recruit for the Crusaders and for the AVB. One of the news reports says Jinny Hutsall is eighteen, not sixteen. They say school records indicate that the Hutsalls moved around a lot and that she repeated eighth grade and frosh. News reports also say that Jinny was involved in a number of episodes at her other schools. The victim of anti-Crusader cyberbullying at one. The victim of a vicious physical attack at another. The fuck? Did Warren Hutsall know about the Reverend's relationship with his daughter? Somehow I doubted that. But then again.

Has Jinny essentially been working as a spy? Smoking out then discrediting agitators like me? Creating dramatic scenarios to create free publicity for the Cause and feed the propaganda machine, just like my mother always said the Crusaders do? Like the whole Red Market thing. Bombing the AVB.

It'd been Jinny's suggestion that we lie at security and say we left our phones at home. She said we could tuck them into our bras and bodices and take some fun bathroom selfies after the ceremony. I should've wondered why Jinny cared about bathroom selfies, when she only ever posted anti-abortion stuff on Crusader forums, never pics. At that point I think I was relieved at the thought of keeping my phone on my body. Like, it's my phone. It also occurred to me that I could get some covert photographs for my blog. I wasn't thinking about outing Jagger Jonze as the total fraud that he is. I was way too afraid to try that on my own. But I did wanna defy him, and maybe post some unauthorized pics of him drooling over some teenaged virgins.

At the Hutsalls' house, when we were getting ready for the ball, no one was mad at Jinny for stealing the Dom Pérignon from the wine fridge and sneaking it upstairs in her Louis tote, along with six crystal glasses.

As she poured the champagne into the flutes, she said, "I can't believe it's actually happening. And don't worry, God will forgive us for the champagne."

Dee worried the alcohol might react with her Wellbutrin but took a glass when Jinny offered.

"Won't our dads smell the alcohol on our breath?" Zara asked.

"It'll be overpowered by the alcohol on theirs," I said.

"Besides," Jinny'd giggled, "champagne isn't alcohol, it's bubb. And I think a little bubb is right for tonight. Plus, I'm so nervous."

I was looking at her, like, Last night you were getting your ring pearled by Jagger Jonze, and now you're nervous about getting a pearl ring from your dad? Seriously? I was also thinking, Do you know that I know your secret, Jinny?

"Rory? Champagne?"

I took the glass. I'd hardly slept the night before and spent most of the morning worrying if Jinny and Jagger knew I filmed them and what they might do if they did. Any moment I'd expected her to ring the doorbell and storm up the spiral staircase to confront me in my room. What would she say? I still don't know. I wonder if I'll ever know.

Jinny wanted to make a toast. Ugh. We formed a circle, held up our sparkling glasses and waited as she blinked back some tears. I felt like such a poser. Jinny couldn't believe this night was actually happening? Me either. Or more, I couldn't believe I was actually going through with it.

Jinny began her toast, "To the Lord Jesus Christ Our Savior." I know she saw me cringe.

"We are so grateful for Your blessings, and so stoked to make this pledge to You tonight. Forgive us for the bubb, Lord."

We all giggled.

"Please watch over us. Especially Rory. We know You move in mysterious ways. May tonight be a turning point for our friend."

The girls thought she was teasing, but I knew Jinny meant every word.

I tipped back the champagne, liking the way it bit my tongue, and fogged my brain, and made me hate Jinny a little less. Well, until she bent down to fix the strap on her pretty Lacroix sandals. And then I was just so jealous. My toe was swollen from trying to move my dresser to get my camera and I couldn't wear my sandals. I had on sneakers.

Mr. Sharpe had bought Fee a pair of the Miu Mius she wanted, but on the day of the ball she texted me that they didn't fit! She'd bought them weeks earlier, when she and Delaney went dress shopping, but now she couldn't get her feet into them and so she was gonna have to wear her white Keds. It never occurred to me, like, oh, obviously, Fee is pregnant and retaining fluids and that's why her lips seem plumper, and her tits fuller, and her feet grew a size. Nope. I just thought that's why we shouldn't try on shoes in the morning when we're at our skinniest and least hydrated. Thank God we both ended up in sneakers. We'd never have made it to Javier's in heels.

Jinny had been encouraging, watching Fee and me lace up our sneakers in her room. "No one can see your shoes anyway. And sneaks are better for dancing."

We never got to the dancing.

After the vow ceremony, our little group had dispersed again. Sherman joined a group of dads I didn't know, to smoke cigars outside somewhere. Jinny snuck up behind me and whispered into my ear that she was going out to the limo to get the other bottle of champagne she'd stashed in her tote. She pulled me out to the hallway to conspire. We definitely didn't wanna get caught with alcohol, so she said we should meet in the farthest bathroom, out back behind the gym on the other side of the school.

"Bee and Zara are doing portraits with their dads," I said, pointing to the photographer's line. "Not sure where Fee and Delaney are."

I told her I'd text the other girls about our bathroom meet and she said, "Oh my God, don't pull out your phone, Rory. And don't text anybody—just in case somebody hears the buzz. And we can't all go out there at the same time. It'd look suspicious."

"Okay."

"I'll tell them."

"Okay."

"Head over there now. Dom and I'll see you in a sec."

Dom and I? Making jokes? With me? Was she drunk? "Okay." I was glad to have an excuse to leave the ballroom.

"The one behind the gym," she reminded.

"I know."

I started down the long hallway that led to the door that led to the path around back to the gym on the other side of the school. That's when I saw Fee, sitting on a bench with her head in her hands.

When I sat down beside her and put my arm around her shoulder, she shook me off. "I'm okay," she said.

"I'll drive you home if you want."

"I can't. It's okay. I'm okay."

But I could see she wasn't. "Where's Dee?"

She shrugged.

"Sure you don't wanna go home?"

"Mr. Tom'd be pissed. You know how much this night cost?"

"But you're sick."

"I'm okay."

I told Fee about Jinny and the champagne rendezvous back in the gym bathroom, and how we needed to be cagey. She told me to go on ahead because she had to find Mr. Tom to say sorry about her ring not fitting. And also, he wanted to get their portraits done. Whatever.

Heading to the gym bathroom, I started to play that crazy-making game of Does Jinny Know I Know? all over again. What would I say if she stepped to me? I'd started to compose an explanation the second I dropped my camera. *No idea what you're talking about, Jinny. I was taking video of the roses outside my window to send to my aunt Lilly. You thought I was filming you in your bedroom? What? No! Why? Were you waxing or changing or something? I didn't see anything, Jinny. I swear.* I could sell that. I felt, even then, as if my life depended on it.

A few dads were out by the basketball courts. I smelled cigar smoke, then heard Sherman laughing, and decided to take the long way around, through the elementary school's playground. It took forever, and the whole time I kept thinking I heard footsteps behind me in the dark. I had this feeling that if I was in a horror movie, people would be yelling at me from the audience: Are you stupid? Don't go! Don't go!

When I finally got there, the bathroom door was locked, or stuck. So much for that. I took my phone from the secret hiding place in my bodice, but no texts. I was about to message Jinny and the rest when I heard a noise on the other side of the door, something metal clattering against the porcelain sink. "Hello?"

There were quick footsteps, and then Fee shouting from the other side that the door was stuck and for me to pull. I did, and together we managed to open it.

"Where were you?" Fee asked. "I've been here for five minutes."

"I took the long way. How'd you get here so fast?"

"Mr. Tom needed to talk to Reverend Jagger about something. Where is everybody?"

"I don't know."

"Should we text?"

"No. Can you imagine how mad the dads would be if they knew we had our phones?"

I dragged a waste can over to hold the door open so we wouldn't get locked in. I hadn't got a good look at Fee, but now I could see that her eyes were puffy and swollen. She took her little makeup bag out to do a reapply. I remember telling her that she shouldn't put her metal clutch on the damp countertop. It could get rusty.

Then I asked, "What's going on, Fee?"

"You said Jinny was bringing champagne."

"What's going on with you?"

"Nothing."

"Not nothing."

"I just feel sick, Ror. That's all. Something with my gut."

"That's all?"

"Mr. Tom's pissed at me."

"Why?"

"He spent all that money on my shoes and I couldn't wear them."

"So you can return them."

"He's pissed about the ring too. To be fair, I was the one who gave him my ring size."

"He's pissed about that?"

"It was embarrassing, Rory. Everyone was looking at us."

"Okay."

"Plus, I feel like shit."

"Well, don't drink the champagne, then."

"Where's Jinny? Where are the girls?" Fee looked at her phone. "No texts. I've got, like, ten percent."

That's when the smell hit me. "OMG, did you fart?"

"I've got bad rot gut. Don't laugh. It's serious. I feel really weird. I'm, like, peeing out my bum."

"TMI, chica," I said. But I didn't mean it. For me, there's no such thing as TMI. "What else did you eat today?"

"I ate nothing. All day."

Except the chocolate thingies, but I didn't think of that in that moment. "God, Fee."

"I know."

I finally shot off a group text. **Like, where are you guys?** I waited a sec, but no one responded. I just figured that wherever they were, it wasn't safe for them to text us back. That portrait line did look long. Then I wondered if Jinny got caught with the champagne. I wouldn't have hated that.

Fee suddenly hiked up her gown and dove into one of the stalls. I mean, everyone has had pee-bum from nerves or eating something bad or whatever. I felt horrible for her, and for myself because smell. Plus, I knew once Jinny Hutsall got here, she'd make Fee feel gross for being human.

While Fee was in the stall, I realized I had to pee, and that's when I saw blood on my pretty new panties. When I got out of the stall, I found the pad dispenser empty, and asked Fee if she had plugs in her purse, and she freaked. Then Fee flushed and OMG the toilet clogged and started overflowing. We were wearing long white gowns. Don't even. I grabbed Fee by the hand and we ran, screaming laughing, because we're sixteen years old and it was all just completely insane. On the way out the door, I accidentally kicked the trash can that held it open. The can fell and the door slammed shut behind me.

"My purse!" Fee said, not laughing anymore. "I need my purse, Rory." She was frantic—way overreacting.

We tried the door, but no way we were getting back in there. We looked around, but no Jinny. None of the girls were anywhere in sight. "Where is everybody?"

"Let's wait on the bleachers," I said. "We'll get your purse later."

We ran off, but she was still obsessing about her purse.

"Your ID is in there, right? Someone'll find it and get it back to you. It's Sacred Heart High, for God's sake."

"No ID." Fee shook her head as she realized this. Now I know the look on her face was relief.

We stopped and sat on a bench from where we could see the

bathroom door in case the girls showed up. We waited. Then Fee pulled out her phone. No signal. Fucking mountains. She doubled over from stomach pain. "What the fuck is going on with me?"

"Maybe you've got that flu. Come on, let's get you home."

We got up off the bleacher and started in the direction of the Grand Ballroom, but Fee had to stop to barf.

That's when the group texts started blowing up our phones. I read the texts out loud.

DEE: **Haps in the parking lot.**

ME: **What?**

ZARA: **What?**

BROOKLYN: **Come outside you guys.**

DEE: **Pastor Handsy tweeking.**

Then I typed. **We coming.**

Even though I'm a cross-country runner, I actually hate walking. And Fee was sick as shit, so we took a shortcut behind the Olympic swimming pool and back through the trail behind the tennis courts, and up over the ridge on the north side of the parking lot. I kept reading the group texts aloud:

ZARA: **Somebody in a backseat.**

DEE: **OMG! Making out?**

BROOKLYN: **Banging at the Ball!**

ZARA: **Just dads here.**

ME: **Perf. Incest at the AVB. Pls take vid.**

ZARA: **Yola and that guy from St. James? He lives close.**

DEE: **It's serious. Jinny calling for help.**

ZARA: **Fee? Rory?**

ME: **We're coming.**

ZARA: **Where you???**

DEE: **OMG. Where you guys?**

ZARA: **See you Dee. See me by our limo? Waving. OMG.**

DEE: **Ppl crying.**

ME: **Crying?**

ZARA: **Camy Jarvis just fainted.**

BROOKLYN: **Can't see ANYTHING!!!**

ZARA: **Rory and Fee where u guys?!!!**

DEE: **Hurry up, Ror. They're looking in your Prius.**

Something shifted. I could feel the dark energy that rose up to the ridge as Fee and I followed the path to a spot overlooking the parking lot. I listened to my inner voice telling me to stay hidden in the shadows of the rock and brush, and pulled Fee back with me.

We could see the crowd that had gathered below us. All of the dads in tuxedos and little virgins in gowns making a wide white circle around my Prius. We could hear the deep-throated murmurs of the fathers radiating up to where we hid. There was something—a person—moving around in the backseat of my car. It was one of us, one of the brides. You could see the white dress. Was someone really having sex in my car? Appeared so. Should the fathers have shielded their children from what they were about to see? Prolly.

The buzzing from the crowd got loud, and then—

Oh. My. God. Jinny Hutsall emerged from the backseat of my Prius, her freaking gold hair blowing in the wind, so fucking glamorous in that white gown. And I'm thinking, Oh my God, Jagger was drilling Jinny in my backseat and they've just been caught! For a sec I felt relief: Jinny will leave and be dead to us. And the Reverend? He'll get fried for it, and that felt like justice.

We waited, along with the rest of the crowd, to see who was

fouling Jinny Hutsall in the backseat, but no one else got out of the car. There was only beautiful Jinny Hutsall. But wait . . .

There was this collective gasp as people grasped that she was holding something in her arms—a small white bundle wrapped up in her blood-streaked pashmina.

Then the whispering started—so loud we could hear it from where we hid: *It's a baby. Oh my God it's a baby. She's holding a baby. That's a newborn baby in her arms.* Did I hear that or did I say that? Or was it Fee who said it? I remember that we shared a look and kept to the shadows and Fee took my hand and squeezed it as we watched the scene unfold—and that's what it felt like: a scene from a movie, not life—and not MY life.

We watched from the distance, me wishing I had my long-lens camera, as Jinny rolled the pashmina back to reveal the pallid face of the thing. A baby. A still baby. A dead baby? Fee squeezed my hand hard. So awful and sad, and it just killed us to see. Fee whispered, "What the fuck is happening right now?"

We couldn't see it, and I didn't know it at the time, but on the security cam footage they just released, of Jinny Hutsall holding the tiny infant wrapped in her bloodstained white pashmina, a fat tear rolled down Jinny's cheek. For a minute the whole thing looked like a photo shoot for a horror movie or fashion magazine. Fee was still squeezing my hand so hard it hurt.

No one seemed to know what to do. Jinny clutched the bloodstained thing to her perfect tits. Then, out of nowhere, a couple of Jinny's brothers showed up to keep people—even the dads—from getting close to Jinny and the baby.

The crowd suddenly parted like the Red Sea and we could see Jagger Jonze running toward Jinny. Seeing the still baby in her arms, he fell to his knees. Jinny said something to him that we couldn't hear. The crowd watched, silent, mouths agape, as Jagger Jonze lowered his head for a ten count then raised it and cocked it like he heard a voice. Then he stood and set one palm on the baby's forehead as he lifted the other hand to God.

Jinny Hutsall raised her free hand too, and that's when it came—a tiny cry.

Fee and I fell into each other's arms. I thought I might die from relief that the bloody thing was alive.

But my car! Who in the name of God would put that baby in my car? The crying got louder. And louder. It didn't really sound like a newborn, but it was soon drowned out by the sound of clapping and cheering from the crowd.

Fee wanted to go down there and join our gang, and find out what the fuck was happening. I didn't know exactly what was happening, but it appeared that Jinny Hutsall had pulled a dead baby from the back of my car and that Jagger Jonze, and Jinny Hutsall, had miraculously resurrected the baby. Somehow, someway, this didn't look good for me. I made her stay put.

"We gotta go see what's going on, Rory."

"No. No. This isn't good."

"Ya think?"

"Fee, this is . . . Something really wrong is happening. This is bizarre."

Fee doubled over then, taken by a gut cramp, otherwise I think she would've pulled away from me and run down.

Jinny—holding the tiny baby with one arm—model-walked the way she does at least five car lengths to where a skinny, dirty, blond, methy teen boy was being held by two of Jinny's five strong brothers. Where did this kid come from?

"Mine. She mine," the boy yelled through his tears. He appeared genuinely tortured, and not very smart. "We thought she dead. She weren't breathing."

"He put that baby in the Prius!" one of the brothers who was holding him shouted.

The other brother shouted, "I saw him too!"

The methy teen was sobbing. "She weren't breathing . . ."

The brothers patted the guy down like they were law enforcement. One found a huge roll of bills in his coat pocket, held together with a rubber band. "Where'd you get this money?"

"It was in the backseat," the teen said. "They said they'd leave it in the backseat."

Jagger Jonze held up his hand for silence. "Who said?"

The words floated up to us almost as if the whole thing were being amplified. Like a stage play. Scripted and acted.

The twitchy teen boy said, "She texted me to leave it in her car. The one with the turtle decal."

There were murmurs, heads shaking.

"Who texted you?" Jagger seemed believably bewildered.

"One of the runners," the boy said.

"The runners? Did you just say runners?" Jagger Jonze paused. "Are you saying there's a runner in our midst?"

The crowd went dead silent.

"This is Rory Miller's car," Jagger Jonze said, confused.

"I didn't get the name," the teen said.

"Are you saying that Rory Miller is a runner?"

Jinny Hutsall turned to the crowd and repeated the line.

Then one of Jinny's brothers prompted the teen. "And Feliza Lopez too."

"I don't know—I didn't get any names."

Fee and I just looked at each other. Holy freaking insanity.

Jagger took the baby from Jinny, cradling her against his shoulder. We could feel the heat from the mob, waves of fear and outrage. Emergency vehicles screamed in the distance.

The baby's cries somehow rose above it all as Jagger Jonze walked through the crowd with the tiny thing, swaddled so that you couldn't see its little face. Then he lifted her in the air like Simba from freaking *Lion King*, which seemed like a bad idea, and gestured for Jinny's brothers to let the teen go.

It seemed like another bad idea when he placed the baby in the arms of the twitchy father, who'd basically just admitted he'd try to sell her for parts.

Sherman. I spotted him weaving through the crowd. At first I thought he was trying to find me, to make sure I was safe, and to tell me he'd take care of everything. But nah—he was fleeing the scene. Sugar Tits' Mazzi pulled up to the security gates at the edge of the campus. And Sherman was gone.

All of a sudden, two more of Jinny's brothers came steaming toward the crowd from the walkway that leads to the gym bathroom where we'd almost been locked in. Her brothers looked freaked, having obviously failed to find us trapped. I saw one of them shake his head at Jinny.

Jagger called out to the crowd, "Find them!"

We could hear sirens, first responders closing in. We didn't exchange a glance, Fee and I, as we turned. We ran back the way we came, skirting the ridge, past the pool and the soccer field and the gym, then up the path that leads to the mountain hiking trails behind the school, tripping over roots and rocks and branches, on our way, although I didn't know it at that point, to Javier's cabin.

We didn't get far before the earth rocked under our feet and we fell on the rocky trail. Earthquake? We got up and looked back toward our school. Smoke was billowing from a corner of the gym. It took a minute to register that a bomb had just exploded in the bathroom. The bomb, Jinny's bomb, had torn a portion of the roof off and flames were shooting out of broken windows and skylights. No time to say Holy Shit.

We ran. And ran. And kept on running. Fee was a soldier—gutting it all the way. Thank God for five years of cross-country. And thank God for full moons.

We heard barking dogs—police dogs, we figured. I pulled Fee toward a nearby creek, and we hiked up our dresses and waded through to throw them off our scent. On the other side, I grabbed a baseball-sized rock, smeared it with menstrual blood then hurled it as far as I could back across the creek, into the brush in the direction of the school—I'd seen a TV show about a murderer on the run scattering rocks with his scent to confuse the dogs. Fee grabbed a rock and spit on it, then hurled it—pretty good arm actually—too. We carried on throwing rocks saturated with our scent until the barking got too close. Then we climbed higher into the hills, through spiky bushes and spiny grass. Each summit we made meant another descent, over dry, crumbly rock and patches of hoary-leaved briar.

We'd been running for I don't know how long when I realized we were headed in the direction of our gardener's cousin's house in the hills. Just about then, we stumbled into a hot zone for cell. The group texts started blowing up again.

I knew about pings and there was no way we were gonna respond. We stopped, though, and I read the texts aloud to Fee.

BROOK: **R u guys reading these texts? Omg you guys? What have you done?**

DELANEY: **Runners? You guys?**

ZARA: **ppl gonna shoot you. Turn yourselves in.**

BROOK: **Turn yourselves in, Ror.**

DEE: **There is a million-dollar bounty on you.**

BROOK: **True. Reverend Jonze just put it on Twitter.**

ZARA: **Go to the police. God have mercy on your souls.**

DEE: **Can't even believe this? Why would they do this?**

ZARA: **Ror has no God. Fee has no guap.**

DEE: **My dad SO MAD.**

ZARA: **OMG you guys. Just got trend alert. We're everywhere.**

Fee and I looked at each other in the moonlight, scratched and pale in our filthy, torn gowns. Wait. What?

BROOK: **We're on TMZ right now. Turn it on. We look amaze in our gowns. Frowny face that Ror and Fee ruined the Virtue Ball.**

DEE: **Turn yourselves in!**

ZARA: **My mom says Shelley has to be involved. Not surprised. Commies.**

BROOK: **Your parents are getting death threats. Turn yourselves in!**

ZARA: **Oh my God you guys. This is crazy!**

FINALLY, JINNY HUTSALL: **God's will be done.**

Fuck.

"We gotta get rid of our phones," I said.

"No!" Fee said.

"Yes. They'll be able to track us."

I remembered there was another shallow creek up ahead. I snatched Fee's phone from her hand and ran, planning to drown my phone and hers. Only there was no water at all in the once-raging creek. I smashed our phones against a rock and buried them in the mud. Fee just looked at me.

"Oh my God, Rory. This can't be happening," she said. "I don't understand any of this. Why would they say that about us? Why would that guy put that baby in your car?"

"I don't know. It doesn't make any sense."

All of this time I've been worried that the baby was real. After watching the footage, though, I'm sure that it was a prop—animatronic. You could tell by the jerky motions, and the face. I have no doubt someone's gonna find that mechanical newborn somewhere online for sale to the movie industry, or to eccentric people who want to pretend to be mothers. It's gruesome, but less gruesome than the thought that they used an actual baby for that stunt. What the fuck crime category would that fall under? Whatever happened, the "miracle baby" has not been found.

Fee and especially Paula have been watching the windows and doors while I've been blogging. The cops? Security company? Still no sign of either. But every time we hear a siren on the Pacific Coast Highway, which is every ten minutes, we flinch, and wonder if we should head back to the closet.

Social media and news outlets are now dissecting the security cam vid. At least some people are suggesting that thing in my backseat was a prop, like the fake fetuses Jinny brought to the courthouse in Pasadena. And the methy teen? Obviously an actor. A pretty good one. Some of the dads that were at the ball are still claiming they saw us grab that baby that was not a baby from the father and run with her into the hills. Others say the methy teen dad just sort of disappeared. No one has come forward with any information about the baby. Interesting that there is no crowdfunding to find either the methy teen or that child.

Holy war. In a war, there must be villains. And the villains have to die. But we didn't.

One of the images I just saw was of Jinny's brother, Garth, who maybe isn't her brother at all, emerging from the girls' bathroom much earlier in the day. Long before the event. But Garth and the other Chippendale dudes can't be questioned because—guess what—they're nowhere to be found. So Garth planted the bomb? Fuck you, Garth.

Paula just asked me to stop writing so we can go check on Fee. I hadn't even realized she'd left the room.

Fee wasn't anywhere on the main floor. We found her sitting on the marble floor of the dark master bathroom.

"You okay?"

She wouldn't look up. "No."

"Fee?"

"I had really bad cramps . . . not stomach cramps, but cramp cramps. I was hoping there'd be blood. I was hoping I was having a miscarriage . . ."

"Oh, Fee . . ."

"I didn't."

"Okay."

"What am I gonna do, Ror?"

I really don't know.

There was a noise outside. I checked out the bathroom window but couldn't see anyone on the beach. No vagrants near the fruit trees. Maybe it was Monty next door, swatting at the raccoon. Paula said she was going to look out the windows downstairs.

I sat on the bathroom floor next to Fee. "Malibu Sunset," I said.

She half-smiled.

"I got your back, Fee. And if you wanna . . . I mean . . . we'll find a way . . . There's still lots of time."

"There isn't that much time, Ror."

"There's lots of time."

"I've missed three periods."

Wait. What? "How is that possible?"

"It just is."

"But—"

"At first I just thought, oh well, sometimes I miss my period when I'm stressed, and I've been stressed. Then I wasn't counting, and I missed the second, and— I don't know. I was in denial, I guess. I just kept thinking no. And then . . . last week, like, my boobs are so swollen, and I feel different . . ."

"Wait. Are you saying you're, like, three months pregnant?"

"Something like that?"

"Something like that?"

"Ror . . ."

"But we just met him. We just laid eyes on him for the first time, like, five weeks ago."

"The father is not Jagger Jonze." She looked into my eyes. "It's not him."

I don't like being wrong, but I have to say I was relieved. But if not him, who?

"He said there was no way I could be pregnant because he pulled out . . ."

Oh my God. "*Who* pulled out? What are you saying right now?"

"I don't . . . I don't want to get him in trouble."

"You don't wanna get who in trouble? Fee?"

"I love him, Ror. And he loves me. And it's complicated, but we're gonna be together."

I blurted, "Dante?"

"No!"

"Miles? Is it Miles?"

"Ror?"

"Fee? Who the fuck got you pregnant?"

Fee paused for a long time, and then, without looking at me, she whispered, "Mr. Tom."

I shut up. His name hung in the air between us. Like a storm.

Mr. Tom. Tom Sharpe? The father of Fee's baby? No. Just. No. Tom Sharpe? Fee had this way of looking at him, this respectfully adoring thing I always thought was daughterly love. And he doted on her to the point it made his own daughter jealous, but I thought that was because maybe Fee *was* his kid.

Finally I go, "You're being one hundred percent serious with me right now. Tom Sharpe is the father of your baby. You had sex with Tom Sharpe."

"Yes."

"If you're joking, it's not funny."

"Not joking."

"And he knows."

"I told him a few weeks ago that I was afraid I might be. But he said I was stupid, because I couldn't be, because he pulled out."

"Oh God."

"And before the ball yesterday, I told him I took the test."

"Jesus. So that's why he was so edgy?"

"He thinks I cheated on him."

"What?"

"He said if I was pregnant, how could he be sure it was his?"

"What?"

"Jagger Jonze told Mr. Tom about what I did with Dante. So now he thinks I'm a slut."

"Why would Jagger Jonze be discussing you with Tom Sharpe?"

"Maybe he wanted to make sure Mr. Tom was protecting me?"

"That's what you call it?"

"Kills me that he thinks I've cheated on him. The thing with Dante happened before we—"

"Cheated on him? What are you even saying right now? He's married. And you're like his kid."

"I'm not. I'm his soul mate."

She said it. *Soul mate.* "Oh my fucking God. That's why you were crying after the vows? Because he accused you of cheating on him."

"Well, yeah, that, and because I'm pregnant, dumbass."

"Okay. Well. This is just fucking ridiculous."

"Do you think he told Jagger Jonze? I saw them talking. Do you think he told him I'm pregnant?"

It hit me that Tom Sharpe might indeed have told Jonze that Fee was knocked up. It occurred to me that Tom Sharpe might somehow be involved with Warren Hutsall, and Jagger Jonze, and everything that happened tonight. It occurred to me that it wasn't Jagger who needed to get rid of the evidence—it was Tom Sharpe. I couldn't tell Fee my new theory. Just. Too. Evil.

"I fucked everything up," Fee said.

"Oh my God, Fee."

"It's my fault, though. Do you understand?"

"No. How did it even . . . ?"

"The first time?"

"Oh my freaking God, there was more than one time?"

"We were alone in the house. He was helping me with math at the kitchen table and it just kinda happened. I wanted it to."

·I could only shake my head.

"It's not his fault."

"People say him and your mother. . ."

"I'm not his daughter, Rory."

"You trusted him. He betrayed you, Fee."

"It was consensual."

"You're sixteen. It doesn't matter if you jumped him and gyrated all over his face, he's an adult."

"It matters."

"He raped you."

"If people find out, his whole life will be ruined. And don't say *rape*. He loves me, Rory."

"Kinga?"

"That marriage was a huge mistake. He loves me. And we're gonna be together."

Paula startled us when she appeared at the bathroom door to say she'd checked around downstairs and all was quiet. With no clue what Fee and I had just been discussing, she sat down on the floor beside us and said, "Don't be sad. Help is coming soon."

When Fee said she wanted to rest awhile, Paula and I tucked her into the downy bed in the master bedroom and crept back down to the great room.

Paula is at the window staring at the beach. I couldn't wait to grab the laptop and write down what Fee had just told me.

It doesn't make any more sense seeing it in print. Tom Sharpe. Fuck. Me.

Fee was right. Her soul mate's world will be destroyed if this gets out, and the lives of all the people around him. Imagine Delaney, who's already lost her mother, and who already hates him for being a cheating fuck, discovering that her father impregnated one of her teen besties. She'd have to double, maybe triple, her meds. Kinga'd be suicidal. No, homicidal. Tom Sharpe would go to jail. And Dee's little sister would lose her father. Jesus motherfucking Christ.

Paula is pointing out the window right now. I think that homeless family might be back.

I whispered, "Back away from the window, Paula. We can't go out there again."

She's not backing away from the window, though.

She's saying, "Rory. Please to stop typing."

"Is somebody there?"

"Yes."

"Who?"

"Jesus."

I knew. Before I even looked up from the computer. I knew Paula had just seen Chase Mason. He'd come in through the beach entrance, and the security siren didn't go off and the yard didn't flood with light.

By the time I got to the window, he was standing on the deck, smiling. *Rory*, he mouthed. I opened the door and let him in.

We didn't move toward each other, though I have to say I wanted to.

I go, "I got your message."

"Figured you would. Corinthians."

"And Larkspur."

"Good catch."

"Also, Aunt Lill would never wear pink. Or a V-shirt. Or a ball cap."

"We were counting on you being bugged by all that."

Paula moved in the shadows, startling Chase, who hadn't seen her when he walked in. I reached out for Paula's hand. She moved forward to take it, her eyes on Chase's face. "This is Paula, our friend. Paula, this is Chase Mason. He's come to help us."

"Hey Paula."

"Hey Chase Mason." Paula's eyes lit up. "Chase Mason."

I told Paula to run up and tell Fee.

Once we were alone, I opened my mouth and said, "Chase, I—" But I couldn't finish, because I started crying.

And that's when he kissed me. Chase Mason kissed me. Maybe it was just to stop me from crying, I don't know, but I was so sorry when he pulled away, and so glad I'd showered.

He goes, "Was that okay?"

"Um. Yes."

"You've been wading through some shit, huh, Rory Miller?"

"Knee-deep, Chase Mason."

I noticed the raccoon outside—same raccoon or a friend—scaling the trunk of the grapefruit tree, and thought about the alarm.

Before I could ask, Chase said, "I disabled it. Sorry it went off before. Must have been scary as shit."

"You know about that?"

"My uncle routed the security response to my phone, so as soon as I got the alert, I let them know it was a false alarm."

We moved into the great room, where we could see each other in the moonlight. I told him about Paula and how she'd been abused and that she was illegal, and orphaned, and that I wasn't going anywhere without her. I told him about Javier, and the hot, stinky shed, and about the copter crash, and tumbling down the crevasse, and Monty with the broom. I also told him I'd written down pretty much everything that has happened in my whole life on this pink laptop. And especially I told him about Jagger Jonze and the whole stupid fucking AVB. I couldn't stop talking. So he kissed me again.

He goes, "It's okay. Everything's okay."

Even with Chase in front of me, it was hard to let go of the feeling it wasn't. "Okay."

Then I kissed him. And the word *swoon* came to my mind, and when we finally parted, I needed to sit down on the sectional.

He joined me. "I've wanted to do that . . ."

"I've wanted you to wanna do that," I said, or something equally stupid.

"But you vibe with the Christians. And I just didn't know . . ."

"Yeah."

"So after this is over?"

"Yeah?"

"You and me? We'll, like, read some books together and see where it goes?"

I laughed. For real laughed. "Sure." Then I asked, because I knew he'd know, "My mother?"

"She's coming. She's on her way."

I saw my mother's face in the moonlight. Her eyes. Her smile. Of course Shelley was coming for us. But hearing it from Chase? Oh my God. My chin started to quiver.

Maybe Chase was worried I'd start bawling again, because he kissed me once more and said, "Stay strong. There's more to come."

"More?"

"It's gonna be meta, Rory."

"Oh."

"People are gonna wanna talk to you."

"The authorities, you mean?"

"The press. Everybody will want to hear your story."

"It's all in my blog. Everything. It's all in there."

He glanced up at the clock on the wall and turned back to me, serious. "Your mother's in a coast guard boat headed this way right now. It'll take about an hour for them to get here. There'll be a guy with her, driving the boat—a friend."

"Okay."

"They'll take you up the coast. Not sure where. Your aunt Lilly will be there, waiting in a van."

I was so relieved at the thought that I'd be seeing my aunt Lilly. "Where will they take us?"

"They talked about getting you to Vancouver. That's all I know right now."

"Fee and Paula too, right?"

"Fee and Paula too."

I had to know. "How are you . . . like, why are you . . . ?"

He paused. "My sister."

"The one who died in the car crash?"

"It wasn't a car crash."

"Oh."

"They'd just passed the six-week fetal heartbeat restriction in Iowa. She was eight weeks. I found her bleeding in the garage."

I had no words.

"When we moved here, I just wanted to forget it happened. But I'd hear things at school. Like, these girls who were, you know, in trouble, and they needed help, and a safe place to go. And it's just so stupid, because it's so hard to get birth control, and anyway, I listened and I got connected and I got involved and . . ."

"You've been involved in this . . . since you were fourteen?"

He nodded. "Your friend? Feliza? Is it true? She's really pregnant?"

"It's true."

"The father?"

"I can't . . . just not right now. The fucker isn't gonna get away with it, though."

"The fucker know she's pregnant?"

I nodded.

"I can help her find a way to do what she needs to do if she makes that choice."

We heard the blades of a copter overhead and watched as it banked out over the ocean on its way toward the Santa Monica Pier.

"The bounty hunters are still out there," I said. "Even though Jagger and Jinny and her dad have all disappeared."

"After the Feds and media sort this shit out, even the Crusaders'll have to change their hymn. Don't worry about the bounty hunters. We got you."

"Okay."

Chase got a buzz and checked his cell phone. "I gotta go," he said.

"Really?"

He took my face in his hands. "Rory, it's okay."

"Okay."

"I'll see you in a few days. Or maybe a few weeks. Trust me."

"I do." I actually do.

He looked at the clock on the wall before sending a text back. Then he said, "In one hour. Stroke of midnight. You take Fee and the kid, and you go out to the beach. Don't stop. Walk straight out to the ocean."

"Stroke of midnight."

"They're lighting off fireworks at the pier. There'll be thousands of people and crowd control issues. Everyone'll be distracted."

"I wonder if Paula's seen fireworks."

"She'll see them tonight. From the boat. Just get to the boat."

"Okay."

"You'll have to wade out into the surf a bit."

"It'll be cold."

"It'll be cold, but when you get to the boat, they'll have blankets and boots and all."

"For Paula too?"

"For Paula too."

"What about my laptop?"

"Take it. You won't have to swim, but put it in a ziplock or something. My uncle must have one in the kitchen. When you get where you're going, keep writing. Your story isn't over. Right?"

"Right. I need to write the prologue."

He started to leave, then he came back and we held each other like lovers at the airport, and he whispered into my hair, "This is gonna sound lame."

"What?"

He put his lips to my ear. "I fucking love you, Rory Miller."

I looked into his eyes. "I fucking love you too, Chase Mason."

He stepped back and brushed the hair out of his big brown eyes. "See you on the other side."

And he left.

I can't wait to see my mother, and Aunt Lill, and Chase again, and to feel safe, and right, and, well, not normal, but not this.

After Chase left, Paula appeared at the stairs. By the way she was grinning, I figured she'd heard a fair bit of our conversation.

"We are going to be safe?" Paula asked.

Safe. Yes, safe. That's what people need. Safe. Fuck the notion of happy. People need to be with people they can trust. Families they can rely on. Have husbands who don't cheat. Father figures who don't abuse. People need to live in countries with leaders who are honest. With roofs over their heads and clean water to drink. Safe.

"Yeah, Paula. We're gonna be safe."

———

Paula and I went up the stairs to tell Fee about my mother being on her way in the coast guard boat.

She was curled up near the top of the bed, and hardly reacted when I told her that we have to leave in less than an hour. That we gotta head out to the beach at the stroke of midnight.

"Shelley's coming."

She just nodded and looked out the bedroom window at the ocean.

"Fee. What's going on, Fee?"

"I just need a minute."

"You have time for a quick shower."

"Stop telling me to shower."

"My mother's on her way. We're saved, Fee. You're hearing this, right?"

"I am. And it's good. I'm really happy about it, Rory. I'm super-relieved. I'm just so tired."

"Me too, but Fee, Chase Mason?"

"I know."

"You know he kissed me?"

She grinned, and there for a sec was my bestie. "Wha. . . ?"

"Many times," Paula blurted, then put her hand over her mouth.

Fee teased. "Thought he was a joystick?"

"Actually, I've been thinking that's a sexist, shaming word, and really, if we don't want guys to call us hos and sluts, we shouldn't call them joysticks."

Fee rolled her eyes. "Not now, Ror."

"I'm just saying—"

"Save it for your blog."

Paula nodded. "Write it in the blog."

Fee goes, "So, we've got an hour?"

"Less," I said.

"And we get in a boat."

"Yes."

"And go where?"

"Vancouver? Not sure yet."

"Until when?"

"Until whenever."

"Okay."

"Come back downstairs, Fee."

"Okay."

"Don't give up. We're almost there."

"Okay. Just gimme a minute."

I wanna give her space and time, but we don't have time and I'm kinda scared of the vacant look in her eyes.

OMG—I heard voices outside. Gotta check.

My heart leapt for a sec because I thought maybe Chase had come back. I definitely thought I heard voices at the side of the house, but when I looked out, there was no one. No hissing raccoon. No old couple with a broom. Must've been my fingers on the keys. I've done that before—thought I heard footsteps and realized it was my own typing, or my heartbeat.

What Chase said is true, I know. It's not over yet. Still, I'm feeling surprisingly positive. Because I know that one day soon it will be over, and we'll be safe. In a new life. A real life. One that's not a lie.

Paula and I went back up to the bedroom to check on Fee. She was sitting up. She looked different. Determined, and ready to go. Thank freaking God.

"Rory," she said. "Please don't write anything about Mr. Tom."

"Forget about all that right now, okay? You gotta come downstairs and we gotta get into our blocks—you know—like Brook at a race. We gotta be ready."

She swung her legs over the side of the bed. "Okay. Just . . . please tell me you didn't say anything in your blog about Mr. Tom?"

Fee needs to be deprogrammed. How do you have sex with, and get freaking pregnant by, a man who is kinda like your father and still call him Mr. Tom? Did he get off on that? Pig.

"I did write about him," I said. "But I'll edit it out later. Okay?"

"Promise?"

"Promise." I am lying. I am sorry.

Paula noticed that the old-school phone on the bedside table was crooked on the hook. She tipped it back into the cradle and showed Fee how the dial works, putting her little finger in the hole and letting it spin back. Fee didn't even smile. Anyway, we don't have time for this.

Fee and Paula are standing at the windows in the great room now, looking out at the ocean for the lights from the boat.

"You think people will ever forget?" Fee asked.

"About us? Of course."

"By senior year?"

"Well, I don't know about that, but eventually."

"Eventually," she repeated.

Paula has packed up her Patriot Girl doll in the backpack. She's standing at the window shifting from one foot to the other, anxious to go. Me too. I told Paula she could go out on the sand in her bare feet, since we'd tossed her shoes out with the rest of our dirty clothes, and Chase said they'd have boots and blankets for us in the boat. So Paula's dream will come true. She'll put her feet in the sand. And taste the salty ocean. And she doesn't even know it yet, but she's going to have the most amazing life. Fee too. We're gonna get through this. That's a vow I mean to keep.

They just started the fireworks, which sounded like an explosion, and we all went a little PTSD until we saw the spray of red, white and blue lights bursting out over the pier. Paula is loving the fireworks.

I know we'll have to talk about the AVB and our escape with the police or whatever, but here's another vow: I'm not talking to the press. I'm not gonna tweet about it. I'm not gonna post pics. I'm not going on news shows. No comments for TMZ. I'm gonna let my blog speak for itself. I know it's TMI in places.

I wrote the truth. It's all I have.

Will people forget about us? Yes. We won't trend forever. Thank God. Because fame sucks.

So weird to be wrapping this up, getting ready to put my laptop away in a ziplock. This thing has become like a vital organ. Like I should be transporting it in a cooler. I don't wanna stop writing. So much more to say.

Thanks again, Nina. And Mr. Javier. I hope God heard Paula's prayers and that you are okay, even if you did bring the police, which I don't think you did. And thanks to all the people who believed in us all along. Thanks to Kim and the rest for talking about truth. And thanks to all you women who put on wedding dresses and took pics running away in smoke. I would follow you all on social, but I'm shutting down for a while.

Delaney? Brook? Zara? When Jinny's spell is broken, and maybe it already has, you are going to feel like a bag of dicks. But I forgive you. For you kneweth not what you sayeth. The Hive. Forever. I love you guys. Because that is human. And I'm still that.

Sherman. It occurs to me that my father might have had something to do with my mother's escape. He's a lawyer. He knows people at the courthouse. Maybe he saw to it that she got keys to her cuffs, or arranged for the car that took her away from the police van. I don't care if that's magical thinking. I'm gonna hold on to that little nugget until I hear different. And if you didn't help, Sherman? I'm gonna choose to believe that you thought about helping, and that you tried to help, and that I haven't left your thoughts since the whole thing happened. I'm gonna believe that you've been aching with fear and worry for me, and for Shelley. I hate you, Sherman, but I love you too.

Hurry up, Mommy.

Paula just said she can see the lights from the boat in the distance. Prayers do get answered.

It's almost time.

Fee just said, "God be with us."

Paula said, "Amen."

God? Um.

I will write a long-ass update when we get to Vancouver, or wherever they take us, and hope this next part of our journey is not eventful.

I am filled with hope and faith and optimism. In this moment, on this night, I feel joy.

‐ᬍᬊ‐

THIS LITTLE LIGHT

BLOGLOG: Shelley Miller   11/29/2024—3:08 PM

My beautiful daughter, Rory Anne Miller, aged 16, was shot to death in the early hours of this morning. Also dead are Paula Hernandez, 10 years old, Feliza Lopez, 16, and her unborn child, gunned down on the beach near Paradise Cove, California.

Rory and her friends were making their way through the sand to the coast guard boat where I waited, when they were struck by multiple gunshots fired at close range. I was a witness to their execution. A supporter who was driving our rescue boat captured the shooter.

According to the news, cell phone records indicate that the man who shot these innocent children was contacted by Tom Sharpe, of Calabasas, California, three times in the hour before we arrived. Phone records also show that a call was made from the Malibu beach house where the girls sought refuge to Tom Sharpe's cell phone, approximately fifty minutes before they were killed.

I've read the contents of Rory's blog, twice, and I'm posting this uncensored version in its entirety. I think that is what my daughter would want.

Rory Miller didn't believe in God, but she believed in truth, and honesty, humility and humanity. She was relentless in her questioning of herself, and of our world. She had so much to live for, and so much to give, and will be sorely missed by me, by her father, Sherman Miller, and by all who knew her and loved her.

Rory died in my arms, with the moonlight reflected in her eyes. Her last words were, "Mommy. I. Love."

The Crusaders continue to flood the Santa Monica Pier in celebration of what they call justice. I hope that when the truth is revealed, their calls for God's will to be done will become cries for mercy on us all.

Please share Rory's story.

For Feliza. And Paula. And Rory. And all of the other girls.

Lest we forget.